Do
Good

Other Books by William Sayres

Nonfiction

    Sammy Louis:
      The Life History of a Young Micmac
    Social Aspects of Education:
      A Casebook. With Edward T. Ladd

Fiction

    Sonotaw

William Sayres

Do
Good

Holt, Rinehart and Winston

New York   Chicago   San Francisco

Published, July, 1966
Second Printing, August, 1966
Third Printing, November, 1966

Designer: Ernst Reichl
87710-0116
Printed in the United States of America

To Chris and Billy

Do
Good

I

"These Peace Corps people," said María, "are they expensive?"

"What do you mean, expensive?"

"Do they cost much? Per unit, of course. I don't think we would need more than one."

"Why do you need one?"

"El Tambo has one. So does San Isidro. It would be nice to have one of our own."

I leaned cautiously back in the squawking wooden chair until my shoulders rested against the wall of the adobe hut. "I don't think they sell them," I said. "They more or less give them away. You have to give them back after awhile."

María nodded, and went on chopping the broiled guinea pig into the rice. "I suppose they might wear out rather quickly in this climate. If one wore out, would they give us another?"

"They might. If it were only the climate that wore him out."

"We would not be demanding," she said, wiping a plate with a fold of her long black dress. "It takes little to divert us."

"You sound as if you wanted him as something to play with. Like a toy."

"Oh, no," she said, filling the plate with rice and guinea pig. "We could learn much from him. *Gringos* are full of

9

knowledge. Very helpful. Very energetic." She put the plate on the table.

"Thank you," I said, pulling my chair over to the table. "I didn't know you thought of me that way."

"Oh, yes," she said comfortingly. "You will start any day now. Any day now." She wiped a large spoon on her dress and put it beside the plate. "Everybody knows how *gringos* are. One of these days you'll tell us all kinds of helpful things. And we'll all be rich." She smiled at me, her teeth startlingly white in the thin mulatto face.

"No less than myself." I started eating the rice-guinea pig mixture. As always, I felt vaguely sad doing so; as a boy I had kept guinea pigs as pets.

Romelio Vasquez, the local police inspector, lived at one end of the pueblo; the *cantinas*, where some of the men would be assembling now for music and drink, were situated at the other end. The dirt road leading from one to the other was considered to separate them as much as connect them, and in keeping with this outlook the road was regularly cluttered with such obstacles as chickens, dogs, and donkeys tethered only by a faith that they would not want to go anywhere unurged. Some sixty huts were ranged loosely along the sides of the road, and in the middle of the pueblo was a plaza with a small church and two smaller schools (one for boys and one for girls). María had once told me that it seemed only fair to have the law concentrated at one end of the pueblo and sin at the other, with the church and schools serving in their central position as a kind of buffer which might keep sinners from the law and vice versa. "A long time ago," she had said, sweeping the black snake off the patio as she did every morning (except that on Sundays she often let it sun there an hour longer before sweeping it off), "I imagined that the naming of a police inspector at one end of a pueblo would cause *cantinas* to spring up almost automatically at the other end."

"It lends a kind of balance," I had said, wondering why

the snake put up with the daily indignity of being swept into
the underbrush; was it possible it came even more for the
ride than the sun?

"Now," she had continued absently, "I realize that it is
rather . . ." She had trailed off, her attention seemingly
swept into the underbrush with the snake.

"What?" I had prompted.

"The other way around, of course."

As I walked along the pueblo road toward the *cantinas,*
where the taste of the guinea pig might be cancelled by the
taste of *aguardiente* and by the smell of strong tobacco, I
passed Sebastian Cruzeros, who sat in the doorway of his
aunt's hut working on one of the posters he produced for
political demonstrations in the city. "Cuba *si, Yanqui no,*"
he said amiably.

"Remember the Maine," I said in the same spirit.

"*Como?* What is Maine?"

"A secret weapon," I said. "We have our slogans too."

"If monkeys could talk," he said philosophically, "even
they would have their slogans. Can you come in for a moment?"

"Certainly."

"My aunt has been worrying about Señor Wally Frank
again."

"I will try to comfort her," I said. Since my arrival in
Melita fourteen months ago I had received three publications with some regularity: the *American Anthropologist,*
sent to me as a dues-paying member of the American An-
thropological Association; *Mad* magazine, for which I was
indebted to a friend of mine who had entered a gift subscrip-
tion in my name as a going-away present; and the Wally
Frank monthly pipe catalogue, which had followed me so
faithfully for so many years with so little encouragement
that I had succumbed at last, with the result that Sebastian's aunt, who was the only local pipe smoker, had been
enrolled in the Wally Frank Pipe-of-the-Month Club. I had
not really expected the pipes to arrive, but arrive they did:

11

all kinds, from a General MacArthur "I shall return" corncob through imported briars of various intriguing shapes
and reputed virtues to a water pipe whose smoke was now
filtered through pure *aguardiente*. Sometimes I had paid
duty, sometimes I had not; but not a single pipe or catalogue
had gone astray until three months ago, when all communication from Wally Frank had ceased. Doña Victoria had expected it; as the catalogues had so candidly admitted, poor
Señor Frank had been unfortunate in his purchases, finding
himself time and again with a surplus of pipes he was forced
to sell at a loss. While she loved to have me read to her the
catalogue descriptions of the items offered at great sacrifice
—as she listened raptly, her tongue would click in sympathy
at the repeated bunglings of his agents and in appreciation
of the amazing values available to those who acted at once—
she predicted that he would soon be destitute, reduced to
standing on a street corner with a cigar box full of ill-
matched stems and bowls. Now it seemed that this had indeed
happened, and though I tried to reassure her from week to
week, she was all but in mourning for him. Some nights she
would sit up late by candlelight, as if at a wake, drinking
sugar cane beer and puffing on the water pipe, cursing between puffs and swallows the incompetence of his agents. She
was almost eighty, and her mind was not consistently clear;
she had wild dreams about Wally Frank which she reported
in detail. To her, Wally Frank was the greatest North
American who had ever lived; he was a saint, a martyr, and
now he had been betrayed. Her nephew tried to suggest that
this was the fate of the just in a capitalist society, and that
a revolution was necessary to avenge him. However, she had
never been particularly impressed by Sebastian's political
inclinations, and when her moods were at their darkest she
would let him know she suspected that the communists with
their Godless underhanded ways were responsible.

Sebastian now followed me into the hut, fanning himself
gently with the poster. His aunt sat in a rocking chair fash-
ioned by the local carpenter, José Ramirez, who had been in-

spired by a picture of the *gringo* president *Juan* Kennedy
rocking away on the cover of an old magazine he had seen
in a city barbershop; José had considered it a remarkable
achievement for a *gringo* leader to appear so unbusinesslike,
inefficient, and comfortable, and he concluded that such a
chair must have exceptional powers. He had constructed six
and a half rocking chairs before the inspiration left him; he
had sold two, including the one in which Doña Victoria now
perched, and on an experimental impulse had incorporated
the others into an outhouse which was distinctive though
not wholly satisfactory from the standpoint of tidiness.

"No news, I suppose," Doña Victoria said glumly.

"None," I said. "Which means no *bad* news, you understand. As far as we know, Señor Frank has as many pipes as
ever."

"That's the trouble," she grumbled. "He has too many
pipes. Somebody comes along with a new kind, he buys thousands too many. Thousands. And then he has to sell for almost nothing. He's too generous. They should put him away
for his own good." She rocked furiously. "Maybe that's what
they did. Maybe they put him away for his own good."

"I really don't think . . ."

"Or maybe they just *said* it was for his own good!" she
interrupted loudly, glaring at me. "It's those agents of his,
they'd do anything to cover their mistakes." From a fold of
her dress she took out the General MacArthur pipe and began to fill it from a stockpile of cigar remnants which she
kept in a clay pot. As she tamped the tobacco down
she watched me suspiciously. "You haven't been keeping
your mail to yourself, have you?"

"You know I wouldn't do that, Doña Victoria," I said
soothingly. "After all, it's not only you I have to consider."
It was true. While I retained nominal possession (though all
were free to look at it) of the *American Anthropologist*, especially since it was very good for pressing ferns, I passed
along my copies of *Mad* magazine to Sebastian, who found
it very helpful in his poster work. Many of the figures that

13

appeared in his posters were taken from *Mad*. Since these were in many cases caricatures of well-known (though not to Sebastian) and highly affluent persons, a typical poster showed a peasant leader who looked like Nelson Rockefeller or Cornelius Vanderbilt shouting a call for freedom from economic enslavement to a crowd of such fellow peasants as Henry DuPont, Princess Margaret, and Henry Luce. He did not consider the magazine very funny. Presumably among the contributing reasons were that he could not read English; that the schoolmaster and visiting priest, whom he distrusted on principle, *did* consider it funny; and that he had somehow acquired the idea that it was put out by the U. S. State Department.

Doña Victoria was now puffing vigorously on the General MacArthur pipe; the General himself could not have looked more formidable. I had never seen her standing, but she must have been close to six feet tall, a foot higher than her nephew, and her shoulders were hung like a wrestler's. It was said that when the moon was full she could fell any man in the pueblo with a blow, and I had seen her swing so viciously at Sebastian that the rocker would spin almost completely around. Her aim was as poor as her eyesight, but once she had connected on a downward rock and Sebastian had been unable to pronounce certain words for months. As usual, she was wrapped in something blue that could have been a dress or blanket or both, with only her long arms free and her angry witch face uncovered. She was a terror; yet people were fond of her, and Sebastian spoke lovingly to her alone of all the people in the pueblo. It was curious to watch him bobbing about her, treating her both gently and fearfully as he might a baby gorilla. I know he admired her strength; he seemed to be drawn to it as if it were the legacy she would leave him when she died. I would almost have said that if he had had it, he would not have bothered making posters, but this would doubtless be an oversimplification.

"As soon as you hear anything," she said between puffs, "report!" There was something about that five-star pipe . . .

"At once, my general."

She chuckled. Then she closed her eyes and her voice turned inward: "Oh, I could lead them," she said meditatively. "I'd know how to lead them, I would." She began to rock as if to a slow marching beat. "The enemy would be . . . *there!*" She jabbed the air with the pipe. "And I'd be . . . *here!*" Another jab. "And I'd . . . I'd . . ." She laughed craftily. "I certainly would . . ." She began to slice the air, as if chopping off heads. "Oh, the fools!" She stopped slicing and resumed puffing, picking up speed in the rocker. Her eyes were on something no one else could see, and as she puffed and rocked, like an engine freed from its freight for an open run toward a far but familiar horizon, the night rain began.

Sebastian touched my arm. "A word," he whispered. "A word before you go." He nodded toward the doorway.

The rain was not yet heavy, but I would have to hurry. There were already spatterings of mud on the cane mat outside the doorway. "What is it?"

"There are rumors," he said carefully. "Is the so-called Peace Corps going to send anyone here?"

"I don't know," I said. "It's possible. We seem to be in one of the—excuse the expression—target areas. But . . . *Quién sabe?*"

"There would be trouble."

"From whom? Surely you're for peace?"

"Ah . . ." He turned his palms up, as if to concede a point that had no meaning. "Peace, yes . . . but not propaganda, Señor."

"Surely it is not my private illusion that you make posters?"

He smiled. "Ah, but that is not the same thing."

"Neither is the Peace Corps." I offered him a cigarette.

15

He laughed and took the cigarette. "Ah, Don Guillermo." His face seemed to joke with itself. Of all his visible possessions, his face was the most impressive. So fortuitous was the blend of white, Indian, and Negro characteristics that I could imagine him being received as alien or native—depending on his mood and purpose—in any part of the world. The blue and gray *ruana* that covered his shoulders was so large—it reached almost to his ankles—that one half expected him to throw it off at any moment, as if at an unveiling, and show an identity thus far concealed only to build up suspense. He had once told me, however, that he wore it only because his aunt had made it for him years ago and became violent whenever he suggested putting it aside; she was waiting for him to grow into it, though he was now in his middle thirties. He lit his cigarette and blew smoke into the rain. "At least you no longer smoke *gringo* cigarettes," he said lightly.

"I can't afford them," I said. "Besides, I've come to like these very much." By now the taste of the strong dark tobacco and sweetened rice paper had become so satisfying that milder cigarettes seemed tasteless. I turned up the collar of my khaki shirt. "I'd better go," I said.

He sighed. "Perhaps I can join you later. Though you understand . . ." He nodded toward his aunt, who was still going full tilt.

"I understand."

"Would you like a poster to shield your head?"

"Thanks, but the rain is still light. It's very generous of you, though, to offer one of your posters."

He winked. "It would not hurt my cause if you were seen carrying my poster, Don Guillermo." He patted my arm and grinned. "A fair trade, no? I'll smoke your cigarettes and you carry my posters."

"It sounds so fair I'll need time to think it over. If I have to decline, there's always the priest."

"Yes," he said soberly. "There's always the priest."

"Hasta luego, Don Sebastian."

"Hasta luego, Don Guillermo."

I stepped into the rain. The wind was rising, and I hurried along the road toward the *cantinas.*

The largest of the three *cantinas* was owned by Alejandro Torres. Unlike most of the local structures, which were made of wattle-and-daub, adobe or bamboo, and had thatch roofs, the Torres *cantina* was made of brick and had a tile roof. It was said that Alejandro prospered because he so obviously enjoyed his own offerings. Whether it was bottled beer over the counter, sugar cane beer (*guarapo*) or corn beer (*chicha*) under the counter, or the more potent *aguardiente* brought proudly to the table, Alejandro was as spirited a consumer as dispenser. It was not just that he drank—Alejandro himself said that if medals were given for drinking, the pueblo would long ago have vanished under the weight, though I believe he was judging on the basis of rather too small a sample—it was the *way* he drank, the flourishes and exuberant noises, all testifying to the delights to be had at his tables.

As I came in Alejandro was winding up the Victrola, which had run down in the middle of a bolero. The fidelity of some of the recordings in his collection was such that it was often difficult to tell exactly when the machine was running down, but he would part with none of them. He did, however, have several superb classical records which, I understood, had been appropriated during an unfortunate fire at the Soviet Embassy in the city. Some fascinating combinations were to be heard: a scratch rendition of "Venga, venga, cha-cha-cha," for example, sandwiched between Shostakovich and Stravinsky. The week before there had been a remarkable dance by a thirsty couple who had carried their mambo well beyond the appropriate record and had reached the third movement of Shostakovich's Fifth Symphony before what I thought was a rather spectacular collapse.

17

There were seven men sitting at two tables. They waved me over, and I took a chair between Ernesto Sandoval, the schoolmaster, and José Ramirez, the carpenter. The pint bottle of *aguardiente* on the table was nearly empty, and I signaled for another.

"So," said Ernesto. "Where is your notebook?"

"In such unforgettable company," I said, "I need no reminders."

"In that case," said Ernesto, pushing the bottle over, "you will doubtless be able to keep in mind the very important lesson I give you now." He tapped the bottle. "This interesting item has in it a mysterious substance which, for purposes of discussion, we may call alcohol."

"Ah." I examined the bottle. "Is it possible?"

"You will note that it looks exactly like water."

I held the bottle close to the candlelight. "Amazing," I said. "When did you first notice this?"

"Just now." He cleared his throat modestly. "However, it does not taste like water."

I tasted it. "More like licorice," I said. "Is there no end to learning?"

"None," he said. "It's all known as civilization."

We all nodded wisely.

"Tell me," I said, "does this liquid produce any effects?"

"None whatsoever," said Ernesto. "One can watch it for hours and feel nothing."

"Perhaps," I suggested, "if one were to drink it?"

"Ah," said Ernesto, "who knows what would happen then?" He rubbed his round forehead as if it were a balky crystal ball. "As a service to civilization, perhaps we ought to find out." He peered closely at the bottle. "However, in some strange fashion, most of the liquid appears to have departed."

"I will work my magic," I said, holding out my hand for the bottle Alejandro was bringing.

"You are a sorcerer, a *brujo*," Ernesto said admiringly, as I put the bottle on the table.

Alejandro beamed at us, his great dry lips quivering in a perpetual invitation to have one more.

"*Carajo*, fat one," said José. "You forgot the glass."

Alejandro began with a giggle and ended with a mighty guffaw. He plunged a hand into one of his enormous pockets and pulled out a shot glass, which he placed in front of me. "Forget?" he said happily. "We elephants never forget." He slapped José on the back and lumbered off to wind the Victrola again.

"A delicate creature," said Ernesto. He filled the glasses.

"At least he supports local trade," said José. "He promised to let me build his coffin." He picked up his glass. "A house would be easier."

"You had better start at once," said Ernesto. "Considering his size and your diligence, it would not be surprising if he decomposes before you finish."

"I would," said José. "But there is not that much wood in all of Melita."

"Then tomorrow we must plant some trees," said Ernesto. He raised his glass. "A toast," he said, "to the trees."

We toasted the trees.

Ernesto raised his glass again. "To teachers," he said. "To teachers everywhere."

We toasted teachers everywhere.

José raised his glass. "To the *campesino*," he said. "To peasants everywhere."

We toasted peasants everywhere.

"One more toast," said Ernesto, "and then you must continue without me. It would not do for the schoolmaster to be found without dignity." He smiled and nudged José. "Let us drink to the Peace Corps, my friend."

"Why not?" José said. "I'll drink to anything." He downed his drink and scratched an ear thoughtfully. "What sort of thing would that be?"

The music was so loud now that conversations were half-shouted, and the smoke was so dense one could hardly tell who was half-shouting at whom. Ernesto had been gone over two hours, but José kept appearing through the swirls, his smooth ageless face as expressionless as the wood he worked. "Have I had too much?" he would ask, his face gliding out of the smoke at me. "Have I?"

"Not that I can see," I would say, trying to focus on a face that had already slipped back into the smoke.

Other faces appeared. Alejandro, like a walrus waddling out of a snow bank, would burst into view, brandishing a bottle or ash tray or rag as if he were ready to thrust it into someone. His bristly close-cropped (for cleanliness, he said, though his huge moustache dripped and shed freely) hair was wet as a bath-brush with sweat, and when he bent over the table it seemed about to scrub me down. "So nourishing," he would say, his dry lips quivering as he uncorked a bottle. "So full of power." Watching him fill my glass with an eager flourish, I had a sensation of being introduced to the first watering place. "Truly the blood of giants." Muttering his little phrases, he would stare at my glass with an expression of such primal thirst that I felt my own throat parch; if he had stayed at my table I would not be able to write this. But there were other throats to work on, and off he would go to other tables, sowing thirst wherever he went.

The number and identity of my companions at the table kept changing. Sometimes I would be alone; sometimes I would feel like a participant in a spirited game of musical chairs (an illusion enhanced by the way the Victrola kept running down). Saturnino, Roberto, Antonio, Frederico, Ricardo, Tomás, Jorge, Secundino, Jaime, Francisco—the faces of *mestizaje*, the heirs of centuries of racial and cultural mixture came and went, swaying in the smoke to marred music. I filled glasses; other hands filled mine. Voices rose and machetes appeared; voices softened and cigarettes appeared. The red cement floor was wet and muddy from the feet that came in from the rain, and when the Victrola ran down the sound of the rain on the tile roof seemed to press us

20

all closer together, as if the music had been a shield against nature. Pieces of talk drifted through the smoke.

"It's the priest's business how often he comes. If you think . . ."

". . . in such a hurry to bury her. *Pues,* they'd just put the grass in her nostrils when . . ."

"You can't trust them. Once they get you in a hospital, all they want to do is cut . . ."

"Do I lie? Do I lie?"

". . .so many hangovers they called him *El Guayabo.*"

"Her godmother was calling for her. So I told her if she ever said anything . . ."

". . . eight goats, one after the other . . ."

"Do I lie?"

A patch of pink brushed by my table: women had come in, and dancing had begun. The patch of pink belonged to a young pale girl named Rosa Linda Perico, who had come from the valley two months ago to help old Visenta Ambato, the curer and midwife (and, some said, witch); the two were distant cousins. Visenta would probably come in later to fetch her. I could hear Constancia Robles, the rather frenetic widow, laughing in a corner; her friend Justicia Luz, a brooding spinster with a certain Theda Bara appeal, was doubtless being intense elsewhere in the room. There were seldom many women in the *cantinas,* and usually no more than two or three couples dancing at any one time, so the customary masculine commotion was not often seriously disturbed. Still, the presence of women added a new potential: for fun, for trouble.

Two faces emerged from the smoke. José and Justicia, like a two-headed creature of sorrow, nodded at me sadly. "She says I have," José said.

"Have what?" I managed.

"Had too much," José said mournfully.

"He is ready to fall," Justicia said. "Remind him that tomorrow is Sunday."

21

"Tomorrow is Sunday, Don José," I said.

"I have never claimed otherwise," José said.

"Do you know what he pretends to want?" Justicia said balefully. "On the very threshold of Sunday?"

"Something unseemly, perhaps?" I said.

"I have never claimed otherwise," José said.

"He proposes to measure me," Justicia said, rolling her eyes as if imploring lightning to strike any hand that would move to measure her.

"Well," I said, "he's a carpenter, after all, and maybe he wants to build you something. You can't expect a carpenter not to measure things every now and then."

"No man measures me," Justicia said slowly, sagging slightly against the table. She had obviously been to one of the other *cantinas* first.

"I'm sure he won't measure you against your will," I said reassuringly.

"I never claimed otherwise," José said. He slipped back into the smoke, and Justicia sagged a little further against the table. She stared at me as if she were practicing the climatic lesson of a hypnotism-made-easy course, and belched loudly.

"That did it," I said. "I'm yours."

Her eyes rolled and she sagged still further, her masses of black hair spilling onto the table.

"Enchanting," I said. "But kindly keep your hair out of my glass."

She slumped into a chair and cleaned out my glass, refilling and emptying it twice to make certain nothing was in it that should not have been. "You like my dress?" she asked heavily.

"It has a life of its own," I said. Her abundantly perfumed violet dress looked like a discarded slip attached to a broken umbrella.

"Made . . . made it myself."

"Don't tell me how," I said. "I already have my suspicions."

"Suspicions," she repeated slowly. "Reminds me . . . some . . . something to ask you." She leaned forward. "Is another *gringo* coming?"

"So the rumors have it," I said. "But I know nothing personally."

"He would not be a missionary, would he?"

"I hardly think so."

She looked relieved. "Would he be rich?"

"Probably not."

She looked disappointed.

"He might well be young and tender," I suggested.

"Young and . . . mmm." She patted her lap; another look had appeared.

José returned from the smoke. He had an unopened bottle of *aguardiente*, which he dangled in front of Justicia. "The ruler waits," he said.

"No man measures me," she said, eyeing the bottle.

"It is painless," he said. "I have only the finest instruments." He put the bottle in a coat pocket of his unpressed blue suit, so that the cork protruded an inch from her nose.

"Mmm," she said. "I might let you show me what you have."

"It would astound you," José said.

"That is all but unbelievable," she said.

"I have never claimed otherwise," José said.

The music was louder than ever and the smoke thicker. Shapes came and went; the dark drab suits of the men carried flashes of female color. Glasses and bottles clattered and clinked, and voices were now sharp, now ponderous. "All that for ten pesos?" someone boomed, and a high giggle followed. ". . . last time the ruts were filled in!" someone complained, and mambo percussions answered. "Almost thirty-five," I found myself saying. "An interesting age," someone assured me. "Thank you," I said gratefully. "As long as you can move," said someone else, "*every* age is interesting," and an argument followed. "*That's* the way to move," someone said, and for a moment I thought I was back in the argument; instead I was dancing with Rosa Linda. I tried to say something profound to her. "You smell like a clover field," I said. "You," she said, "smell like chewing gum." I nodded wisely; great truths were being traded. I felt dizzy . . .

Out in the night rain, I stumbled along the road toward my room. A few late candles burned in paneless windows, and the wind was cold.

II

"Heavens!" María said. "They've sent a skeleton!"

We watched the slender figure trudge up the small rise leading from the highway to the pueblo road. He wore a well-cut conservative brown suit with matching tie and shoes, and carried a suitcase. "It's partly because he's somewhat tall," I said.

"There'll be no bed to fit him," María said, straightening her gray broomstick skirt and giving her beautiful teeth a quick wipe on the sleeve of her white fiesta blouse.

"Don José can build one," I said.

"With rockers, perhaps," she said, smiling.

The kitchen fires of the pueblo, started in the morning chill, were largely unattended. The converted Ford truck that carried passengers and produce between the city and the capital of the *municipio* had not had such a waystop turnout at Melita since the archbishop, whose car had been stolen in the city, had paid a visit almost two years ago. Even Doña Victoria, who had come to nurse the notion that it was Wally Frank himself who was coming, presumably to explain the delay in shipments, had insisted that she be carried to the arrival area. There she sat, on a barrel overlooking the highway, puffing on the General MacArthur pipe. Romelio Vasquez, squeezed into his blue uniform for the occasion, was all crispness and authority; the night before, he had asked Sebastian to prepare a document the visitor could

25

fill out, since it seemed only proper to have him fill out *something*. Sebastian had produced a truly imposing document, calling for all sorts of suitably irrelevant information, and Romelio now held it proudly, ready to present it as if it were the key to the pueblo. Ernesto was ready to make another presentation: the only volume in English in the small school collection; it had remained there unread for many years, and how it got there in the first place no one could say for certain. It was entitled *The Chadwick Sisters: A Tale of Honor*, and had been privately printed "because of the importunities of dear friends" in 1892. The only other item to be formally presented was a bottle of Alejandro's own special mixture, made up of the assorted leavings of his customers over a period of several weeks—he usually reserved the mixture for himself, and having tasted some of it once, I thought it just as well. I had told him at the time of tasting that I suspected it might be a trifle smoother if he did not include what was spilled on tables, but he had answered rather logically that it would take too long to fill a bottle if he did not take advantage of small accidents. Apart from these formal presentations, it was said that Constancia and Justicia were planning to make an informal gesture later on, but there was neither confirmation nor denial from the two ladies themselves.

Romelio touched my shoulder. "Please accompany me, Don Guillermo. I do not know how, ah, fluent he is, and it would be embarrassing if he thought I was about to have him arrested and torn to pieces by this mob."

"Yes, that might be embarrassing," I said. "It's the little misunderstandings that are often the most upsetting. But he's doubtless quite fluent; it's not as if he were somebody of importance."

Romelio chuckled, and led the way to the top of the rise. The new arrival put down his suitcase and came toward us with a nervous smile and extended hand. "I'm Peter Bradley," he said. "I seem to have been expected."

"Shake hands with *him* first," I said. "He's the man in charge." I made flowery introductions. "Don Romelio is the local Eliot Ness, so behave," I added.

"Who is Señor Ness?" Romelio asked.

"A famous officer of the law," I said. "Possibly he shot too many Italians, but nobody's perfect."

Romelio shrugged. "We must shoot what is given us to shoot," he said. "If we listened to every complaint, we would not get to shoot much of anything." He frowned menacingly at Peter, then laughed explosively. "You will find we jest a little here," he said kindly. "Of course, part of it is serious, and it is well to learn which part."

"Remember that," I said.

Romelio cleared his throat. "And now . . ." He presented the document. "Please fill this out within forty-eight hours."

"And then what do I do with it?" Peter asked.

"Then?" Romelio looked thoughtful. "Oh, just leave it. I'll be around to pick it up one of these days."

"But be sure you fill it out within forty-eight hours," I said.

"You must be the, um, anthropologist," Peter said.

"Um, yes," I said. "Welcome. And don't worry."

"Thanks." He looked uncertainly at the waiting crowd. "Do you happen to know where I might stay?"

"It's been arranged," I said. "The local carpenter has a large extra room he uses only seldom for certain, so to say, measurements. He insists on offering it to you."

"You're positive he won't need it?"

"If he wants to use it temporarily, I'm sure he'll let you know. Now get your suitcase; you have some people to meet."

"Doña Victoria," I said, "may I present Mr. Peter Bradley. Mr. Bradley, Doña Victoria Hortensia Salazar de Campo."

"What was that name again?" she snapped.

"Mr. Peter Bradley. Don Pedro might be more convenient to say."

"Not *his* name," she said. "*Mine.* It has such a nice roll to it, and I almost never hear the whole thing any more."

"Doña Victoria Hortensia Salazar de Campo," I said as grandly as I could.

"It makes me tremble to hear it," she said. "What I could have been!" She closed her eyes and tasted her name silently. Then she opened her eyes slowly and glared at Peter. "Where are they?" she challenged.

"Where are what, Doña Victoria?" Peter asked, his schoolboy face reddening.

"The pipes, young man, the pipes!"

"What pipes?" Peter asked anxiously.

"His name is Bradley, not Frank," I reminded her gently.

"Exactly!" she said. "I knew the moment I saw him there was something wrong. Are you one of his agents, young man?"

"I don't think so," Peter said, backing up a step.

"Don't run away, young man," she said. "I'll crush you if you take another step away!"

"I won't," he said gamely.

"Now," she said confidentially, leaning closer and jabbing at him with the pipe stem, "are you his bastard son, young man?"

"Whose, um, bastard son would that be, please?"

"Aha!" she said, poking him under the ribs. "You don't deny it, eh?"

"I . . . I'm not really sure what you're asking me to deny, Señora."

"Look at it this way," I said helpfully. "Are you *anybody's* bastard son?"

"Oh," he said, "of course not." But Doña Victoria was not listening. She was staring triumphantly at a small bulge in his suitcoat.

"Pull it out, young man!" she cried.

He gaped at her. "Pull it out?" he said weakly.

"Reach in and pull it out!" she ordered. "Show it to the world!"

"I . . . I don't understand," he said, flushing and looking quickly at his fly. "Pull what out?"

"Don't hide it!" she said excitedly. "Hurry up and let me see it! Then you can come to my house and see all of mine."

He was trembling, but he looked determined. "I just couldn't," he whispered.

Understanding came to me at last. "Certainly you can," I said.

He looked at me in astonishment. "I can?"

"Why not? You *are* carrying a pipe, aren't you?"

"Yes, but . . . *yes!*" Shaking in relief, he took the pouch from his inside coat pocket and handed it to Doña Victoria. "You unzip it," he said, his voice breaking on "unzip." "The pipe's in the bottom part."

She screeched delightedly and extracted the pipe, a lustrous briar with curved stem; I might have expected a collegian with the proper quota of sophistication and idealism to have such a pipe. "Ah, you beauty!" Doña Victoria said.

"My father gave it to me," Peter said.

"Of course he did," she said, her suspicions of paternity confirmed. "He's making them better than ever."

"He didn't make it," Peter said. "He just . . ."

"I know, I know," she said impatiently. "He didn't make it *himself*, it would take him forever to turn out all the . . ." She trailed off and began sniffing the tobacco. "But his *people* make such . . ." More sniffing. "Sweet as the crotch of a powdered baby, young man."

"Sweet as the . . . ?"

"That's where most of the powder is, you know. You'll let me try it, won't you?"

"Please help yourself," Peter said.

She filled both pipes, pausing to give him an exuberant jab in the ribs. "Ah, it's good you've come," she said.

"Congratulations, Pete," I said. "You're about to smoke your first peace pipe."

"What did you say was in it?" Peter asked, looking at the froth seeping from the bottle around the heavy cork.

"Whatever you like," Alejandro said expansively. "And a little besides."

"I've never seen anything quite that color," Peter said.

"And you never will again," Alejandro said proudly. "Each one is somewhat different. Yet there is a certain constancy of taste."

"I've only tasted it once," I said, "but I can well believe it."

"Go on, *joven*, sample it!" Alejandro said, gazing soulfully at the bottle, his great dry lips straining toward the seepage.

"I would, Señor," Peter said, "but my stomach is a little uneasy from smoking so much so fast. You see, Doña Victoria . . ." He blanched and took a deep breath.

"She tried his pipe and had him try hers," I explained. "Don Pedro is accustomed to pipes which have been treated now and then with what are called pipe cleaners. So when he smoked her pipe, there were certain juices that came through . . ."

"Please!" Peter said, holding up his hand. "Doña Victoria was. . . . very . . . kind." He cupped his mouth.

"I am confident her juices are of the highest quality," said Alejandro reassuringly.

"A rare old vintage," I suggested.

Peter groaned and sat on his suitcase.

Alejandro looked concerned. "A swallow or two of my little present might help," he said, lowering his huge body to the ground next to Peter and stroking the bottle. "Look at it, Pedrito, look at it," he said softly. Operation Thirst had begun.

I turned partly away; *my* stomach needed no such treatment, especially not at this early hour. Even so, the murmurs and sighs, the small drummings of eager fingers on glass and the whispers flowing with the gentle persistence of a mountain spring—these were sounds that began to persuade me that the first and last object of life was to satisfy thirst. I glanced at Peter; with an expression of surprise on his face, he was drinking . . .

"Excuse me," Peter said, trying to focus on a page of the book Ernesto had just given him. "I can't seem to read this Spanish."

"It's English," I said. "Your native tongue, you may remember."

"I remember very little, my . . . my good, good friends." He reached out to steady himself, finding only the posterior of a placid donkey. He smiled politely at the donkey. "My, all these beautiful animals right out in the open."

"I think he will do, Don Guillermo," Ernesto said. "He has a certain capacity for foolishness."

"A very important capacity," I said.

"Who could believe such a *gringo* is out to exploit us all economically?" Ernesto said.

"Not to say politically," I said. "Or socially, for that matter."

"Brittania rules the waves," said Peter happily.

"Yes, he will do," Ernesto said. He rubbed his long graceful hands together. "If he survives."

"Go home, *Yanqui*," Sebastian said hospitably. "The trend is to the left, no?"

"The trend," said Peter emphatically, "is to freedom!"

"He appears to have you there, Don Sebastian," I said.

"Oh, we will have fun," said Sebsastian gleefully. "Will you model for my posters, Pedro?"

"Should I?" Peter asked.

"You'd be in distinguished company," I said. "But I advise a strongly worded no."

"No, no, a thousand times no, Señor," Peter said with elaborate courtesy.

"Oh, he's a good one!" Sebastian said, shivering ecstatically within his tremendous blue and gray *ruana* as if he were a butterfly getting ready to throw off the cocoon. "What a pleasure it will be to convert him! Or . . ." He shrugged.

"Or what?" I asked.

"Or destroy him," Sebastian said coldly.

Stares and smiles and stares and frowns and stares: Peter met them all with courtesy and warmth. Whether he managed this because of Alejandro's present or in spite of it, I could not say. His suit, watch, shoes, necktie, suitcase, and freckles were examined curiously. One old woman was so enchanted by his freckles that she kept touching them, dutifully saying "with your permission" each time. She evidently could not make up her mind whether he wanted them or not, and finally gave him ambiguous assurance that "sulphur baths would help"—presumably either to make them go away or increase in size and coverage, according to his wish. Dogs sniffed his shoes warily; more accustomed to bare feet as tough as leather than stockinged feet inside leather, they were uneasy—only such outsiders as the priest, teachers, and myself went about in such things. Still, outsiders meant little extras in food, and there were tentative waggings of tails to go with the nervous yips and whines. The children seemed the most delighted; shy and reserved at first, they were the most responsive once the formalities were out of the way. His height was a wonder to them; an inch or two over six feet, he was even taller than Doña Victoria and myself, who pressed six feet—in most of South America, five-footers were far more common than six. Laughing and chattering, the children clustered around him, seeking contact; yet a word from a parent would send this one or that scurrying from the cluster to wait respectfully for another word—children here were much better behaved than their northern counterparts, with spankings as unnecessary as conscious psychology. Not many words were sent into the young cluster, however; the firmest of my early impressions of Peter Bradley was that he liked children. He knew how to chuck under chins, to tickle, to lift for the high view, to hug without thought. Again, I could not discount the possible effects of Alejandro's gift, but I had come to trust the credo, *In vino véritas,* more than I did most. Whatever the essence of Peter was, drink would not diminish it. A child held high went a long way with me.

At last we came to José.

After I made introductions, my attention was diverted by a request for a cigarette and an invitation to a baptism. When I turned back, José was saying cordially, "Should you die, you would be at the very source of the finest coffins and crosses to be had. Of course, there is no obligation on your part. With or without your order, I will happily attend to your wake."

"José is full of good works," I said.

"I have never claimed otherwise," José said.

"Do you have an easy-payment plan?" Peter asked. "Go now, pay later?"

"Mm," José said. "I believe you will fit in well here, *muchacho.* Especially in one of my coffins. I always guarantee a perfect fit. Sometimes, you understand, I have to compress the customer a bit, or leave out one of his more trifling parts, but eventually the fit is perfect." As usual, he was deadpan; he reminded me of the late Fred Allen, except that his skin was smooth and clear—his face always looked freshly shaven, though in fact he never shaved.

"He doesn't give trading stamps," I said. "But he's otherwise satisfactory."

"Trading stamps?" José said. "Have I failed without knowing it? What are trading stamps?"

"Little things you lick and turn in for magnificent treasures," I said. "Tickets to Babylon and El Dorado, some say."

33

"Have you licked any personally?"

"Not lately," I said. "But thousands of my countrymen are doubtless licking them this very moment."

"To think of it," José said, "perhaps your government will some day give us these trading stamps instead of money." He sighed. "Then we can sit in the sun all day licking stamps."

"On rainy days you would have to lick them inside," I pointed out.

"Or leave them outside," José said. "From time to time we could look out and watch our work being done."

"You have great insight, Don José," I said.

"I have never claimed otherwise."

We came to José's home, an adobe structure with tile roof and cement floor. There was a bedroom on either side of the main room (which was a combination living room and working room—it was difficult to tell which pieces of furniture were to be used and which to be sold, especially since José moved them from one category to the other on impulse), with the kitchen and patio in back. In consideration of his guest, José had replastered the inside walls with the finest cow dung to be had, and the air was still rather chewy. The room offered to Peter was the largest, and had been used to lay out the pieces—wooden and, it was said, quite unwooden—with the most formidable dimensions. José had tidied up the room conscientiously, except for two unfinished coffins and parts of a *trapiche*, a fruit press whose primary local use was in the production of sugar cane brew. He indicated these apologetically. "There seemed to be no place else to put them, *muchacho*. But if they disturb you, out they go, ready or not."

"I'm sure we can live together in harmony," Peter said graciously. He put his suitcase on the wide slat bed. "After all, it was their home before mine."

José nodded. "Some things do have a way of staying put," he said. "There is a peculiarity about the bed which I would call to your attention, but it escapes me just now. It periodically comes to my notice." He looked at the bed thoughtfully. "Perhaps it will not trouble you after all. It seems to occur only under certain conditions."

"May the powers that be preserve those conditions," I said fervently.

"And protect the innocents at the same time," José added.

"Meaning me," Peter said with what I considered genuine regret. "I have a somewhat unfortunate confession to make."

"By all means, wait for the priest," José said. "We are not to be confessed to, *muchacho.*"

"Above all, not us," I said.

"I have never claimed otherwise," José said. "There are urges that afflict some of us in such an interesting and . . ."

"Irresistible," I suggested.

". . . irresistible way," José continued, "that we give in to them not only freely but rather systematically. This, after all, is the age of science, no?"

"Yes," I said. "Research is the keynote."

"For me," Peter said sadly, "it's still all theory . . ."

"Mm," José said. "But progress reaches even the innocent, no?"

"Yes," I said. "It is the true test of progress."

"I have never claimed otherwise," José said. "Whatever it was that was said."

Peter sat on the bed. "There is a peculiarity, you say?"

"Not wholly unpleasurable, as I recall," José said. "All that comes to me at the moment is that it quickens one." He sat on the bed next to Peter. "I don't suppose you feel quickened?"

"Not really," Peter said. "Perhaps I'm insensitive."

"No," José said comfortingly. "My impression is that a female contributes something to the sensation." He fastened a loose button on his fly. "If you think your government would approve, I will be happy to speculate."

"My government," Peter said, "would probably approve

35

Red China before it would approve what you may have in mind. Not that I presume to speak for my government *or* for the condition of your mind, Señor."

"Mmm," José said. "How well he speaks. I can still remember the *gringo* hordes of yesteryear who could only say, 'Me no understand' and 'How much?' " He stood up and looked out the small window. "It was such a treat to hear them." He breathed deeply; the smell of corn bread baking came from the hut across the road. "There they were, *muchacho*, the bearers of civilization, saying over and over again, 'Me no understand' and 'How much?' " He came back to the bed. "Such a treat to hear them."

"And you hear them no more?" I said.

"Now that you mention it," José said, "it seems to me they are not wholly gone. Not wholly." He looked closely at me. "I take it you would not claim otherwise?"

"I would not claim otherwise."

He nodded and sat on the bed again. "And I do not claim to have summed them up," he said. "Some of my best friends have been *gringos.*" He winked at Peter. "*Gringos* are just as good as people, no?"

"I hope so," Peter said.

"There are many who hope so, *muchacho,*" José said. "And I always stand ready to tell them that *gringos* should have equal rights with everybody else. That's what I always stand ready to tell them."

"I have always felt I could count on you to tell them that, Don José," I said.

"You may continue to feel so," he said graciously. "After all, *gringos* have a certain merit." He looked idly at one of the coffins. "In their place, of course."

Peter put the last of his shirts in the coffin—José had suggested using it in the absence of a bureau—and stretched. "All unpacked," he said.

"At least the Peace Corps doesn't overload you," I said. "Most people bring far too much—things they don't need, things they can buy more cheaply after they arrive." It seemed strange to be speaking English; I had not been alone with a fellow countryman for over fourteen months.

"I . . . I wanted to talk to you about that," he said slowly.

"About what? Overloading?"

"No. About the Peace Corps. You see . . ." He glanced out the window toward the hut where José had gone to dicker over some corn bread. "I don't want anyone to think I'm . . ." He faced me. "The fact is, I'm not here officially from the Peace Corps. That is . . ." He paused.

"You're an undercover agent for the John Birch Society?" I prompted.

His quick grin as quickly became a frown. "It's not easy to tell. It started with the Peace Corps, but . . ." He looked out the window again. "I was sort of a borderline trainee all along—right through the six weeks at Rutgers and the final month down here—and finally they . . . well, they wanted to send me back."

"Why?"

"Partly my health—I barely got by the physicals up there, and down here I couldn't seem to get used to the diet and altitude; I lost over ten pounds in three weeks." He smiled feebly. "You can see I'm pretty much of a string bean."

"What else?"

"The other thing was . . . I guess I had too many doubts."

"About what?"

"Oh, the whole business, I suppose. Sometimes I'd think it was the greatest thing we ever tried to do, and other times . . . well, apart from everything else, the pettiness used to get me discouraged."

"Pettiness?"

He nodded. "Big people acting little. And little people trying to act big. And all the backbiting . . . " He leaned against the window sill. "Oh, there were some big ones who really *were* big, and some little ones who didn't turn out to be so little after all. And even the others—or most of them anyway—might have been all right individually, or with people they wanted to be with, or in a different sort of job. The trouble was, there they all were, all these different types, thrown into the same pot. Right on top of us."

"No wonder you're thin."

He smiled. "Oh, it was partly funny, I know. We had these professors from all over the country, and they'd tell us one thing, and then some business types would come in from Washington and tell us not to believe all that ivory tower stuff. And the Spanish prof got pretty defensive about not being a native speaker—though he did well enough, I thought—and he had all the native speakers on the staff barred from his class because he said they were an upsetting influence. He made it a general ban—I couldn't tell if he was trying to be tactful or just evasive—but there was really only one native speaker on the staff, and he wasn't a native speaker in the sense that he learned it down here; he'd grown up in a Spanish-speaking colony in the New York City area. He—the last one—was *muy macho*—a real man in the Latin sense—and it wasn't all sweetness and light between him and some of the milder academic souls. I remember once, though, there was this delegation from Washington that came and pestered all the souls about the program, and he told the delegation to get the hell out of there and stop interfering. The point is, they all had *something*, and probably more if you could take them one by one, but they kept bumping into each other and sniping at each other until you wondered where the Cold War was supposed to be."

"But you didn't seem to want to drop out," I reminded him.

"That's just it," he said. "Somehow it all *worked*; I mean well enough so we wanted to stay with it. Even when I was most griped, I hated to think that they might let me go. It wasn't just pride, either; there was an excitement about it all that none of us had ever had before. It was a *big* thing we were in on, and all the confusion in the world couldn't touch that. Maybe the confusion even added to the excitement. All I know is, no matter how exhausted or edgy or depressed I'd get—and I used to go to bed after the daily bombardment so riddled with unrelated facts and conflicting advice that I wondered if some genius in Washington had found the secret of absolute disorder—there was still this feeling of excitement that carried me through. I was over-stimulated, I guess."

"And now?"

"I'm still trying to hang on, I suppose. I'm afraid I've embarrassed them; they didn't want to tell me flatly I was out—they're pretty sensitive about their problem children, and seem to work overtime trying to avoid doing anything that might backfire. I can't say I blame them; after all, nobody knows *for sure* about anybody else. And they can't pretend there isn't a spotlight on the operation. Sometimes you just can't tell if you stand to lose more by kicking somebody out or leaving him in. Either way there's a spotlight to worry about. That damned spotlight . . ."

"What about it?"

"I can't look back on the program without thinking of that spotlight. It was so much a part of the whole experience it seemed to go with the training, like a special course on how to get along with people you don't know and can't see. It was there for the staff too, and I guess it was tougher on some of them than on us. Some had stayed in the ivy shadows so long it was a real shock to them. Wherever you went and whatever you tried to do, you couldn't be sure you wouldn't run into a camera or a microphone or just a long sharp pencil ready to shaft you into saying something that might or might not come out in print the way you said it." He shook his head. "I never realized before how much you were at the mercy of some of those fellows. Most of them were fair enough, but there were some real crackpots."

"Such as?"

"Well, there were some extremist publications that twisted what you said to make out the program was racist or subversive or about to collapse—that sort of thing. We used to post some of the articles on the bulletin board; they were good for laughs, but they were frightening too. They reminded you of all the pressure groups taking potshots at the program and trying to undermine it. No matter how crazy their viewpoint seemed to you, you had to remember it was deadly serious to them, and if some of them had their way, you'd be strung up or clapped in jail tomorrow."

"Or exiled," I said. "You might even find yourself down here."

He chuckled. "Sometimes it all seems like a madhouse, doesn't it? But it isn't. It's just a lot of different systems of logic, I suppose."

"Someone might say that's what you find in a madhouse."

"I guess so. Still . . ." He trailed into thought. A light rain had started, and I could hear a few old voices calling children to shelter; those who were kept largely indoors by age were the first to call others to them. The least sign of rain was for them a promise of loneliness eased, and I had often seen their faces like so many framed death masks in the hut windows as I walked along the pueblo road; their eyes were turned to the clouds, urging the dark ones closer. Peter's face was now pressed close to the rain, and he was breathing deeply. I could not mistake it: it was the look of a child of the city who was discovering the smell of wet earth.

"I . . . I felt so strange suddenly," he said at last. "I was going to say something more about the spotlight, and then I felt as if all at once I had come out of it, and for the first time in almost three months was free of it. But then . . . then I realized that I wasn't free of it at all, that I was right in the middle of it. The pueblo's the spotlight now, isn't it?"

"I'd say that depended on your system of logic."

"Yes, but . . ." He reached out and touched the rain. "It

seems so odd to go right through a window this way," he said dreamily. "As if an absence of glass were something just invented."

"The pueblo's full of inventions like that," I said. "Wait till you fall in what we call a mud hole. You'll want to send a special postcard to the home folks about that."

"Maybe I will," he said defensively.

"Just be sure you mail it, then," I said. "Don't drop it on the road. It might fall into evil hands."

"Thanks," he said drily.

"Remember," I said, "you heard it here first."

"Yes, Sahib."

"Remember also," I said, "we have some of these inventions in the States."

"I wasn't being critical," he said. "And I didn't think I was being patronizing."

"You were just being enchanted," I said. "That's what you were being."

"Is that so bad?"

"Not especially. It's good of you to show me your child-like sense of wonder. Just don't use the word 'picturesque.' "

He looked at me curiously. "You *do* get angry, don't you?"

"There goes your child-like sense of wonder again." I took out my cigarettes. "Yes, I get angry."

"I'd like to find out what makes an anthropologist angry."

"I don't get angry as an anthropologist," I said. "I get angry as a person." I lit a cigarette and inhaled the strong sweetened smoke.

"I'd still like to find out why," he said. "There are other things I'd like to find out. Maybe they all go together."

"Maybe. I take it that's why you're here?"

"Yes." He turned back to the window. "I'm not exactly disowned, but I'm here more or less on my own. It was all worked out with my parents. It's even possible the Peace Corps may pick me up again formally after awhile. But . . ."

41

"But what?"

"I suppose it goes back to those systems of logic we were talking about. I got to the point where I couldn't be sure I was doing what was right. Just because somebody else believed it was right wasn't enough. There were beliefs to spare about the Peace Corps, and . . . well, I couldn't honestly say I wasn't being sold a bill of goods. Maybe all of it was just something to keep the natives from getting restless. So . . ."

"So," I said, "you're here. Are you planning to help the natives?"

"Oh, I can be helpful, I guess. I have, how they say, skills. But before I wish them on anybody, I want to learn more about help—what it is, what it isn't."

"You've picked some interesting questions." I went to the door. "Lately it always seems to be raining when I leave a place. Maybe I shouldn't stay so long."

"Or leave so early," he said.

"Nice of you to put it that way," I said. "In case I didn't make it clear: welcome."

III

The machetes were busy in the plaza, cutting the grass close to the ground for the run of the *vaca loca* that night. The *vaca loca* was a fiesta creature—the skull of a cow or bull mounted on a hooded frame that concealed the carrier. The horns were wrapped with rags soaked in kerosene, and when the plaza was sufficiently filled with celebrants, into their midst would charge the *vaca loca* with skull lowered and horns blazing. Those who had drunk too much to dodge were felled, and those who had drunk too little to play were scattered, but those who had drunk just enough became *toreros,* slipping the wild charges with *ruanas* or coats for capes.

I wandered over to Ernesto, who was just taking his third swing at the same clump of weeds. "*Hola,*" he said, straightening up. "Personally, I think the machete is overrated." His long dark hair, usually so neatly combed, hung wetly over his forehead under a mat of cuttings. "At least I know why I'm a schoolmaster."

"So why don't you stop all this and go teach somebody something?" I suggested.

"I would," he said, "but I seem to be in charge here." He waved his machete toward Sebastian. "This morning, at least, I represent the established order, and it wouldn't do to leave the field to revolutionaries. Not that I plan to represent anything tonight, you understand." He watched Sebastian with interest. "I feel almost inadequate when I see such form."

"He's closer to the ground than you," I said consolingly.

"In more ways than one, I like to think." He casually flipped his machete so that it stuck in the ground. "Another of my amazing but useless feats," he said rather sadly. "Nevertheless . . ."

"Nevertheless what?"

"What, after all, is usefulness? Sometimes it seems quite useless."

"That's another amazing feat," I said. "To be so deep so early."

"Amazing but useless," he said. "Nevertheless . . ."

"I think you have something going," I said. "Nourish it, and it may last forever."

"You may take notes on it if you wish," he said magnanimously. "You *used* to take notes on almost everything."

"When I started out," I said, "I used to lose too much if I didn't take notes. Now I find I lose too much if I do. Have you seen Peter?"

"Only from afar. He's probably off somewhere considering things. Yesterday he was considering plants, I understand. Today—*quién sabe?* Perhaps a cow and her ticks."

"Why not?" I said. "A sense of wonder must be nourished, Don Ernesto."

"Personally," he said, "I have never considered a tick. Other things, yes, but never a tick. I'm not criticizing ticks, Don Guillermo. Nevertheless . . ."

"Nevertheless?"

"My personal feeling is, if a tick must be considered, let another tick do it. A parochial attitude, you say?"

"I didn't say."

"Then you thought. You considered. You considered my refusal to consider any and all ticks, and you concluded . . ."

44

"I concluded I'd better ask somebody else where Peter is."

Ernesto pulled his machete from the ground. "When you find him, you may tell him he's welcome to join our little group in considering the ways of grass." He slashed moodily through a small patch. "At the same time, you should advise him not to. The ways of grass are not nearly as interesting as the ways of, say, women. You would agree?"

"It seems probable."

"I'm afraid it's a probability that hasn't occurred to your young friend in the week he's been here. Why does he stay to himself so much?"

"I don't know," I said. "I'd guess he wants to check the borders before moving all the way in. He may be shy, too."

"You don't consider you ought to help?"

"Just now he distrusts help, Don Ernesto; giving it, taking it. He prefers to make his own moves, and I for one say what I said about the cow and her ticks: why not?"

"You are either tolerant, Don Guillermo, or lazy. Or perhaps they are not so different; perhaps tolerant people are mostly those who are really just too lazy to do anything about anybody. There are certainly some in the world who ought to have something done about them."

"Such as?"

"The more I consider," he said, "the more I suspect that a few *gringos* would be included. Among others, of course."

"I'm glad you added that of course."

"I could do no less," he said, "for one who has stopped taking notes."

The church at the far edge of the plaza was a lime-coated square brick building with an adobe bell tower and cement floor. It was only twelve years old, and some of the women of the pueblo still complained, as if it were yesterday's mistake, that it was a sinful shame to have run out of brick before the tower was started. Others, however, were of the opinion that the adobe was closer to heaven by right, and that such expensive frills as bricks were doing the devil's work.

The *fiesteros*, who were in charge of the fiesta arrangements, were in the church now, putting everything in order for the arrival of the priest that afternoon. The *fiesteros* belonged to the local *cofradía* or church brotherhood of the Sacred Heart of Jesus. The fiesta commemorating the Sacred Heart was usually held a week or two after the official observance date of June 20th, since the priest served other pueblos in the area. This year it was being held only six days late, which seemed rather too early to some. Doña Victoria, who had not finished patching her fiesta dress (she had great difficulty threading a needle, and would let no one do it for her), had in fact grumbled loudly out the window at me on my way to the plaza; in her judgment the priest was coming with indecent haste, much in the manner of a lover pressing himself on a woman before she has had a chance to warm up.

As I approached the church, José and another *fiestero* came out for a smoke on the steps. I waved to José and he left the steps to meet me.

"Have you seen Peter?" I asked.

He brushed church dust and cigarette ashes from his black suit. "No," he said, giving a final flick to his fly. "He has been all but invisible to me. Of course, I have never claimed I could see especially well. But since he lives with me, one would have thought . . . still, I've been busy with my churchly chores, and . . . on the whole, the answer *does* seem to stand as no. Has he stolen anything from you?"

"Nothing."

"Just what he has stolen from me, Don Guillermo. I say it happily"—he spoke as a pallbearer might speak to a relative of the deceased—"though I confess I have long had a lingering hope that a *gringo* might steal something small from me." His frozen face seemed to soften momentarily. "Ah, the mad little desires we all have. Even so . . . " He dropped his cigarette on the grass and scrunched it under a sandal. "Even so, the point is . . ." He reached in a back pocket and pulled out a half pint of *aguardiente*. "At my stage of life I have come to believe . . ." He took a swallow and produced an incredibly flat belch. "If a man does not steal from you, why look for him?"

"Every day I learn something from you, Don José."

"It is nothing to be ashamed of, Don Guillermo. Almost everyone learns something from me. I have never claimed otherwise. But if you try, you can forget it painlessly." He took another swallow and offered me the bottle.

Early as it was, I would have sampled it, but José had an interesting habit of spitting back into the bottle during a swallow, and it was said that anyone drinking with José should have either two glasses or a separate bottle. Only Alejandro, who rejected nothing related to thirst, drank freely from the same bottle with José and it was suspected that in such bouts Alejandro gave as good as he got. "*Gracias*, no," I said. "I have had great quantities of orange juice this morning, and somehow, looking at that bottle . . ."

"You have a certain sensation?"

"Yes, it definitely is a sensation. A kind of . . ."

"Turning?"

"Just the right word, Don José. Yes, definitely a turning. Time and again you score."

"My interest in measurements has given me a certain precision," he said modestly. "If there were a little more Spanish and a little less Indian in me, I might be rich."

"I thought you were proud of the Indian."

"Ah, it is one thing to be proud, and another to be rich. Besides, I am not really so proud." He took another swallow. "I am proud mostly in self-defense." He put the bottle back in his pocket, and looked toward the church. The other *fiestero* had gone inside. José sighed. "There's another pound or so of dust to absorb, so I'd better . . . the way the dust in there settles on me, I feel like one of those vacuum cleaners they have in the city . . . some people seem to have a talent for drawing dust . . . sawdust, church dust . . .

47

what can one do with such a talent?" Muttering, he moved away.

Two vendors from the city came into the plaza: one sold candy, the other religious pictures (some of them cut from magazines and framed). It was too early to expect much business, so they sat by their large baskets and talked. A photographer arrived shortly afterward and set up his equipment; he would be taking family portraits later on. He half-heartedly solicited the other two, who returned the solicitation, and the whole business was shrugged off with mutual relief.

Romelio bustled into the plaza and, with a show of efficiency especially remarkable because he neither touched anything nor seemed to look directly at anything, inspected the baskets and the photographic equipment. Today he would be on a perpetual inspection tour: candy, religious pictures, tripods—whatever he came across would have to pass muster. Whenever he rested, he faced the sun, drawing a gleam to his badge and the shiny black visor of his blue cap. He never rested long, however; there was always something to catch his eye, and off he would go to check on it. Just what he might find in candy and cutouts, no one could say, but when he passed, people nodded in approval: justice was being done.

Romelio came to the tree under which I sat, gave the tree a quick once-over, did the same to me, and paused just outside the shade, letting his badge and visor shine at me as if readying me for the third-degree. "So," he said, "you just sit."

"I confess," I said. "What's more, I've done it before."

"If I had a form, I'd make you fill it out."

"Why don't you just take fingerprints?" I suggested. "You wouldn't need a lot of long forms for that. You wouldn't even have to go over them; you could just put them in a box and refer to them from time to time."

He smiled. "So I could, so I could. Where's your young friend?"

"I've been more or less looking for him myself."

"By sitting under a tree?"

"It's something I've learned here: the long way around is often the best, and usually the most interesting. Sooner or later he'll probably come to the plaza, no?"

"*Sí.* Everything comes to the plaza today. If you see anything illegal, report to me."

"Within forty-eight hours?"

"Unless you become sick."

"Tonight is the night for sickness, Don Romelio. What about you, *amigo?* Are you going to break the law a little?"

"I never break the law, Don Guillermo. I break heads that break the law."

"How amazing that people still walk and talk around here! Is it possible we have our own special laws?"

"It is possible. Anything is possible." He smiled again, but there was something behind the smile that reminded me I had twice seen him crush a man's skull. It was not that the crushings had been unprovoked—one of the men had gone berserk during Mass and had attacked the sexton; the other had started on a drunken rampage with a machete in each hand—but the almost casual manner in which Romelio had struck had impressed me. There had been a sort of easy gusto about it that the Anglo-Saxon would tend to find callous and even cruel. Yet with the passing of the months I had come to think of the gesture as closest in kind to a shrug: there were forms to be observed, and death after all was everywhere.

"So you will not join us tonight?"

"I did not say that, Don Guillermo. I said I never break the law. I also said anything is possible. So it is possible I may join you."

"If you do," I said, "you must permit me to buy you a legal beverage with legal tender, and we will drink to the law."

"It is possible." He took off his cap and polished the visor on a sleeve. "Your young friend," he said casually, "he is old enough to drink?"

"The letter I had from the consulate said he was twenty-two."

"You had a letter from the consulate?"

"A very brief one, Don Romelio. It just said he was coming and anything I could do for him would be appreciated. It was almost a form letter."

His eyes flashed interest. "Your government is very efficient."

"Not so efficient, Don Romelio. He came before the letter did."

He put his cap back on and let the glare find my face. "Ah," he said soothingly, "that may be the fault of our postal service." His voice had a hypnotic remoteness and seemed indeed to be coming right out of the sun. "Tell me, Don Guillermo, does your friend have . . . how shall I say . . . diplomatic immunity?"

"Not as far as I know, Don Romelio."

"So that if I should have to . . . take action against him, there would be no . . . official obstacle?"

"Not to my knowledge. He hasn't done anything wrong, has he?"

"Not yet. No, not yet. But . . ." Romelio hesitated, then went on very carefully. "To be frank, Don Guillermo, I am a little worried about this *gringo*. He is perhaps too . . . intense, no?"

"Perhaps it is only that he is young."

"Perhaps. But . . . it seems to me there is too much intensity and too much . . . innocence in him. These are not so bad in themselves, but put together . . . and in a strange country . . . to me these are warning signs."

"So?"

"So," he said, speaking very formally now, "I do not want you to blame me too much if . . . at least you will know I will not have acted on impulse."

It occurred to me that perhaps he was using the sun as a shield more than a weapon now: he could not be seen saying what he was reluctant to say. I had learned early how much aggression was carried in courtesy; lately I had come to be sensitive to the amount of courtesy carried in seeming aggression. "Would you have me speak to him, Don Romelio?"

"What could really be said? He has wronged no one, bothered no one. I would not wish to make him even more intense. However . . ."

"Yes?"

"If you see him, share your tree with him. If he could learn to relax . . ."

"One and all are welcome to tap my great laziness," I said. "But it is a difficult thing to give away. There's little demand for laziness these days. Still, I'll offer it freely."

"Good. I suspect we can do little, really, but wait."

"I'm waiting."

"And watch."

"I'm watching."

"And be ready to move. To protect him, if possible."

"And if necessary."

He nodded. "You seem to think he will be able to . . . save himself."

"It's my hope, Don Romelio."

"I join you in that hope," he said in a voice that hid well whatever hope it held.

Shortly before noon María brought me a pot of *sancocho*, the potato-yuca-platano soup-stew, which served as the area's chief dietary item. She was wearing her white fiesta blouse with a brightly patterned skirt she had made from material Sebastian Cruzeros had presented to her shortly after my arrival in the pueblo. Sebastian had wanted to look me over in my pueblo quarters, and the gift had given him access. María still did not know—or pretended not to know—the origin of the material, but it was actually a collection of cuts from flags which had been on display during an international soccer tournament in the city. The tournament had ended in a riot, and the flags had disappeared. As María bent over to hand me the pot, she could have been saluted from any direction by millions.

"I was afraid you might take your siesta *before* lunch," she said. "You are so enterprising."

"Enterprising!?"

"Certainly. You *gringos* always want to get ahead. I could just picture you taking your siesta before everyone else." She brushed her long hair from her thin mulatto face and tried to look serious.

"Oh, come now, María! I really *am* busy, you know."

"I could tell at once. You are busy thinking up ways to make us all rich." Her beautiful white teeth caught the sun Romelio had left.

"I did that yesterday," I said. "I'm working on something else now."

"Am I permitted to know?"

"I'll confide in you. I'm busy losing my identity."

"Ah, in some ways you have," she said. "But in other ways it's clear you're you."

"I've failed again," I said, taking the lid from the pot. "I'd better go back to making you rich." I sampled the *sancocho* with the large wooden spoon in the pot. "After lunch."

"And your siesta."

"It's these full schedules that have kept me from success so far," I said, leaning back against the tree. "Is there no one to lift my spoon for me?"

She laughed. "One to lift it, and one to turn it." She knelt by the pot and sniffed it. "There is a little too much potato, but it is not so bad, is it?"

"Like everything that comes from your kitchen and heart, María, it is truly good. If it were not for the memory of your poor husband, I would propose at once."

"You have no memory of my husband," she said drily.

"But I do." She stood up. "Besides, you put my kitchen before my heart."

"With me it is the last that is best, María. The first shall be last, you know, and the last first."

"At least it helps keep the poor in their place," she said, smiling.

"Even so, it could be true, you know."

She shrugged. "If it is, that's one thing. But it's another thing to hear from the high place that the low place is mine, and that my time to move up is after I'm dead. I've had better offers, lover."

"See how important the last is? You called me lover."

"I am too old for consequences. If I were not, I might be under that tree with you."

"It could be pretty messy, with the *sancocho* and all. Still, there's an expression we have which may make no sense whatever to you, especially since I'll say it backwards: all these potatoes and no meat."

"I understand what *carne* has to do with carnal," she said. "I am not the last in understanding. But you need someone a few hundred years younger, *Guillermito*. Someone like Rosa Linda Perico, no?"

"As Don Romelio would say, it is possible."

"I imagine even you are capable of behaving like an animal," she said mockingly.

"As Don José would say, I have never claimed otherwise."

The church bell rang; the priest had arrived. As he strode into the plaza, followed by the musicians who had come on the same bus, the *fiesteros* came from the church to greet him formally. Children and dogs hovered near him with special curiosity; since he came to the pueblo regularly only for the four fiestas celebrated locally, he was a near-stranger to many. He was a lean, brisk figure with the face of a hungry scholar determined not to eat. His black robe cracked in the sharp wind. Usually the wind seemed to rise with the people from their siestas in the early afternoon—today, with so many siestas deferred, it seemed to have been brought by the priest as a sign of his power. He was a walking whip.

José, every inch a pallbearer, led him into the church. In a few minutes the priest came out alone, nodded at the trimmed grass, looked coldly at the three entrepreneurs (the seller of religious pictures had told the candy vendor earlier that he wanted to get his offerings blessed by the priest, but now he just cringed), and started out of the plaza with a crisp decisiveness, as if he had had quite enough of the pueblo and would return to the city as fast as the wind he had produced would carry him.

He paused by my tree. "Don Guillermo."

"In the flesh," I said humbly. "If I may be forgiven the use of the word."

"You are not forgiven," he said. "There will be much to count against you in the end."

"You say only what I believe, *Padre.*"

"Of course," he added, "there may be a residue we can count for you."

"You give me great hope, *Padre.*"

He came closer. The wind seemed fiercer than before; leaves swirled about his robe. "I have heard there is another American here."

"We are all Americans, *Padre.*"

"I use the term as the *Yanquis* use it. Only for themselves."

"As some *Yanquis* use it, *Padre.* It is a custom. It is not meant to give offense."

"It gives offense nonetheless. As you say, we are all Americans. Those who speak as if it were otherwise are helping to ensure that it *will* be otherwise. The difficulty is . . ." He frowned.

"Go on, *Padre.*"

"The difficulty, Don Guillermo, is that we are not really the same kind of Americans. Our own development has been quite different from yours. In many ways we are closer to other parts of the world than to you. You must . . ."

"Yes, *Padre?*"

"It may seem curious to say that these days it is the strong who must be especially careful not to offend, but I believe it is so." He plucked a leaf from the air and glared at it, as if it had sinned in leaving the tree for a wild ride in the wind. "It will not be easy to hold things together . . ."

"Yet we must try, *Padre.*"

"Yes," he said, his voice suddenly softened. "We must try." He dropped the leaf and the subject and curtly went on, "Is the boy Catholic?"

"I didn't ask him, *Padre.*"

"You wouldn't," he said. "His name?"

"Peter. Peter Bradley."

"Peter," he said meditatively. "The weakest and strongest saint. Some would say, some would say. Where is he?"

"Saint Peter or Peter Bradley, *Padre?*"

He looked at me quizzically. "I see you cannot help wading in sacrilege."

"I feel almost pushed into it, *Padre.* Perhaps it is the Devil."

"Or foolishness."

"Yes, *Padre.*"

"Where is Peter Bradley?"

"I don't know, *Padre.* He takes walks."

"Why?"

"To consider things, I believe."

"What things?"

"Oh, plants, ticks, odors . . ."

"Ticks?"

"It is only a supposition, *Padre.* He considers all kinds of things. Perhaps God."

"Ticks and God," he murmured. "Why do I listen?"

"You have a great tolerance, *Padre.*"

55

He shook his head and sighed. "Unfortunately, I have my own perversities to deal with."

"I trust they will be forgiven, *Padre.*"

"I wonder." He looked thoughtful. "Speaking of perversities, do you still receive that abysmal magazine?"

"*Mad* magazine? Yes, *Padre,* it persists in coming. I seem to be able to do nothing about it."

"And you still pass along the copies to Sebastian?"

"Yes, *Padre.* Do you object?"

"On the contrary, it gives me a certain access to him. In fact, he stays remarkably close to me while I read."

"Why is that, *Padre?*"

"I believe he wonders what I find so funny. I tried to explain it to him once, but . . . who can explain? Then, too, he suspects there are things besides humor in it that you and I can get but he can't—secret things, perhaps from your State Department." He looked at his watch. "I may as well stop by before the procession."

"He's probably there. He finished with the grass a little while ago, so he might be resting."

"It's not so much what he's resting from as what he's resting for that worries me." He sighed. "I hope it won't be too wild tonight." He turned away.

"Give my regards to Doña Victoria," I said. "If she seems a little upset, it's because her dress isn't ready."

He nodded. "The rest of her usually seems ready for anything."

"No less than you, *Padre.*"

"I wonder," he said, looking down the pueblo road. "Lately it's been . . ." His voice was lost in the wind.

The church bell rang again, and light from lanterns and candles began to grow behind the windows. The bass drum started to boom from the steps, drawing people into the plaza. A few entered the church for rosaries and prayers. I left my tree and followed. José came out, shaking his head. "They're all saying rosaries to the beat of the drum," he shouted at me. "Why don't you have the drum stopped?" I suggested. He looked at me blankly. "I don't claim it's wrong," he said.

I went inside for a short prayer. The benches were neatly arranged, the dust and cobwebs had been largely exorcised, the walls and air were still damp from the watering down, and the smell of burning kerosene and wax was strong. María was in front, lighting a candle, probably in memory of her husband, whose only fault—according to her—had been a love of misery. Five old women were huddled close together on a side bench: a lump of musty wrappings, vibrating with the drum. Two rows behind them an old man knelt, head bowed, scratching his crotch. Three younger men— brothers—sat stiffly in the middle of the church, obviously uncomfortable in their homemade suits, sweat spreading from their armpits. A young boy came in, nervously crossed himself backwards, emitted a shocked belch and crossed himself the right way twice over for good measure. A young girl sauntered in, spilling a temporary surplus of chastity left and right, carrying her virtue up front to the largest unlit candle, which she ignited as if she were putting torch to the prototypical penis. On the way back she noticed the old man scratching his crotch, and spat disgustedly in the aisle.

Outside again I ducked under the backswing of the drummer and sat on the steps, watching people go in and out. Suits and dresses were largely drab in color and haphazard in cut and fit. Faces were constrained, with the conformity of impending ritual. The hubbub of the talk died out as the talkers approached the steps; the drummer swung as if his job were to crush talk forever. The three other musicians came up and tried to say something to the drummer; he could neither hear what they were saying nor could he bring himself to stop thumping long enough to make it possible. Finally the three ranged themselves beside him and joined in raggedly with cornet, clarinet, and French horn. The noise now exploding above me drove me from the steps; I wondered what it added to the saying of prayers inside.

57

The priest came into the plaza to get the procession started. With the help of the *fiesteros,* he rearranged people into a double file, women on one side and men on the other. The schoolboys and schoolgirls had assembled at their respective schools, and now they came over, led by their teachers (Ernesto carried himself with such dignity I suspected he had done a little preliminary research on the properties of *aguardiente*), to head the files appropriate to their sex (although an oversized boy named Enrique Ramírez—a distant cousin of José—confused things momentarily by slipping into the female line and goosing an old woman who laughed delightedly). Between the files the priest took his place at the front, with the four *fiesteros* who were to carry the image in the middle and the musicians bringing up the rear. Unfortunately, they did not bring it up very successfully, since the clarinet player gagged on his instrument when it was caught by the backswing of the drummer, and the rest of the procession had gained fifty yards before he was able to blow without losing anything. Still, the procession was at last under way, and the priest was careful not to look behind him.

The procession circled the plaza, threatening briefly to lap the clarinet player, who straggled behind his colleagues until a small stone from Enrique's slingshot spurred him. Candles were produced from pockets and shawls, to be lit as soon as the circling stopped. For a time it seemed that it would never stop, since the priest was apparently thinking about things of such consequence that he could not slow down. Faster and faster he went, until Doña Victoria, who was being virtually carried by her nephew and the police inspector, swore at him so loudly that several of her contemporaries looked fearfully skyward, as if expecting the retributive bolt from heaven instantly. The procession slowed, with a certain amount of bumping as the files closed up, and came to a stop outside the boys' school, where the image now resided.

The small statue representing the Sacred Heart of Jesus

regularly "visited" the homes of the *cofradía* members in succession, with each brotherhood member receiving it in the afternoon and taking it to the home of the next designated member the following afternoon. The travel schedule was so arranged that the *fiesteros* would know exactly where the statue would be on any given day; as soon as they were notified of the fiesta date by the priest they could, if they chose, make preparations to have the procession stop at the appropriate home and transport the statue from there to the church. On two past occasions, however, such preparations had misfired: once the specified home had been a good three miles from the church, and the wind and rain had been so heavy that the procession had arrived only to find that the hut had been swept down into the river, and the statue was not recovered until two weeks later, when a fisherman downstream pulled it in and promptly began shouting in terror; the other time, the family dog had dragged the statue from the home while the procession was forming, and had buried it in a place he either could not or would not reveal to the harried *fiesteros*—it was later discovered with the help of a divining rod by a curer who was found using the statue for black magic. Since then the statue was placed in the boys' school well in advance of the fiesta. The efficacy imputed to the image had not at all been diminished by its misadventures. On the contrary, its survival through such trials was regarded as not without significance. It was said to be no accident that it had found its way to the hands of a fisherman, or that it not only had outlasted the forces of evil but had even maneuvered them into an act of rescue.

The image bearers entered the school and the priest told people to light their candles. There was a great fumbling for matches, and a few curses at inconsiderate gusts. The end of the afternoon had become the beginnings of night, and the priest called on people to hurry up with the candle lighting. "We'll never find our way back to the church without those candles," he said, and several old women tittered appreciatively. The image bearers came out of the school with the statue, housed in a freshly painted red box on a wooden platform with handles for the carriers. The platform was decorated with artificial flowers and a blackboard eraser which one of the bearers now noticed and quickly carried back into the school.

An old man with a bell rushed up and made apologetic clangs to the priest. "You'll never guess where it was, *Padre*," he said, and everyone within earshot leaned closer to find out where it was. "It was right there on the shelf where I'd left it," the old man said, and the listeners leaned back disappointedly. The old man was Procopio Fernández, the sexton, currently under treatment in a city clinic for a disease about which nothing was locally known but much speculated. The priest waved him to the front of the files.

Procopio held his bell up high until the image bearers were back in position, then rang it authoritatively and the procession started again. It had suddenly become wholly night—dusk was a momentary thing here—and with the moon hidden the only light came from the candles, each held close to the sheltering coat or shawl ahead. Halfway to the church Procopio rang his bell again and the procession stopped—not all at once, since the danger of being singed by an abrupt stop was too obvious to too many. Three of the musicians began to sing a hymn, with the fourth accompanying on the clarinet. Five men (including Alejandro, whose face in the uneven candlelight might have been that of a man plagued by thirst in the flames of hell) commenced to set off skyrockets, lighting them with the candles at a pace oddly consonant with the rhythm of the hymn. There were murmurs from the files; whether intended as a reaction to the skyrockets or participation in the hymn I could not have said. The sky was wild, and now the moon, as if provoked out of hiding, appeared over the church. The clarinet stopped three bars before the singers did; the bell was rung, and the procession moved on.

When the procession reached the church, Procopio gave his last ring. The image was carried into the church and placed near the altar, while another hymn was offered without clarinet and skyrockets. Then, as the priest waited outside to note any who failed to enter, the church filled for the services.

Men and boys (If I mention males first, it is because they unequivocally came first here.) moved to the right of the church, women and girls to the left. While the males saw to it that their heads were uncovered, the females saw to it that theirs were covered; in a few families the man simply tossed his hat to his wife. Some seemed confused by the benches, which were not part of the regular furnishings of the church but were brought from the schools on special occasions. A local mark of pride was endurance in kneeling; those who felt up to it knelt, while the others sat hunched over as if the difference were without distinction.

The liturgy I found as soothing as always: a humming that let feeling replace thought. I reminded myself that I was not a very good Catholic, especially since I was a Protestant, but then I was a misfit in any liturgy. Still, what I was had little to do with what was, and in my own unworthy way I respected, even loved, what was here.

The priest was now reading the names of those who had contributed time and pesos in sanctioned amounts to the fiesta arrangements. Those named quivered as if strummed. He ended with a more general commendation of all present "for their efforts however modest," and urged everyone to give more (he did not precede it with "even") generous support to the next fiesta. "There's not a soul here who can't afford at least a two-centavo candle," he said, inflecting the word "soul" as if to suggest that its salvation—with the scales of good and bad deeds otherwise balanced—might depend on a two-centavo candle. Then he advised unmarried mothers to get married ("If you hesitate because of shame, it means you realize your need for redemption!"); warned against Communism ("You want to be buried in holy ground, don't you?") for a few minutes, during which Sebastian managed a resonant belch; and exhorted his listeners not to nourish beliefs in ghosts, phantoms, goblins, and other discredited denizens of the supernatural ("Let's not be slaves of superstition.").

José took up a collection, thrusting his long-handled pan under eyes as they opened from prayer, and rattling the pan under eyes that seemed closed suspiciously long. Sebastian put in a button; then, when the pan came near him again, surreptitiously dropped in a peso.

The final words of the priest were strangely soft, with the simplicity of the counsel ("Help one another . . ." "Be as children . . ." "Respect the gifts of God . . ." "Do not forsake your family . . .") given a certain majesty by the gentle directness of the voice and the stateliness of the lean figure whose face no longer seemed hungry.

At the conclusion the musicians played (Was it my imagination that they sounded better than before?) on the church steps as the people filed out. Except for the music —which itself was slow and subdued—and the shuffling of feet, there were no sounds to disturb the pervasive peace of the departure. People moved as if in a dream, as perhaps they were, and the priest walked with a dignity which seemed to be only a few minutes old, yet which also seemed to have been with him forever. The smell of candles and lanterns burning in musty air seemed to follow us all outside, as if the essence of the church—for a moment, at least—had been sent into the world to flavor it.

The people waited beside the steps, watching the priest move slowly down them. Some reached out to touch him, and others just reached out. The music stopped, and the musicians looked at each other as if wondering why it had sounded so good.

The priest moved beyond the crowd, then turned, his hand raised to bless those who watched. Light from the church doorway touched his hand, and moonlight offered his head a crown. Then, with the air stilled in reverence richer than any I could remember, another light was added.

"Look out, *Padre!*" someone cried. "*Cuidado!*"

Around a corner of the church came the blazing horns of the *vaca loca*, heading directly for the priest. Some of the women shrieked, and a few of the men shouted to the priest to dodge, but most watched dumbly, paralyzed by the astonishing sight. The priest seemed too startled to move at first—his hand was still raised, blessing chaos—then he glanced behind him, and whirled to confront the charge. Like a creature of hellfire, the *vaca loca* streaked toward the priest, who strained to move out of the way, but whose feet, invisible under the black robe, seemed now to be lost.

Less than ten yards from the priest the *vaca loca* staggered, and with a shudder tried to change course. But now the priest had found his feet, and like two persons who seek to pass each other in a corridor but keep moving in the same direction, fire and robe zigzagged together in a brief bizarre dance.

An instant before collision the *vaca loca* dove to the ground, vanishing for a moment under the robe as if good had swallowed up evil. Then the horns, still ablaze, came out the other side, and the priest toppled onto the back of the carrier. There he sat, robe askew and eyes remote, as if he were riding the beast of hell backwards through a nightmare.

The *vaca loca* struggled to take off its hood, and at last the blazing horns were free of the carrier.

"Well, Peter," I said, "at least you missed the collection."

IV

Peter and the priest slowly disentangled themselves, each looking at the other warily. There were throat clearings and tentative rumblings, but neither spoke until the disentanglement was completed—one might have thought there was a mutual suspicion that a word from either side could break the spell of separation and make the coupling permanent.

Now they stood apart, circled by rapt watchers. The priest brushed off his robe very deliberately, as if trying to stroke dignity back into himself. Peter wobbled and wavered —there was no dignity anywhere for him—and finally produced a beautifully apologetic, and wholly inappropriate, smile.

Yet, amazingly—almost shockingly—the smile was returned.

"I must say," said the priest, "it's a new experience to be tumbled from a state of grace in such a fashion."

"At least you came out on top, *Padre*," said Peter.

"The church always comes out on top," said the priest wryly. He gave his robe a sharp tug to straighten it. "So you are Peter?"

"Yes, *Padre*, I'm afraid so." Peter's face was even redder than usual—I supposed he had been drinking, but he smelled only of kerosene and grass.

"Peter, Peter." (I thought for a heady, irrational mo-

ment that the priest was going to add, "pumpkin eater.")
"Tell me, Peter . . ." Peter leaned toward the priest, obviously ready to oblige by telling whatever he could. "Peter, my boy, may I assume you plan to take the sacraments while I'm here?"

"Yes, yes, *Padre*, all of them, certainly," Peter blurted.

"All?" The robe seemed to ripple; the whip was stirring. "Extreme unction? Ordination?"

"I mean all I'm eligible for, *Padre*." Peter smiled sheepishly; there was no return this time.

"What I particularly had in mind was confession, Peter."

"I'll confess, certainly," Peter said promptly. "To anything." He shook his head and grabbed air, trying to recall the last two words.

"To anything?"

"Anything I'm guilty of, I mean." Peter tried to stop wobbling; it *did* seem to put him at a disadvantage. Still, I somehow found myself liking him more than ever.

"Is it much, Peter?"

"Oh, yes, *Padre*. I'm really an impossible person. I sin left and right."

"Left and right?"

"And up and down. Especially up and down. In my thoughts, I mean. I do almost nothing *physically*. But oh, *Padre*, I persist in thinking about it!"

"This is not a confessional, Peter," the priest said drily. "If you wish, you may see me tomorrow. Early."

"Yes, *Padre*, early."

The priest tapped the ground with one of his invisible feet. "You *are* Catholic, Peter?"

"An inadequate one, *Padre*."

"Like one or two others, Peter, like one or two others." The priest looked around at the circle of watchers. "I'll expect a reasonably"—he said "reasonably" as if he suspected that reason had very little to do with it—"complete explanation of all this tomorrow, you understand."

"You see, *Padre*, it all started when I . . ."

"Tomorrow," interrupted the priest firmly, looking again at the circle of watchers. "Though I suppose I'll be one of the last to know, at that." He sighed. "I doubt I'll sleep much; I feel too stimulated. I feel . . ." The circle tightened. "Never mind how I feel. Why should I bother about my feelings? The important thing is . . ." He looked intently at Peter.

"That I'm sorry, *Padre?* I am, you know, deeply and . . ."

The priest waved the rest of it away. "No, Peter, the important thing is to know . . . when a warning is being given."

"Yes, *Padre,* I'll keep it in . . ."

"No, Peter, no," the priest said so softly I could scarcely hear him. "Not for you, Peter. For me."

The fiesta night had exploded. Skyrockets swooshed and boomed, music shrieked and thumped from the *cantinas,* and in the plaza the *vaca loca* was running wild again, exhausting a small cast of carriers. Peter, Ernesto, José, and I made our way to Alejandro's *cantina,* stopping first at José's home to pick up a little table he had built to carry with him on fiesta occasions when existing facilities elsewhere were apt to be overused. We managed to set it up in a temporarily deserted corner (someone had thrown up rather violently there, but we were patient), and soon enough Alejandro had brought over a mop, bottle, and glasses, and was busy scrubbing under the table while we were busy pouring above it.

"Ah," Ernesto said happily, "it's so good to have a reserved table."

"If one must collapse," said José, "far better to do so under one's own table."

"It's undignified to collapse under strange tables," Ernesto agreed.

People kept bumping into the table, and there were many who paused to stare with heightened interest at Peter. Sebastian looked at him so keenly I wondered if he were planning to sketch him for one of his posters; he said nothing, however, and I suspected he had not yet decided whether Peter were less dangerous or more dangerous than before.

"So," I said, patting Rosa Linda's behind as she snaked by, "what happened, Peter?" Alejandro gave the floor a last swipe and hurried away; he had been unusually quiet.

"A funny thing happened to me on my way to the plaza," Peter said in a magnificently deadpan voice. "It seems . . ."

"That's the trouble," Ernesto said philosophically. "It always seems. It never is."

"I have never claimed otherwise," José said.

"Let's drink to it," I suggested. We drank to it.

"Have I told it already?" Peter asked.

"I can't be certain," Ernesto said. "Shall we vote on it?" We voted on it. By democratic process, we determined that Peter had not yet told it.

"I'd been out in the fields," Peter said, "trying to figure out why people planted in vertical rows instead of horizontal—there's too much runoff in vertical rows, you know, and erosion's quickened . . ."

"And your story's retarded," Ernesto said. "Please keep these asides—fascinating though they are—to a minimum."

"Sorry," Peter said. "I also looked into the grazing pattern . . ."

"Aha!" I said. "So you *were* considering cows. And doubtless ticks."

"Ticks?"

"Never mind, Peter," I said. "But please get out of the fields and back to the plaza."

"That's just it," he said. "I didn't get to the plaza; not directly, anyway."

"You seem to get nowhere directly," José said glumly. "Not that I'm complaining; my whole life has been . . ."

"*Please*, Don José," Ernesto interrupted. "Proceed, Peter."

"As I was getting ready to start back," Peter said, "Don Alejandro came by, and we got to talking about cows, and he

67

told me all about the *vaca loca.* I don't quite understand it, but the more he talked, the thirstier I became."

"He was put into this world to make people thirsty," José said. "He could talk about dissection and embalming, and it would make you thirsty."

"So," Peter said, "on the way back we stopped at a place where some drinking was going on, and . . ."

"That would be Visenta's place," Ernesto said. "She's a witch."

"The lady *was* rather homely," Peter said.

"I mean she's a *professional* witch," Ernesto said. "A real *bruja.* She has an amazing assortment of spells and charms. Some say Alejandro owes his thirst power partly to her; she's a cousin of his. She's also a midwife and curer. She aborts very well."

"She what?" Peter asked.

"Every now and then Alejandro sends a girl in trouble to her. Not really very often; there isn't much stigma to illegitimacy around here. What happens is . . ."

"*Now* who's breaking into the story?" José said. "Not that I'm complaining; as I've often said, it isn't . . ."

"It certainly isn't," Ernesto said quickly. "Forgive us both, Peter, and please continue."

"So some of the people there offered me a drink, and another, and . . ."

"And before you knew it your trousers were gone," José said solemnly.

"No," Peter said. "But they told me I shouldn't be so aloof, that I ought to take part in things, to join in and . . ."

"Set fire to the priest," José muttered.

"They were really very nice," Peter said a bit tartly. "Very friendly. They told me I could participate in a . . ."

"Noble custom," Ernesto finished, sighing. "The words 'opportunity' and 'honor' were mentioned, perhaps?"

"Yes, they were, but . . ." Peter looked seriously at Ernesto. "It wasn't just a practical joke, was it?"

"No, it wasn't *just* that."

"Wasn't it true about the opportunity and honor?"

"It wasn't *un*true, Peter. Let's just say it was a mixture. We're a mixed people with mixed ways. *Verdad,* Don José?"

"You're the teacher," José said.

"I accept your reassurance," Ernesto said. "So, Peter?"

"So after Alejandro left we drank some more and talked some more, and one thing seemed to drift into another, and suddenly there I was, and there the priest was, and . . ."

"Here we are," Ernesto said, raising his glass.

This was another procession, a faster procession, with no bellringer to stop it. Light colors and heavy shapes whirled by, and I remember telling myself I ought to draw a sample by grabbing every third one. I came up immediately with Rosa Linda. "You're not very random," I said.

"Qué dice?"

"You're so pretty I wish you weren't so young," I said. "On the other hand, if you weren't so young, you might not be so pretty." Her dark hair hung almost to her waist, and I wondered—only wondered—what would happen if I tied it to my chair.

"I plan to stay pretty," she said. "Visenta gave me a charm to help."

"Nobody should live with a witch on purpose," I said. "Come live with me, and *I'll* exploit you."

She giggled; I hated giggles, but not hers. My course at Harvard on field techniques hadn't told me what to do about young apprentices to witches, and at the moment I was rather glad it hadn't. The scientific method had its virtues, but it was a poor thing to tuck in at night. I was professionally compulsive only to a point; then a small, still voice said, "What the hell, what the hell." Which is probably why I wasn't rich and well-known, and why I was still here. Not that I was at all dynamic, or ever really *did* anything, but I kept feeling that if anything shattering was going to happen to me, it was far more likely to happen here than at East

69

Cantaloupe University. I had such a tremendous drive for anonymity that only here—where I was known as an outsider—were passing forces at all likely to bump me briefly before moving on. And even here I often felt all but invisible; it was as if I had burrowed into the culture to hibernate, and emerged wearing part of it. Whatever my success (if it could be counted as success) in adapting, I was a total failure at pigeonholing. Once, when I was lying in the plaza on a clear, sunny day, with children tumbling over me and María approaching with a pitcher of cool spring water, with the sight of the mountains in the distance and the smell of clover all around. I asked myself what ethnographic category could ever hold such a moment, and ended only by kissing a little girl who came too close and chalking it up not to surrogate parenthood or informal recreation patterns but to a sudden feeling of great love.

The trouble with so many ethnographic and ethnological monographs seemed to be that somewhere in the process of classification and analysis the people were lost. What we so often ended up with was a file of systematically impaled —and quite dead—butterflies. Statistically we could show that they hadn't been whirlybirds, but . . .

If I seem to criticize, I'm criticizing myself: here I was, after many drinks and with Rosa Linda and her long, long hair right in front of me, not only able but unable *not* to think about social anthropology; I was myself contaminated, perhaps impaled.

"You look fuzzy," she said.

"I *am* fuzzy," I said. "Now run along and let me draw the next ball."

"*Cómo?*"

"There's a bucket full of red and blue balls," I explained. "An equal number of each. How many balls must I draw— I'm blindfolded, you see—before I can be certain I have two of the same kind?"

She reflected. "Where is this bucket?"

"Far, far away."

"Then why not leave it there?"

"Because I'm far, far away too."

"Is your young friend far, far away?"

"I don't know where he is," I said. "I don't think he knows either. But I think he's going to find out." I paused. "He's not too much older than you. Perhaps you're interested in helping him?"

"I'm interested in many, many things. Even fuzzy things." She scratched one of her beautiful knees. "I do not come here to be bad, you know."

"Oh? Tell me where you go to be bad, and I'll meet you there."

She giggled again, and shook her head. "You are a terrible man. Go play in your bucket of balls, terrible man." She patted my face—a little hard, I thought—and slipped away.

Next I came up with an old rheumy man named Ildefonso Isabella, who hawked and spat with grim abandon. "It wasn't I who did it," he said crossly.

"Did what?" I asked.

"Whatever you're accusing me of." He spat viciously on the floor. "Somebody's always accusing me of things I never even had a chance to do." He picked up my glass and emptied it. "If I weren't of royal blood, I'd strike back." His private —and often public—conviction was that he was a descendant of Queen Isabella. And maybe he was, maybe he was.

"All I'm doing is drawing a sample," I said.

"Leave me out of whatever it was you said," he grumbled, pouring himself another drink from our bottle. "Leave me out of it entirely." He emptied and refilled my glass. "It wasn't *I* who knocked over the priest, you know."

"I'm sure he didn't mean to . . ."

"Funniest thing I ever saw," he said in a voice as sour as his breath. "Shameful. Shameful he didn't finish him off." He quickly downed another drink. "In case you're listening, God, I didn't mean that." He slammed the glass down on the table. "But I couldn't help it if my neck was stiff."

71

"Your neck was stiff?"

"So stiff I couldn't bow my head to pray. And after the service he asked me about it . . ."

"The priest?"

He nodded vigorously; clearly his neck wasn't stiff now. "He asked me, and I told him, and he *doubted* me. I could tell. It didn't matter what I said, he didn't believe me. Oh, I could tell."

"I didn't notice anything like that," I said.

"Oh, it didn't happen today. It was another time. Four years ago. Almost exactly." He wiped his nose on a sleeve thick with past wipings. "It's an awful thing to be doubted by one's priest."

"But four years ago . . ."

"Oh, he hasn't forgotten. I can tell. He looks at me in that certain way, and . . ." He sniffled and wiped again. ". . . *accuses!* It's no pleasure, no . . . things I never even had a chance to do."

"I thought it was about your neck."

"My what, Señor?"

"Your neck. You said it was so stiff you couldn't bow your head to pray."

"And so it was. I suppose you hold *that* against me, too." His voice was bitter, recriminating. "Four long years ago, and you hold it against me today."

"But I wasn't even here four years ago," I protested.

"All the less reason," he said sharply. "Do you think I *like* being seized for something I did four years ago?"

"I didn't seize you for that."

"Oh?" He looked at me suspiciously. "What did you seize me for, then?"

"For my sample."

"I had nothing to do with it. I wasn't even near it at the time, and . . ."

"I haven't lost one," I said. "I'm putting one together."

"Then leave me out of it entirely." He hawked and spat. "I'm always being tampered with for one thing or another, and lately it's been worse than usual. If it weren't for my royal blood, I'd . . ." He paused to produce a smile of secret knowledge.

"You'd what?"

"I'd warn you about your friend, Señor." His long nose, reddened by the wiping, began to drip again. He let the drops form and fall, as if the way to let out secrets were a drop at a time. "Oh, I'd warn"—drop—"you"—drop—"to"—the next drop was slow in forming, and he shook his head to hurry it up. If his nose had suddenly gone dry, he clearly would have been disappointed. The drop finally fell and, as if unwilling to take a chance on the next one, he finished in a rush. ". . . look out for Visenta. And others. There are plans for your friend. Oh, yes." He took an enormous, spotless handkerchief from a pocket and dabbed very lightly at the tears of pleasure in his eyes; the handkerchief was evidently for use only above the nose. "Oh, it won't be gentle, no." He chuckled and dabbed some more. "He *would* accuse me, would he?"

"He accused you of something?" I was beginning to feel quite dizzy; I decided this would be a small sample. What, I wondered, would be the central tendency in a sample consisting of Rosa Linda and Ildefonso? On the average, they were . . . what? "Just what did Peter say?"

"Peter? Who's Peter?"

"Pedro. My friend. The one you were talking about."

"Oh, *that* one." The tears of pleasure were streaming from his eyes now, rolling unchecked down his bristly cheeks; he returned his handkerchief to his pocket, apparently to keep it from any serious risk of a smudge. "The way he knocked over the priest was something to see, wasn't it? Funniest thing I ever saw. Oh, he's a brave boy!"

"I thought you said he accused you of something."

"I wouldn't doubt it at all." His anger came back. "Anyone who'd knock down a priest is capable of anything, *I* say! Shameful. Things that happened years ago, and he's ready just like *that* to use them against me!"

73

, I'm sure he doesn't think badly of you."

ᴅ the less reason to talk against me!"

ᴊut he doesn't. I'm sure he'd say nothing that wasn't
ᴏd about you."

"Oh?" He reflected. "He must be peculiar, then. *I* know
how people talk about me. Things I never even had a chance
to do!" He shook cautiously, as if he were held upright only
by a thread he could not chance breaking. "I've even been
accused of mounting Visenta. Mounting!" He let his teeth
rattle in indignation. "I don't ride witches at my age!"

"What about her plans?"

"What plans?"

"Never mind," I said, feeling relieved. "For a moment I
thought you said she had plans for Peter . . . for my
friend."

"Oh, *those*." He clapped his hands and swayed in delight.
"Oh yes, *those* plans!" He began to laugh . . .

We were moving now—with the "we" changing continu-
ally—from brightly lighted *cantina* to dimly lighted hut,
from the night of the pueblo road to the flash and flare of
the plaza. Here and there lay a celebrant asleep—one
learned where to watch for them, so that one could step over
or around them without inconvenience to anyone—or two
celebrants who had passed from public to private ritual—
one did not often see these, but it was largely a matter of
knowing where not to walk. Somewhere Peter had acquired
a large blue *ruana*, which covered him almost as effectively
as the robe had the priest, and a high straw hat with a tre-
mendously wide brim; all in all, he looked like an initiate of a
curious monastic order. I later learned that the *ruana* had
been the entire back wall of one of the more dimly lighted
huts visited; the regular adobe wall had given way during
one of the not infrequent earth tremors, and after desultory
attempts to patch it the *ruana* had been put up to serve
temporarily. In a magnificently hospitable gesture, the
owner had whipped off his temporary wall and presented it

as Peter was departing (I had been a hut ahead of Peter at the time). Peter told me the gesture had been functional as well: the owner had declared it was a sign of his resolve "to have a proper erection *mañana*." The hat had come from Doña Victoria, who had woven it herself (as usual, once she had got started and warmed up, she found it almost impossible to stop; rocking and weaving and puffing, she would turn out one oversize thing after another, which Sebastian quietly unraveled when she finally slumped into sleep). She had plunked it on his head so fiercely he had not been able to decide whether a gift or a blow had been intended. Later, when a dead bat fell on the brim (it seemed perfectly natural at the moment to have a dead bat come down, and I did not even wonder about it until well after the fiesta—could a skyrocket have caught it?), he concluded that since the brim had protected his face the hat had actually been a very useful gift, and that we ought to go back and thank her properly. We did so.

"I don't want any bats," she said angrily. "Dead ones least of all." She rocked furiously and blew cannonballs of smoke at us; I could tell she was pleased to see us again.

"It's our last offer," I said. "Take it or leave it."

"Really," Peter said anxiously. "Really, Señora, I'm afraid you've misinterpreted . . . you see, I was hit by this bat, and so I thought I ought to come thank you . . . because of the brim, you see . . ."

"*That* should clear it up," I said.

"Of course it does!" she snapped. "A bat fell on him, and the hat I gave him kept it from landing on his face, so he came to thank me for the hat."

"That's absolutely right," Peter said in awe.

"Yes, I think she's got it," I said.

"Why not? It's a common enough story," she said plaintively. "There's never anything new any more."

"Common?" Peter asked, entranced.

"*Absolutamente!*" She blew more cannonballs at us. "The sky's full of falling bats these days. And if it isn't bats, it's something else. It's not safe to go outside anymore." She sniffed the bowl of her calabash (she had once told me her pipes smelled best to her just before they went out, and since the cannonballs made it difficult for me to breathe, I took the sniffing as a good omen), and added, "It's just as bad inside."

As usual, she was wrapped in blue—whether blanketed in a blue dress or dressed in a blue blanket could not be satisfactorily established—and with her considerable height presented a figure strangely like that of Peter in his blue *ruana;* as if she were his Dorian Gray transformation. Indeed there was a curious affinity between them; she obviously liked him (in a way, I suppose, he was her puppy), and he was definitely fascinated by her. With an age gap of about sixty years between them, I would have expected a difference in vigor, but in their case it was Peter who seemed to be the frail one. With her wrestler's shoulders and reckless rockings, she seemed ready at any moment to bound from her chair and scoop up her fragile friend before he was overcome by dust and drifting cobwebs. Of course, part of the affinity was that they were both pipe smokers—the only two for kilometers around. What it was that bound pipe smokers together in their mystic and often aromatic communion was beyond me, but it certainly applied to Doña Victoria and Peter. Even now, as she sucked the last remnants of smoke from the crumbled cigar butts she used as fuel, he was reaching for his pouch to stoke up with Taffy #73, or whatever his candied blend was called.

"What happened to your fiesta dress?" I asked. "Not that what you have on isn't as becoming as always."

"That priest!" she muttered. "Just like him to come before I could finish it." She nodded toward a large basket where she kept such odds and ends as thread, string, pieces of cloth, beer bottle caps (she had a notion these were coins of the devil, and could be used to buy him off if he suddenly appeared one night), pretty stones that children sometimes

76

brought to her to trade for a secret puff on her pipe, locks of hair she claimed were from past lovers (the locks were all mixed together in a little mat she had for years been trying to sell to Visenta as a love charm), and pre-crumbled cigar butts. "It'll just have to wait until next year. If he lives that long." She looked approvingly at Peter. "Serves him right you gored him, boy."

"I didn't gore him," Peter said hastily. "I just . . . we just fell over together; that is, it was my fault, I don't mean it wasn't, but I didn't really . . ."

"I heard you caught him with a horn," Doña Victoria said. "In the groin or some interesting place like that."

"No, no," Peter said. "I just bumped him a little. He didn't bleed at all."

"He wouldn't anyway," she said. "It's the same with all of them."

"With all of them?" Peter said. "Priests, you mean?"

"I mean the ones who run things," she said. "Including priests. They've been bleeding us for years; no wonder they don't need to bleed themselves." Her rocker was still; she stared eagerly at Peter, as if she wanted to throw him what she could before the rocker took her away. "My nephew's a little *loco*, but he's right about one thing: if people think religion's going to keep them from that communism business, they'd better think again. There's too much of . . ." She waved her hand around the room. ". . . of *this*. You know what it mostly is, young man?"

"What?" Peter said.

"Dirt. That's what it mostly is. There's too many living too close to dirt. Dirt walls, dirt floors, dirt pots . . . most of what we have is only dirt, young man. You know why we live in dirt?"

"Why?"

"Because we *are* dirt, that's why. As far as the ones who run things care, that's what we are. Religion's mixed up in it, too. Helps keep things the way they are. It's no accident." She leaned forward and held out her hand for his pouch. "The rich man knows what kind of family to have."

"What kind is that, Señora?"

"One son for the government, another for the military, and another for the Church. If there are others, off they go to the places that count: law, business, *you* know. There'll be influence enough in *that* family! What counts is the way power's kept. That's what counts, young man: keeping power in the family!" She intertwined the long almost flesh-less fingers of her outstretched hand and slapped back the pouch he offered. "They're all in it together, young man! But things grow from dirt!" She slowly separated her fingers and took the pouch. "You know what's growing from dirt right now, young man?"

"What, Señora?"

"Just what they planted, that's what." She began to re-fill her pipe. "I'm old and half blind, and even *I* can see what's growing." She squinted at Peter, as if to emphasize how poor her sight was. "Not that *they* can't see it, too. But why should they change? *Really* change, I mean? Why should they give up what's been in the family so long? Why should they, young man?"

"I . . . I'm afraid I don't know enough about it, Señora."

"What is there to know? Look around you, young man. Then look at the way *they* live. As things are, nothing leads from here to there; they keep the best for themselves, and why shouldn't they? They think it's only right to have it." She tossed the pouch back to Peter. "But even my fool nephew knows it's wrong that nothing leads from here to there. Even fools and old women can ask questions. You've met my nephew, young man?"

"Yes, Señora."

"I think he's a little crazy, and he thinks I'm a little crazy, and the truth probably is we're both a little crazy. Whether it's because he's lived too long with me or because

I've lived too long with him, or simply because I've lived too long and he's lived too seldom, I can't say. But we both know there's something growing; maybe it takes a little craziness to know it, or maybe it's something even craziness can't hide. But it's there. We both know that." She took a candle from the table beside her and lit her pipe.

"Then you agree with him?" I asked.

"I do not!" she said indignantly. "It isn't that *comunismo* business of his that's growing, it isn't really that. Not that fools like him aren't ready to take over the crop! Oh, they're ready, they are!" Her eyes seemed to swell behind the candle flame. "Fools!" The sweet smoke began to shroud her face; her eyes now seemed to be floating, immense and deathless, in a sea of ghosts. She started to rock, still holding the candle.

"I'm not sure I understand about the growing," Peter said. "Just what is it that . . ."

"Fools!" she interrupted, her eyes now closed behind the smoke. Wax dropped onto her hands and into her lap, but she did not appear to notice. Faster and faster she rocked, until the candle went out and only the glow of her pipe was on her shrouded face. "I'd crush them, I would!" She and Peter puffed away, like conspirators of different species, tasting the sweetness of each other's smoke as if this at least were a way they could kiss. "How I'd crush them," she crooned; I could not tell now if the reference was to annihilation or to an embrace. I felt left out; two tall figures in blue filled the room.

"About the growing," Peter said.

"Yes, yes," she said dreamily, assenting to everything, responding to nothing. "I'm the one to do it." The calabash sizzled and bubbled—Sherlock Holmes in one of his disguises, rocking away on the chase. "I was there all the time, all the time."

"The growing," Peter said. There was no longer any inquiry in his voice; he was caught in the cycle of long puffs and short phrases. The air was suffocatingly sweet; I tugged at Peter's arm.

The machete flashed, and the wick—fire still clinging briefly to it—jumped from the candle. "So," someone said, "you *are* sober."

"No," Faustino said, relighting the candle. He was the kind of muscular man who made it appear that great strength was needed to strike and apply a match. "I'm drunk. I can only do it when I'm drunk." He flashed a Burt Lancaster smile all around.

We were in the Medina hut. Faustino, with all his muscles and misplaced charm, was a considerate host: he only sliced up his own things.

"Try it with a cigarette," someone suggested.

"On *your* lip," Faustino said, making his hand tremble so realistically he had to catch it with the other.

The suggestion was withdrawn.

Peter—was he really still there?—nudged me. "How did we get here?" he whispered.

"We probably walked," I whispered back, feeling very clever and relentlessly aware that what I considered gems were probably wasted—the story of my nothing life. "Taxis never run this late." I almost cried at this last bit of hilarity. Here I was, one of the few persons of my time who knew the truth about us, and all I did was try to make jokes. I silently cursed the National Science Foundation and Harvard University for sending defectives into the area; yet I loved them too, because their computers and formulas allowed a tolerance for slobs.

Peter shook his head to clear it. "Did I pass out?"

"Not entirely," I said comfortingly. "You were a little groggy, perhaps. If I believed in trances, I'd say you were in one."

We were sitting on the dirt floor, our backs against a wall that shed lime and dust whenever we shifted. Faustino was the only one of our seven companions who was not seated as we were; he presided at the low table in the center of the room, tending the four candles that supplied the only light in the windowless hut. He tapped the table with his machete, as if he were a scoutmaster getting ready to lead his little troop in song around the good old campfire. Alejandro and José—the walrus and the carpenter, I thought—were in fact humming a dirge across from me, while Sebastian (who had slipped one of his posters under him, and was now sitting squarely on the face of Daddy Warbucks) was whistling what seemed to be a combination of the "Internationale" and "Some Enchanted Evening." The other three were Enrique Tono, a spindly man with fourteen children and a wife reputed to be the most frigid in the history of the pueblo (Enrique was much admired locally); Frederico Salcedo, a short heavy man who had once been the police inspector, and who had been relieved of duty shortly after developing a tendency to arrest local girls under fourteen (one of these was later shown to have been an arsonist, which cheered up Frederico immensely for a while); and Jorge Sandía, a sociably soft man whose chief opinion was that the best things in life were next door (even though he was forever dropping in on people, it should be said in all fairness to him that he usually brought more than he took—he made and very generously distributed excellent candy, bread, and pastry). Those who had worn coats and ties to church had discarded them for *ruanas;* if we looked rather motley, we also looked warm and comfortable.

Faustino tapped the table again. *"Silencio, por favor!"* We were not to sing after all. *"Caballeros,"* he said, "you are not here to watch me do tricks, are you?"

Were we? I had no idea; but Faustino assured us grandly (ah, that smile!) that we were not. "No, my friends, it is not *my* tricks you want to see."

"She is really coming, then?" Jorge asked, rubbing his hands together eagerly. I half expected him to say that it was just what he had thought: the best things in life *were* next door.

"She starts with us," Faustino said proudly.

"*Who* starts with us?" Peter whispered to me.

"I don't know," I whispered back. "But I suspect he's bringing on the dancing girl." Lime and dirt spurted from behind Peter's back. "You may watch from time to time," I added.

Faustino left, and we waited in silence. A jug of *guarapo* was being passed around; some watched it make its way from mouth to mouth. Others stared at the candles. It was as if the fiesta night were by now so deeply rooted in us that there was no need to disturb such moments of peace with a show of cultivation. I began to hope that Faustino would not return, that the quiet was more than a prelude to . . . what?

I looked at Sebastian, in whose brooding eyes the candlelight trembled. Was he thinking of the ways of revolution or the ways of his aunt? Perhaps both. José's eyes were also on the candles; his smooth ageless face seemed like the wax he watched—at his wake there would doubtless be a curious uncertainty among the onlookers as to whether or not he was really dead. Alejandro's eyes, as might be expected, followed the jug. I wondered who was tending his *cantina;* perhaps, I thought fleetingly, the press of business had been so great that he had left it in charge of one who did not take up so much of the space into which customers might fit. Or perhaps . . .

Speculation ended. Faustino hurried in, all muscles and smile. He whispered something to Jorge, and Jorge nodded.

A few seconds later one of the shortest full-grown females I had ever seen came into the room. She was about four feet tall in her low pink slippers, which were her entire costume. Undressing was not a highly developed art in this area, and she had evidently simply left her dress and underthings in the other room. She carried a guitar, which she handed to Faustino, and while he was tuning up she blew out one of the candles and rearranged the other three.

Her proportions were amazing; she looked like a fertility symbol, and I could almost imagine her on someone's mantle with a clock in her stomach. Her face, like her height, was that of a child, and in fact her persistent pout suggested the reluctance of a girl attending her first dance with what she emphatically considered the wrong boy. She made no effort at all to smile, or to move gracefully, or to follow the music Faustino had now begun to produce.

What she now started to do was presumably a dance, but it looked more like a prolonged shiver. It was as if she had pressed an inner button that made everything move but her feet. I had never before seen, and have not witnessed since, such an exhibition of flying flesh. Looking at her, one would have thought she surely had more than the prescribed number of everything. With the candles placed as they were, breasts and buttocks seemed to fill the room—all from this one little female. Sweat rose to her skin and was hurled in all directions; the last spattering of this sort I had experienced had come from a dog shaking itself after a swim. Oddly, the smell was of oranges—I later learned she used orange extract as an ointment.

While I neglected to study Peter's face—my attention was largely drawn elsewhere—an occasional glance indicated that he was in a state of shock. I tried to think of a quip that might induce him to close his mouth at least, but the truth is that I had more than enough difficulty keeping my own lower jaw in place. As she moved faster and faster, I had a sudden image of Doña Victoria rocking faster and faster; it seemed unreasonable that these two should belong to the same sex. I tried to picture the dancer puffing on the General MacArthur pipe, but the only vision I produced had the pipe protruding from the dancer's behind like a wand in a windstorm. I regretted the vision—in my own way I sought purity—but all my efforts to keep my thoughts closer to the world of innocence were dispersed by the spray of this navel (surely) orange juice machine gone berserk.

It occurred to me that I ought to drop a card to the National Science Foundation. What would I say? "Having great time, wish you were here," perhaps.

Peter seemed to be strangling, and I nudged him. "If you can't breathe, close your eyes," I whispered.

"I . . . I can't," he whispered back.

"Then what are you complaining about? Don't you like music?"

"I . . . it's just that she's . . . it's . . . she's the first I've ever seen."

"The first what?"

"You know . . . that way . . . like that."

Whether she heard us whispering or not, I could not say —perhaps she was simply intrigued by the sight of Peter— but now, so gradually that it seemed at first accidental, she moved toward him. The sounds of strangling increased, and I wondered if I shouldn't do something protective. I could think of nothing feasible, however; it didn't seem quite right to stand up and hit her.

She bent over and tugged at his *ruana*. He gaped at her. She tugged again. "Give me please, mister," she said in heavily accented (from "geeve" to "meester") English. It just went to show, I thought, that wherever you went, you were likely to find English spoken.

Though Peter had difficulty understanding what she wanted, in the first place, and moving his limbs, in the second, at last he managed both, and she resumed her vibrations using his *ruana* (which smelled of oranges for days afterwards) as a cape. I don't like to criticize, but she was very clumsy with it, and actually became entangled twice. Still, it appeared that there were purposes other than those that met the eye.

Jorge was the first to find out. Working her incredible way over to him, she dropped the *ruana* over his lap and legs; then, before anyone could say boo (which would have been inappropriate anyway), she disappeared under it.

84

"What's she doing under there?" Peter whispered hoarsely.

"She's not reading the meter," I whispered back. "Outside of that, I have no idea what she is or isn't doing." I reflected. "At least," I amended, "no idea I care to talk about."

It was difficult to tell whether Jorge had expected this visit or not. His expression kept changing from alarm to delight and back to alarm again. Once he turned such a deep red I remember feeling surprised that so much color could come to such pasty skin. Twice he cried "Woops!" This is not a translation but just what he said, although I feel certain he did not intend it as an expression of English. All that we could see of her was an occasional hand or foot, not counting the slipper she threw out (Why only one? I wondered). As for the *ruana*, it was highly agitated. I was reminded of the time a bobcat got under the quilt in my uncle's summer cabin.

At last she emerged. I believe I can say truthfully that the rest of us were almost, if not quite, as limp as Jorge. She retrieved her slipper and tucked something in it before her foot; whatever else she had done under there, she had very probably emptied his pockets. Not that he looked like a man impoverished; on the contrary, he looked like a man who had just invested in a stock of assured and abiding value. He looked a little proud, a little smug, and eminently at peace.

José was next. As the Invisible Woman struck again, I got another distress signal from Peter. "She . . . she's not going to . . . to go all *around*, is she?"

"Who knows?" I said. "Say what you will, it's a dandy little ice-breaker."

The truly astounding thing about the maneuver now in progress (progress?) was José's expression: it did not change at all. The *ruana* was having convulsions, but José's face was as serenely frozen as ever. I reminded myself never to play poker with him (he told me later he had played cards only once in his life, and had done very badly). I was not the only one who was impressed; the other watchers seemed more intrigued by the calm than the convulsions. Sebastian even applauded briefly. When both slippers came shooting out, there were congratulatory murmurs and nods. Evidently the ejection of a slipper was a tribute, and José was a two-slipper man.

Shortly before the dancer (I still call her a dancer; I am not one to accuse on circumstantial evidence) reappeared, there was a struggle of such unique dimensions under the *ruana* that I wondered what new libidinal heights or depths might have been explored. The *ruana* slipped slightly, and the answer was plain: this was the fee-collecting stage, and José—good old inscrutable José—had kept his hands in his pockets.

"Capitalist exploiter!" Sebastian said, fighting away a small smile.

"I have never claimed otherwise," José said mildly.

"It's unfair," said Jorge, though it was not clear whether he meant it was unfair to the dancer or to himself, who had already paid.

"I was only joking," José said in his pallbearer's voice, handing the dancer something which, judging from her surprised smile, she found quite acceptable.

As she looked slowly around the room now, a conservative appraisal of the atmosphere would be that there was a certain amount of suspense in it. Alejandro drained the last of the *guarapo* from the jug, then rolled the jug into the center of the room: evidently he was suggesting a spin-the-jug selection. But she had already chosen: Peter.

She moved very deliberately toward him, as if she suspected that this bird might try to fly. But Peter was in no condition to fly; he could not even wiggle. Petrified, he watched her advance, *ruana* outstretched.

At the first touch of the *ruana* he stirred, and for a mo-

86

ment it seemed that he might protest or run away. But he did not protest or run away. He simply passed out.

"Ah," José said, "he is with us again."

Peter opened his eyes, and at the sight of the unfinished coffin closed them again.

"You are not even partly dead, *amigo*," José said reassuringly. "You are back in your room, and we are with you."

His eyes reopened instantly. "*We?*" he said anxiously.

"Don Guillermo and myself," José said. "The young lady is occupied elsewhere."

Peter groaned. "Am I in disgrace?" he asked.

"Not at all," José said. "You held your ground to the last. You did not retreat, and you did not cry out. What happened to you was clearly beyond your control."

"What do you mean by what happened to me?" Peter asked quickly.

"I mean your unfortunate—or possibly fortunate—loss of consciousness, *amigo*. Would you like a little wine?"

"No, no thank you," Peter said with a shudder.

"Some water, perhaps?"

"No, nothing at all, thank you." He raised himself on his bed, then sank back. "I don't think I'll get up just now."

"We didn't bring you here to get up just now," I said. "I thought you might like to leave a call for lunchtime."

"Lunchtime," he said, shuddering again.

"I didn't necessarily mean you had to eat anything," I said. "I meant I wouldn't disturb you until noon or so."

"Any time," he said. "Any time, as long as you don't bring food. Or drink. Or . . ." He blushed. "Are you sure I'm not disgraced?"

"If a two-slipper man says no, you ought to believe him," I said.

"There is a certain respect for innocence," José said kindly.

"Innocence," Peter repeated softly. "In some ways I feel anything but innocent." He looked at the coffin that held his shirts, and at the window on whose glassless condition he had remarked the first day. "There are so many different kinds of innocence." He smiled. "I enjoyed tonight, I really did."

"On the whole," José said, "you entered in very well, I thought. If I may say so, you became more of a . . . person for us." He cleared his throat—a highly demonstrative noise, for him—and put his hand lightly on Peter's forehead. "If you wish to be sick, don't worry about my floor. There are few substances unknown to it."

"I don't think I'll be sick." Peter smiled again and stretched. "The fact is, I feel remarkably good right now." He closed his eyes.

"Sleep well, Pedrito," José said gently. He winked at me and left.

I started to follow. "One more thing," Peter whispered.

"Yes?"

"Thanks."

"For nothing," I said. "Whatever I did was probably the wrong thing."

"Well, thanks anyway." His voice was very drowsy.

"Have you learned what you came for yet, Pete?"

"No," he said, kicking off his shoes. "But I'm having one damn fine time."

V

The next day Peter said, "I've decided to repair a bridge."

"Oh?" I said, kicking a dud skyrocket out of the way. We were walking along the pueblo road toward the plaza. It was early afternoon, and life seemed to be moving in a slow and brittle way: men nodded as if they dared not incline their heads too far for fear of losing them entirely, and women held their heads stiffly erect as if waiting (in vain, as they knew) for the world to apologize. "Any particular bridge?"

"No," he admitted. "I was hoping you might know of one."

I looked closely at him. He was freshly scrubbed and shaved, and like myself wore clean khakis. Still, he looked tired: the face that usually reddened so easily was now pale, and his pale blue eyes were now quite red. "Frankly," I said, "you sound groggy. What happened to all that rest you got?"

"I'm afraid I didn't get it," he said ruefully. "This morning I remembered I was supposed to talk to the priest before he left. I was rolling over to get a better grip on the pillow at the time. So . . . I got up." He took out his pouch and partly filled his pipe; then, after putting the stem in his mouth and giving it a tentative suck, he grimaced and hastily returned the pipe to his pocket. "As they say back home, I shoulda stood in bed."

"At least," I said, "there was one thing you *didn't* have to confess to."

He smiled. "True. Chicken that I am." A group of children ran by, heading for the plaza with a battered soccer ball. The laughter of the young had its special appeal, of course, but not just then, not just then. "He was really more considerate than I deserved," he went on. "But he gave me what I was feeling like, and I do mean hell. I suppose that's the wrong word; hell doesn't come from priests, does it?"

"I've heard even a glimpse of heaven can be painful as hell to sinners," I said.

"Maybe that's what he gave me, then." He rubbed his eyes. "Light *can* hurt, I know that." A rooster flapped across the road in front of us. "Even so," Peter continued, "I didn't feel that he, well, disliked me. Mostly he just kept looking at me; waiting me out, I guess. But I felt so sick and tired I ended up waiting *him* out. Oh, I made my little confession, all right, but I didn't go on and on the way he seemed to want me to. So after awhile he asked me one or two things about the *vaca loca* business—he didn't really sound as if he wanted to hear much more about *that*—and then he chewed me out, more or less generally. Then he had me say a prayer with him, but I got the dry heaves in the middle of it—what a duet *that* was!—and that's when he chewed me out specifically. So I figured it was time I repaired a bridge."

"That follows," I said doubtfully.

"What I mean is, he said something about mending my fences and tending to my bridges—bridges to God, I think. Though maybe he wanted me to jump off one; I couldn't hear very well with all the racket I was making. Anyway, I got the message, even if it wasn't his. If the Peace Corps can mend fences and fix bridges, why couldn't I?"

"Incompetence?" I suggested.

He shrugged impatiently. "The point is, it's time I went ahead with the sort of thing the Peace Corps does. Not that I can do it the same way."

"Why not?"

"Oh, they're organized. They work in teams, you know.

With each other, with local counterparts. It's all pretty systematic. And I'm not."

"Are you bragging or complaining?"

"Neither. Maybe it just goes with the confession of the day. So where's a good bridge? I mean a bad bridge."

"I don't know. We might try the River Kwai."

"No, seriously. There ought to be at least one bridge that needs fixing."

We had reached the plaza. It looked like an outdoor living room—a community living room—after a party. There was a clutter of colored paper, bottles, cigarette and cigar butts, benches (these had been taken from the boys' school to the church for the services of the night before, and late efforts by two celebrants to return them to the school had brought them only halfway across the plaza before the sense of purpose was lost), sundry stray articles of dress, a chair someone had placed in the middle of it all (I could just picture the lone figure seated in the midst of chaos), and three celebrants who had stayed too long and were still sleeping it off. The soccer game was under way, and what with the visual and auditory commotion I had a strong urge to seek more serene surroundings. "Let's take your problem to the people," I said. "I think I read a directive about that somewhere."

"Memorandum Four Hundred Thirty-Seven, Item Two," Peter said. "Or was it Item Three?"

"Item Two-c, possibly," I said. "We can always split the difference."

"Yes, we can always do that," Peter said. "Now the only question is, can we always find a bridge?"

"You mean the kind that goes across rivers and such?" Ernesto asked. "One end on each side?"

"I knew you'd understand," I said.

"Any particular sort of material?" Ernesto pursued. "What does he do his best work in?"

"What do you do your best work in, Peter?" I asked.

"Oh, I play no favorites," Peter said. "As long as it's broken down somewhere."

"If it's one of ours," Ernesto said, "it's broken down." He thought about it. "There *are* some odds and ends of bridges, but nobody really uses them anymore." He thought further about it. "Whether nobody uses them because they're odds and ends, or they're odds and ends because nobody uses them, I just can't say."

"I suppose I could fix one and see if it's used again," Peter said hopefully.

"You might change the course of traffic for the whole area," I said. "People might go miles out of their way to cross your bridge."

"You could put up a little plaque," Ernesto said. " 'This bridge was patched by Peter Bradley during the administration of . . .' ah, whoever it happens to be by the time you finish."

"You might even put in a plug for the Peace Corps," I said.

"Unless, of course, there's a war on at the time," Ernesto pointed out.

"I'm inspired," Peter said. "Take me to your bridge."

"Immediately," Ernesto said. He was sitting naked on a school bench in his two room quarters at the rear of the boys' school, nursing a huge mug of steaming coffee. He stood up, clapped a hat on his head and said, "You don't mind if I bring my coffee along?"

"I thought a schoolmaster had to be careful about his reputation," I said.

"Ah, yes, but there's no school today, you see."

"In that case," I said, "bring your coffee."

The footpath ended—fortunately—where my wind gave out, and the four of us (José had joined us en route, pledging his willingness to take whatever measurements we might desire, short of the length of the river) rested on boulders and looked at the virtually unmoving waters of the Río Vinagre.

"Regard the river," I said spiritedly. No one bothered to reply, possibly because the river was already being regarded. The bridge had once been a simple but serviceable structure of *guadua* poles lashed together with agave fiber; the poles had held until the far bank had given way, then had become twisted and split. It was a beautiful spot, in a little winding valley about three miles south of the pueblo. The ground was well tangled with bushes and high grass, and here and there were trails that led nowhere. These were attributable to stories circulated by the elders to the effect that riches had long ago been concealed here by the *conquistadores* and their descendants. Every now and then little groups with machetes would come down for a treasure hunt. As far as atmosphere went, a bridge in ruins was eminently suited to the site.

Ernesto, who had decided after all to bring his clothes instead of coffee, threw a pebble into the river and said, "All in all, it's a nice out-of-the-way place to work on a bridge. We're not likely to be disturbed by people going back and forth."

"It's such a harmless river," José said. "Why can't we just leave it alone?"

"Progress," Ernesto said. "Human needs must be served."

"But nobody ever comes here except to look for something that doesn't exist," José said.

"We'll change all that," Ernesto said.

"But why?" José asked.

"Why not?" Ernesto countered. "Just measure the width, please."

"Mmm," José said. "There is a problem; if I put one end of my tape on this side, how do I get the other end to the other side without a way across? Perhaps if you could fix the bridge a little . . ."

"If we could fix the bridge without a measurement, why would we need a measurement?" Ernesto asked.

"That would seem to be *your* problem," José said. "I was talking only of mine. However . . ." He gave the river a careless glance. "Offhand, I should say eleven meters, thirty-six centimeters from bank to bank."

"If he misses by more than two centimeters," Ernesto said proudly, "I'll buy drinks all around. In fact, I'll even buy one of his coffins."

"Did I say eleven meters?" José said promptly. "I meant one hundred eleven, of course."

"Your original estimate stands, my friend," Ernesto said reprovingly. "Surely you don't place a sale above your professional reputation?"

"I have never claimed otherwise," José said. "How does it look, Pedrito?"

"It would not be a difficult thing to do," Peter said slowly. "I could even suggest a number of different styles to choose from. But . . ." He looked around the valley again. "It *does* seem a little ridiculous to put up a bridge in the middle of nowhere."

"Ah, but that might be the very best place for one," Ernesto said. "There'd be no one to break it, and from time to time we could come look at it, and read the plaque, and . . ."

"Who said this was nowhere?" José broke in. "It's somewhere, just like every other place. In fact, it's one of the nicest spots around."

"I only meant there were no people here to use the bridge," Peter said.

"How could there be, when there's no bridge to use?" José asked.

"Yes, but when the bridge is finished . . ."

"You just said you didn't *want* to fix a bridge here," José said. "You don't expect crowds to keep coming to a river bank where there's so little hope of getting a bridge, do you?"

"Yes, but if the crowds were here, I'd want to fix the bridge," Peter said determinedly.

"So you won't make a move until crowds are waiting on the bank, is that it?"

"You mustn't try to confuse him, Don José," said Ernesto. "The point is, he seems to want some assurance that his bridge will be used. *Bueno,* if that's what he wants, I personally promise to lead small groups back and forth across the bridge each and every month or so. Lightly, of course."

"What about animals?" I asked.

"The smaller ones could be included, I think," Ernesto said. "As long as their habits are clean."

"Is it necessary to say that I see little point in having such a bridge?" Peter said, shaking his head as if between fascination and exasperation.

"You bring us here to tell us that?" José said. "It doesn't seem to be much of a gain."

"If Sebastian were here, he would say, 'Who are you to tell us where we must have our bridge?'" Ernesto said. "Aren't you going to let the people decide? Self-determination and so forth?"

"I . . . I suppose we could ask some others," Peter said. "But are you serious about . . ."

"A poll!" Ernesto said enthusiastically. "We must have a poll. What the man in the pueblo road thinks. I've seen some of your magazines; I know just . . ."

"It wasn't that I really wanted to come," José said glumly. "There I was, nails to find, sawdust all over the bed. And I'm led all the way here just to be told there's nothing to be done. I'm not one to complain, and it's possible I'm a better man for being put through it, but still . . ."

"You win," Peter said. "Let's go sample opinion."

"I'm sure that means something interesting," José said politely, "if it means anything at all."

"We'll take you around and make introductions," Ernesto said. "Do you want us to explain about you?"

95

"What would you explain about me?" Peter asked.

"Oh, little things. That you're harmless. That your height is more or less natural where you come from. That you didn't mean to knock over the priest. That your shoes aren't as expensive as they look. Little things like that."

"Whatever you think appropriate," Peter said, sighing. "As long as you don't tell them about that business with the dancer."

"Oh, there's no need to tell them about that," Ernesto said. "No need at all."

"A bridge," said Peter to Tomás Hinojoso. "Across the Río Vinagre."

"*Si*, Señor," said Tomás. "A bridge, you say." His age now exceeded his weight; as he had passed through his seventies and into his eighties, he had shriveled into a little goat of a man, with a white pointed beard and, when he slept (which was often), a high bleating snore. Yet he had been a community leader—a *principal*—during the years of transition from Indian to Mestizo status. His name had been the first on the petition to divide the reservation lands into individually owned plots, the heritage of a language no longer spoken, a costume no longer worn, and ways no longer followed. Now he sat in front of his mud hut, huddled in ragged Western clothes, peering at Peter as if at a creature from outer space. "You *did* say a bridge?"

"Yes," Peter said. "What we'd like to find out is, which one most needs fixing?"

"*Pues,* the one that is broken the most, I should think." I found myself congratulating him. I liked Peter, but I had come to admire the way in which persons like Tomás made us start all over again.

"I don't mean in terms of its condition," Peter said. "I mean in terms of its location. *Comprende?*"

Tomás shrugged. "Condition . . . location . . . Is it a riddle, Señor?"

"No," Peter said. "Where would you say a bridge is most needed?"

"Where there is water to cross, Señor. At least, so one would think." He nodded expectantly at Peter, as if he hoped there would be no disagreement on this.

"Yes, but in what place?" Peter persisted. "What specific place?"

"Specific, you say? Ah . . ." Tomás seemed much impressed. "You have had a good education, no?"

"What? Why, yes, I suppose so. But . . ." He looked wonderingly at the old man for a few moments; the look was returned. "Do you know the Río Vinagre, Don Tomás? The place where people go to look for treasure?"

"Ah, yes, the treasure," said Tomás slowly. "It won't stay hidden forever." He leaned toward Peter and spoke confidentially. "I'll tell you where you ought to look."

"I'm not really interested in the treasure . . ."

"Not interested in the treasure?" Tomás said, affronted. "Are you a vegetable?"

"I hope not, but . . . what I mean is, just *now* I'm interested in the bridge there. The broken one."

"That's the only one there," Tomás said dryly.

"Yes, I know. I was thinking of fixing it."

"Did you want to borrow something? I have a hammer around somewhere."

"No, thank you. What I want to find out is, do you think it's a good idea?"

"Why ask me? You don't even know me."

"I'm going to ask a number of people," Peter said. "I'm starting with you."

"What was the question again?"

"What do you think about having that bridge fixed?"

"Since it's broken, that would seem to be the best thing to do to it, Señor."

"Yes, but is there any other bridge that it's *necessary* to fix?"

"But Señor," Tomás said soothingly, "if it were *necessary* to fix one, it would have been fixed."

"Then you don't think I ought to fix that bridge?"

"I didn't say that, Señor. I think it would be nice for you to fix it. A young man needs exercise."

"It's propaganda," Sebastian said. "You want people to think well of your country."

"Of course I do," Peter said. "But that's no reason not to do it, is it?"

Sebastian smiled. "It's no reason to *do* it, either." We were standing beside the ancient truck that, in its late afternoon role as bus, was to take Sebastian and his posters to the city for a demonstration or two. He had on his special marching hat, a man-of-the-soil straw piece he had had fitted with a protective plastic lining. In his oversize *ruana*, he seemed at once larger than he was and smaller; perhaps the larger self would be dominant to those most readily intimidated, while the smaller self served to protect him against those stronger officials who might hesitate to attack in public such a ludicrously insignificant figure. He was unshaven, but despite rubbings, tuggings, and ointments his beard was a sparse and prickly thing of stubs and scattered whorls.

"Are you going to be known as the one who denied his people a bridge, Don Sebastian?" I asked.

He laughed; he was usually in a good mood at the outset of a demonstration. Even now he may have been picturing himself throwing a brick through the oft-shattered U.S. consulate window. I had heard that he regularly aimed at this one window, as if to spare the consul the inconvenience of ordering replacements of more than a single size. "Go ahead and fix it, then," he said. "Who knows? I may be known as the one who blew up the *Yanqui* bridge."

"I was hoping you'd help us fix it," Peter said.

Sebastian looked more surprised than I had ever seen him.

"Ah," he said thoughtfully, "that's very good, very good. Impossible, but very good."

"Why impossible?" Peter asked.

Sebastian looked at Peter almost tenderly. "So young," he said. "So very, very young."

"Why *not* join in?" Ernesto said. "We won't tell anyone."

"It is a matter of principle," Sebastian said. "Of course, I could picket you, just to keep you company."

"Who could read your signs?" Ernesto said.

"They will know, they will know," Sebastian said. "My position is no secret."

"I thought part of your position was to help people help themselves," Ernesto said. "That's what's being tried."

"What's being tried," Sebastian said, "is propaganda."

"Join in," José said solemnly, "and make your own propaganda."

"Now there," Sebastian said, "is a thought."

Procopio was sitting on the church steps, polishing his bell. "Such a mess," he said, nodding toward the cluttered plaza. The sun was low, and the soccer-players and sleepers had gone, the former to do what the latter had just done. The chair still stood in the middle, as if waiting for its master. "We must do something about it soon." The debris was stirred by a warm breeze, and Procopio watched it sympathetically, as if he could not be expected to remove what was still alive; when it settled down, *pues*, that was the time to put it away. "When I think of all the fiestas we have had . . ." He lit a cigar butt salvaged from the litter and puffed on it reminiscently. He was not as old as Tomás, but he was old enough to have lost six of his eight children in an epidemic over thirty years ago, shortly before the partition of the reservation lands. The other two children now lived in the steaming Valle to the east. He flicked ashes on the steps and looked at Peter with the affection of one who loved youth but did not regret its passing. "So many fiestas, *joven*. You have much to experience."

"I know," Peter said.

"There was a boy your age who set fire to the police inspector one fiesta," Procopio said. "It was only a small fire. We put it out with holy water."

"Remember the bull in the schoolhouse?" José asked.

"Very clearly, Don José. Ah, the poor schoolmistress. He tried to mount her, I believe."

"He was not a normal bull," José pointed out.

"At least he was not queer," Ernesto said.

"Ah, those were the days," Procopio said. "Education was stricter then. Nowadays the pupils only play."

"It only seems like play," Ernesto said. "They learn all kinds of things. Of course," he added, "there's a limit to what I can teach them in two years."

"What would you say," Procopio said to Peter, "if I told you it took me over two years to learn how to ring this bell?"

"I'd say I can well believe it," Peter said politely.

"Well, you shouldn't believe it, because it didn't," Procopio said. "All I did was hold it up and ring it. That's all. It's just a bell, after all."

"Speaking of learning," Ernesto said, "Peter learned how to fix bridges. He does it very skillfully."

"Have you seen him do it?" Procopio asked.

"Not yet," Ernesto admitted.

"Then how do you know?"

"He told me," Ernesto said.

"It may be that what he's learned is how to lie very skillfully," Procopio said. He winked at Peter. "Don't take that seriously, *joven*. If you say you can fix bridges, as far as trust goes I'm also prepared to say you can fix bridges. A valuable talent, however useless."

"I've been hoping to make it useful," Peter said. "There's a bridge around here I've been thinking of fixing."

"That's a good thing to do," Procopio said promptly.
"I don't mean the fixing part. I mean thinking about
it." He spit on the bell and polished it some more. "My
godfather used to tell me that thinking about a job was at
least half the effort. He was right, too. I've practiced to the
point where thinking about a job is practically the whole of
my effort." He gave the bell a tentative shake. "Ah, what a
sound! I tell you, *muchacho*, it's something to be able to
make people move and stop and move again with a tinkle.
Big results at almost no cost to myself. That's the way the
big landowners do it, and that's the way I do it. Do you
know why it's possible, *muchacho?*"

"Why, Don Procopio?"

"Tradition, that's why. People jump at a tinkle if tradition calls for it. It's partly good and partly bad, *muchacho*.
Sometimes I think we're a truly miserable lot here, we've
lost so much of our tradition. But sometimes I think there's
more hope for us than for the unmixed; if we can break a
tradition that kept us Indians, we can break a tradition
that keeps us peasants. Do you believe that?"

"I . . . I suppose so."

"If you do, you're a fool. Still . . . these days it's the
fools you have to watch out for. *No es cierto*, Joselito?"

"I have never claimed otherwise," José said. "The world
is being measured."

"What does that mean?" Ernesto asked.

"It's not easy to explain," José said. "But it has a signi-
ficant ring to it. Like his bell."

"My bell is only a bell," Procopio said. "It is only what
people believe about it that gives it significance. I remember what happened to my cousin Alfredo when the reservation was being broken up: he woke up one morning believing he was Pizarro come to do away with the Indians."

"It was symbolic," Ernesto said with a schoolmasterly
nod. "You see, the Indians really *were* being done away with,
in the sense that . . ."

"It was nothing of the sort," Procopio said. "Alfredo

was the craziest of my cousins, and the competition was keen. He was only a little more *loco* than usual that morning. Just the night before, he'd tried to ply our guinea pigs with *guarapo,* heaven knows what for. It was only a matter of time before he was bound to wake up believing he was Pizarro; he'd already waked up believing he was almost everybody else he'd ever heard of. What a terror he was, though! He had us all running around like whites." Procopio paused to spit on his bell again. "His only weapon was a large portion of a douche basin his father had brought back, along with a lot of other interesting things, from the city scrap heap. But you should have seen him use it, *muchacho!* He was *muy hombre* that day—a real man. He felled twenty-six of us, some more than once. I remember one little old lady who got up four times before she had sense enough to stay down. He only swung at three old ladies altogether, but in those days it took real courage to swing at even one. You know what finally stopped him, *muchacho?*"

"What?" Peter asked.

"Education, that's what. Joselito's grandfather—he was a carpenter like Joselito, but he knew a thing or two—kept telling him over and over again—dodging all the while, you understand—how Pizarro really took his exercise in Peru. It started puzzling Alfredo, and finally he went back to bed to think it over. 'In Peru?' he'd say to himself. 'Pizarro was in Peru?' At the time we thought it was a matter of getting his geography straight; if Pizarro was in Peru, he couldn't be here, could he? But it wasn't that at all. We found out later Alfredo had never heard of Peru, didn't even know what it was; he was just so confused he couldn't bring himself to do anything. So I have a great respect for education, *muchacho.*"

"Mmm," Ernesto said. "Let's get back to bridges."

"I never cross them," Procopio said. "I've stepped on stones, and waded some, but in my whole life I've never crossed a bridge. I don't object to them, you understand;

I've just never been on one. I suppose there are good ones and bad ones, like everything else."

"We were wondering whether to fix the bridge across the Río Vinagre," Peter said. "Or is there another one that ought to be fixed first?"

"Ask a man who's tried one," Procopio said. "You could cut every last one loose and float it into the ocean and I wouldn't care."

"Then you don't think we ought to fix any?" Peter said.

"That's not what I said, *muchachito*. There are lots of things worth doing that I don't care about. Must a man be concerned about everything?"

"You might want to lead the next procession across it," José said.

Procopio held up the bell, as if meeting a tribute with a toast. "Your grandfather would be proud to know the blood hasn't yet thinned out, Joselito. Like Alfredo, I have something new to think about. Yes . . . " He stared at his bell. "I can almost see the crowd and the candles. I'd lead them onto the bridge and stop them there with a tinkle. Perhaps there'd be rain, and a swift current, and the bridge would sway. And they'd all be waiting . . . waiting for me to let them off with just a little . . ." He turned his wrist until the bell rang faintly. "Oh, there's great power in little things, *muchachito*. Yes, it has possibilities . . ."

"You would have to have permission," Romelio said. "You would have to fill out a form, and there might be a hearing, and . . ."

"What's a hearing?" José asked.

"*Pues*, you'd have to come before me and tell me about it, and . . ."

"That's what we're doing," José said. "You're hearing us, aren't you?"

"Um. Perhaps we can overlook that part. There's still the form . . ."

"Where is it?" José asked.

"I haven't made it out yet. You haven't requested one."

"How could we, when we didn't know we needed one?" José asked.

Romelio looked up from the small table that served as his desk. His office had been the bedroom of his three children before his appointment as police inspector, and here and there among the "Wanted" posters and other official paraphernalia were bits and pieces of broken toys. He had brought everything he could from the *municipio* central office, including notices of crimes thirty years old, fingerprint records of persons long deceased, lists of padlock combinations, discarded ink pads, and confiscated counterfeit lottery tickets. His wife was a mild young woman with delicate features and fingers deft (and well practiced) at keeping his uniform clean and pressed. His children—a girl three years old, and twin boys five years old—now slept in a somewhat larger room that had once been rented to Alejandro for the storage of miscellaneous mixes; Alejandro believed in keeping his holdings well spread out, so that in the event of a calamity at one end of the pueblo he would have a nest egg or two at the other. With his appointment, Romelio had decided this was not a proper function for a police inspector's room, and the arrangement had been terminated. For a while, perhaps for sentimental reasons, he had kept a jar of mix in his new office, until one day, finding his ink supply depleted, he had moistened one of the pads with the mix, with the result that wherever he applied the stamp a hole tended to form.

Now he peered at José as if he were watching a hole form in the carpenter's forehead. "I'll prepare something suitable," he said. "There are some things I've always wondered about you; you'll find a few interesting items included . . ."

"*He* fills out the papers," José said, pointing to Peter. "I am merely a consultant."

"There'll be a special set of questions for consultants," Romelio said.

"I'll only lie," José said, sighing. "Will you know the difference?"

Romelio grinned; his smiles seemed to slide easily back and forth between cruelty and good humor. "At least I'll have you trapped in writing."

"Who writes?" José said.

"I'll put it down myself, and have you verify it," Romelio said.

"What's verify?"

"That means you swear it's true."

"If it's a lie why should I swear it's true?"

"That's just it," Romelio said uncertainly. "That's the point exactly."

"What is?"

"*Pues,* that you can't swear it's true. It would be against the law."

"Then I certainly won't do it," José said piously. "You go ahead and put it all down—anything you like—and I promise not to swear it's true. Agreed?"

"Perhaps we ought to go back a little, and . . ."

"You've changed your mind?"

"No, but . . ." Romelio scratched his head. "What was it you wanted to do?"

"I've forgotten temporarily," José said.

"Repair a bridge," Ernesto said. "The one across the Río Vinagre. Or any other one, for that matter."

"You have to know which one, or I can't issue a form," Romelio said.

"That's why we're here," Peter said. "To get your advice on which one."

"My advice?" Romelio looked pleased. "Ah, my advice." He stood up and moved around the room, puttering with his paraphernalia—touching this, straightening that, blowing dust from one place to another. "It's *my* advice you want, is it?" He opened an old book of "Regulations for Local Peace Officers," printed in Portuguese. He thumbed through it sadly. "I keep thinking I can read it, but I can't."

"It *is* uncomfortably close to Spanish," Ernesto said sympathetically. "But even if you *could* read it, Don Romelio, it only applies in Brazil."

"The principles are doubtless very much the same," Romelio said.

"Whatever they are," José said.

"Yes, whatever they are," Romelio said dejectedly. He put the book down—it was bound very impressively, and certainly seemed to be full of principles—and resumed his puttering. After looking into a few reports and pamphlets (one was on the maintenance of patrol cars), he sat down again. "The fact is," he said, "I have no advice."

"Honesty never fails to move me," José said.

"Can't you just give me an opinion?" Peter asked. "Would it be better to fix that bridge or a different one?"

"In my opinion," Romelio said with a shrug, "it would be about the same either way." He swung at a fly with his cap.

"Who else would be a good person to ask?"

Romelio studied Peter's face—it was a tired, red, and very young face. There was nothing of the air of a putterer about Romelio now. He put his cap slowly and deliberately back on his head; clearly it was no longer a cap to be swung at a fly. "Listen, Pedro," he said carefully. "You are well-intentioned, yes. You may even have a certain usefulness . . . perhaps. But if you plan to improve us . . . remember that you are only a boy. As a boy, you ought to be warned, and I am warning you now." He leaned close. "Things are going on here you may not have noticed; *gringo* eyes excel at looking directly, but when it comes to looking indirectly at things they are often blind. There are currents . . . slow currents, like those under your bridge. Does this seem to you to be a pueblo sleeping away its life?"

"I . . . I hadn't thought of it that way, no," Peter said.

"One of your countrymen did. He barely had time to look around, but he was so certain of what he'd seen he didn't wait to look again. A pueblo sleeping its life away, that's what he said we were. He didn't mean only us." His voice was very cold now. "There are things that appear to be asleep that suddenly strike, Pedro. The power to strike forms under the appearances of sleep. If it were not for the appearances of sleep, it would not be permitted to form. Do you follow, Pedro?"

"I . . . I believe so."

"Good." Romelio leaned back and flicked his tongue over dry, almost blue lips. "I tell you this because you have taken time to wonder about us a little. We have had too many intruders and too few friends." His voice softened. "You want to know who to ask next about your fountain . . ."

"Bridge," Peter said.

"*Puente, fuente,* it doesn't matter. I'll tell you a secret: they are much like my forms. It's comforting to have one completed, but . . ." Romelio shrugged. "The only importance for you is that it may lead you to something important. Yet . . . I warn you again . . ." He looked at us carefully, one by one. "You are in good company now; it's time you called on Visenta. Ask her about your bridge, Pedro. Ask her."

"I will, thanks."

"But not alone, Pedro," said Romelio. "Not alone."

It was dark now, and the door of the hut opened to more darkness. Like a needle lowered to a record rim, a voice inside scratched, then caught at the substance of what turned out to be almost beauty—an imperfect cutting of a prayer of perfect faith. I had not been prepared to listen before I saw, and I would have lost the first words had their sound not made me suddenly lonely, suddenly uneasy.

"Whatever you wish," said the voice, "is here to be given you. Pedro . . . Guillermo . . . José . . . Ernesto . . ." Our names came to us as if from the roll call of the honored. The honored dead.

"About this bridge," Peter said so shakily, yet so doggedly I felt I ought to contribute an appreciative chuckle, or at least a smile. But I didn't.

"Do it," said the voice.

"Do it?" Peter echoed.

Silence.

"You *did* say *do* it?" Peter asked.

"I did."

"Then . . . is that all?"

"No," said the voice. "It's the beginning. Come in."

VI

That the room was small I judged only from what I had seen of the outside the few times I had passed the hut; inside I could see only a few vague twists and zigzags, as if the walls were spattered with luminous paint that had all but ceased to glow. That there were rooms behind this I also judged from what I had seen of the outside; the hut was built somewhat like a telescope, widening in stages from front to back. Visenta was of the pueblo without being quite in it; the hut was on a knoll less than a mile from the pueblo road, but the path that led to it had all the appeal of a fuse to a bomb or a line from fishpond to gaff, and I had only walked that path when Rosa Linda had asked me. Visenta herself I had seen only when she had come into Alejandro's *cantina* to fetch Rosa Linda, and when she had hurried past me on the road to deliver a baby (any time after conception) or try to cure something vile with something viler. Such glimpses had left me puzzled; from a distance she appeared homely, even repulsive—yet the nearer she came the less evident was the homeliness, and indeed when she was within striking distance (I thought of proximity to her in this way) she was ominously attractive.

Very probably it was knowledge of what she was and did that made her seem repulsive from afar, since her features were almost classic and her skin clear and smooth—such, in fact, were her features and skin that one suspected the essence of Visenta hiding behind a face she had made to match the tastes of the outside world. I was reminded of the cruel stepmother in one of my picture books: as a boy, I had considered her as ugly as a woman could be; when I had looked again at the pictures as a man I was surprised to discover that she was really rather lovely in looks alone—it was what she represented that had made her forbidding. Now, as I waited in darkness, the image of Visenta in her black shawl and dress scuttling back and forth between the pueblo and her hut mixed oddly with the smell and feel of a honeyed mist that, to me at least, was strongly sensuous.

"About this bridge," Peter said again. It seemed so inappropriate I swallowed the wrong way and coughed loudly.

"Hush," Visenta said. We hushed.

I wondered where Rosa Linda was. I had never been able to find out much about her duties; I knew she kept house for Visenta and helped prepare what were ostensibly medicines, but she would tell me nothing else. Not that I had ever managed to question her closely; her pretty young face and the faintly perfumed hair that hung almost to her waist made ethnographic detachment difficult for me. I often dreamt of taking her away from all this, but I dreamt just as often of enjoying her fully while I was here, and the waking truth was that I did not have enough initiative or confidence to do either. Still, I hoped I would see her tonight; if this sensuous mist got to me much further, I might have a surprise for her.

"I don't want to complain," José said, "but your candles might work better if you lit them."

"There is nothing you have to see," Visenta said soothingly. "You know what we look like."

"I forget easily," José said.

"It's only a sign you don't really care," Visenta said. "As soon as the wine is served, we'll go into the other room."

"You'll tell us if and when we're drinking it, won't you?" Ernesto said.

She laughed softly. "You are so funny, *caballeros.* I'm so pleased to have you all here at last."

"I'd be pleased to see you, too, if I could," José said.

"Hush, hush . . ."

We waited several minutes in silence. Then a glass was pressed into my hand. "I'm sorry about the delay," Visenta said. "The moon was not right."

"I should have known," I said.

"Ah, so funny," she said kindly. "Please drink."

Warning myself that I shouldn't, I did. The wine tasted like shellac, but toward the last of it I found I liked shellac. "I would have clinked glasses," I explained generally, "but the chances of missing were large."

My glass felt heavier; it had been filled again. I lightened it. "I suppose I'm drugged," I said. "No offense, Doña Visenta."

"Ah, Guillermito, you are so harmlessly ridiculous I'm enchanted."

"That I know," I said. "After all, you *are* a witch."

"It was my mother's wish," Visenta said.

"Her death bed wish?" I asked.

"No," Visenta said. "She wished it well before I was born. That makes it even more important, you'll agree?"

"I agree, I agree." I felt so congenial I could hardly bear it. "It was nice of you to approve of our bridge."

"Bridge? Ah, yes, the bridge." My glass was filled again, and I drank without hesitation.

"Where's Rosa Linda?" I asked as casually as I could; my impression was that I was panting somewhat at the time.

"She is waiting for you, dear Guillermito. You must do as much for her."

I tried to concentrate. "There seems to be a definite meaning in what you said; if it would only hold still . . ."

"Exactly, dear Guillermito. If you would only be still and wait, all would be well."

111

"But if I don't, it won't?"

"Please, Guillermito. You are supposed to be very patient, for a *Yanqui*. The serving is almost done."

I thought I heard sounds of pouring, but could not be certain. It occurred to me that I might be alone. "Peter? José? Ernesto? I'm not the only one here, am I?"

"It's possible," José said.

"No, it isn't," Ernesto said. "*I'm* the only one here."

"I just don't understand what this has to do with fixing a bridge," Peter said. "Would it be different if it were a fountain or a well, or a . . ."

"Please, *caballeros*," Visenta interrupted. "You must calm down before I take you into the next room."

"This is one hell of a place to calm down," I said.

"It is indeed," Visenta said. "Darkness and wine should have a soothing effect." She laughed softly.

"Who cares about the next room?" I said. "Let's just stand here forever. Or better yet, let's leave; too much calmness is bad for the liver."

My glass was refilled. "Finish your wine, *caballeros*, and we'll proceed," Visenta said firmly.

The honeyed mist followed us only part way into the next room before it was invaded by the smell of cigar smoke. It had never seemed especially appropriate to me that the odor of a cigar was termed a bouquet, and in this case it was emphatically inappropriate. What I sniffed had a chewy pungency that reminded me of the final stages of one of Alejandro's crude black stogies. Had the moon or Alejandro kept us in the other room so long?

The candlelit table was set for six. I say "set": there was an empty bowl at each place. "Is Alejandro joining us?" I asked.

"Rosa Linda is joining us," Visenta said.

"Then Alejandro had to leave?"

Visenta looked searchingly at me. Her eyebrows had been darkened with charcoal, and her lips reddened with berry juice. It was a shame I had no military secrets to keep from her. In her own grotesque way, she was quite appealing.

"Ah, the cigar," she said finally. "I smoke his cigars myself, you know. He gives them to me sometimes. I *am* his cousin, you understand."

"*I* don't understand," Peter said. "All we wanted to find out was . . ."

"I know, I know, child," Visenta said. "But there are other things to find out. More important things. Please sit down."

Occasionally I had an impulse to say, "I *am* sitting down," but dazed as I was, I knew she knew it, and since I had nothing else to contribute, I bent silently over my bowl (things had come and gone in it) and listened. When all other sensory links failed, my ear could still keep me, even if unwillingly, in the world. Sometimes it functioned so relentlessly I almost resented it; it held too much that did not fit well with what was seen, and I had no talent for reshaping the one to suit the other. Where I saw squalor and hopelessness, I heard humor so light and abundant I wanted to forget it. And there were other things heard that stayed with me too long . . .

". . . nothing to do about it," Visenta was saying. "One burial after another—the babies went first—but they wouldn't come near us to help. It wasn't the only time; we're a cage to keep out of. If it's bad, let the peasants have it, let the little animals in the country use it up, that's the idea. At least I try to cure some of it."

Peter was clearing his throat. I hoped he wouldn't ask about the bridge again. "Then why do you . . . why are you . . . ?"

"Why am I called a witch, child? Because I *am* a witch. Oh, I won't change you into a cockroach; we've enough of those already. But I use what I use to do what I do."

"I . . . I'm not sure I understand, Señora."

"It's supposed to be wrong to hate, child. It's supposed

to be wrong to want revenge. That's what the powers that be say—the *good* powers, of course, the ones with all the good money and all the good land and all the good priests to back them up. But a witch, *pues*, a witch can hate, and I do. I've had enough of the *good* powers that be, child; I'll take the other kind. I'll use what I use to do what I do. Eat your soup."

"I'm really not hungry," Peter said. "What . . . what kind is it?"

"You're afraid of my soup, are you? Well, you needn't be. There's nothing in it I wouldn't eat myself."

"That probably doesn't help much," José said.

"Guillermito's had two bowls," Visenta said.

"And just look at him," José said.

"I'm alert," I said. "I happen to like this position."

"You see?" Visenta said. "But no matter. Don't eat what you don't want to eat. Rosa Linda, take away his bowl."

I raised my head; there she was, in a thin white cotton dress, looking like Elizabeth Taylor before the National Velvet horse was traded for a marry-go-round. "You can have my bowl too, Rosa Linda," I said. "Any time."

She giggled. "Did you like your soup?" she asked.

"I pretended it was you," I said. "You're not a witch, are you?"

"Who knows? Perhaps a little." She smiled, took my bowl, and dodged a clumsy swipe I offered.

"Bring the chicken and rice, Rosa Linda," said Visenta. "And hurry. We're late enough as it is."

"Late for what?" Peter asked.

"For some calls we're going to make. You're coming on my rounds with me."

"It's started raining," Rosa Linda called from a back room.

"Nor rain, nor hail, nor sleet, nor whatever shall keep the *bruja* from her appointed . . ." I began.

"Hush," Visenta said. "Next time I'll give you less wine."

"It was the moon's fault," I said.

114

"Then next time come when there's no moon to be seen," Visenta said. "For some things it's the very best time."

Visenta bent over the baby writhing on a cane mat. The mother sat on a wooden box, holding a small dish of mutton broth. "I can't nurse him," she said, "and he won't take anything else."

Visenta tapped the body lightly with her long fingernails; under the heart she jabbed quickly and tasted the blood she drew. "What do you mean, you can't nurse?"

"I'm dry," the mother said. "I've tried, but there's nothing." She looked suspiciously at us; Ernesto, Peter, José, and I stood by the door, trying not to seem intrusive. The hut was so small this was virtually impossible, though the dimness of the light helped somewhat. There were only two candles, and these were on the household altar in the corner where the baby lay. Every pueblo home had its altar, however simple. Here there was a peso picture of the Virgin Mary on a crude wooden stand decorated with pine tufts and topped by a little cane strip cross. Except for a small bench and a second mat (now rolled up) on which the mother slept, there were no other furnishings. The dirt floor was cold and slightly damp, and the mud walls were windowless. The mother was wrapped in blankets and shawls; the baby had been so wrapped before Visenta had arrived to tap and jab. Before the mother had turned her face to us, she had seemed quite old: a shriveled cluster of rags huddled on a box. Now I could see she was really young, less than twenty, though her teeth were already so rotten and her skin so rough it seemed a pointless technicality to call her young.

Visenta took a packet from a large leather pouch and handed it to the mother. "Rub this on your breasts before you try again."

"What if it doesn't work?"

"Then you might as well burn them off, for all the good they are to you," Visenta said harshly. "Where's Pedro?"

115

"Right here," Peter said.

"Not you," Visenta said. "The father."

"He's still in the city," the mother said. "I think he's looking for work."

"I want him back," Visenta said. "I can have you flowing like a spring if I can work through him."

"Well, I can't get him back," the mother said.

"*I* can," Visenta said. "He's the key—not the baby, and not you." She replaced the coverings on the baby. "The blood's all right."

"I was afraid there might be an evil spirit . . ."

"Phagh! Just because I'm a *bruja*, people expect me to see evil spirits everywhere I look. The child needs milk; I'll send over some he can take right away."

"Where will she get it?" Peter whispered to me.

"I heard that," Visenta said. "I sneak it from nursing mothers."

"You don't *really*," Peter said.

"Just leave the wheres and hows to me," Visenta said. "Though I don't mind telling you how I'm going to get the father back."

"How?" Peter asked.

"Fear," Visenta said proudly. "I'm linking the baby's life to his, and letting him know about it. If anything happens to the baby, the father can expect the same; agony for agony, death for death. That's where a little hate comes in handy; I'm arranging for revenge in advance. Oh, he'll come back quick enough, you'll see."

"I don't much want him back," said the mother.

"All the better," Visenta said confidently. "There'll be a little suffering all around, then. You can't let a man in you without expecting to pay for it."

"I've already paid for it," said the mother.

"You've barely begun," said Visenta cheerfully.

"I told her not to send for you," the man grumbled. "I hardly feel it these days."

116

"Who cares what you feel?" Visenta said. "If you'd stop passing it on to her friends, she'd let you feel any way you like. Drop your pants."

"I will not," the man said. "It's only a touch, and I've never hurt anybody with it."

"No? I know a few deformed children around here who might disagree."

"They're not mine," the man said positively. "I picked up two things in the city: syphilis and timing. I know when to strike." He winked at Peter. We were standing in the back patio; the man's wife had sent us all out. She had made it clear that she did not want to talk about it or hear about it: she just wanted it stopped.

"You strike with a string," Visenta said contemptuously. "Drop your pants."

"Not for a witch," the man said. "You might make it disappear."

"That might be better than letting *you* go on making it disappear," Visenta said.

"*I* make it disappear?" the man mused. "Oh yes, so I do, so I do. And reappear, too." He smiled. "Now you see it, now you don't." He nodded amiably at Peter. "Speaking of tricks, *muchacho*, that was a good one you pulled on the priest."

"It was all in the timing," Peter said.

"Timing, yes," the man said appreciatively. "There's nothing like timing."

"It's time to drop your pants," Visenta said impatiently. She rummaged around in the leather pouch. "I'm going to give you something that's even better than your wife's friends."

"You are?" the man said with quick interest. "Not that almost anything wouldn't be better than *some* of her friends."

Visenta took out a jar and then unscrewed the lid. "This is better than *any* of her friends. It's all in the way I work it in."

"He's going to get a treat instead of a treatment," Peter whispered to me.

"I don't know if I ought to let a witch do anything like that to me," the man said doubtfully.

"It takes a witch to do it right," Visenta said. "Just place yourself in my hands; there's more to be had from me than from anybody." In the moonlight that had come with the end of the rain, her face had the pale softness of smoke, and her darkened eyes and stained lips had a predatory intensity.

When we were on the pueblo road again, Peter asked her, "Will that really cure syphilis?"

She shrugged. "I wasn't trying to cure his syphilis."

"Then what . . . ?"

"What was in the salve? A little something to help him keep what he has to himself."

"I don't understand."

"Any undue friction will cause a rather horrible burning sensation. Does that seem cruel, child?"

"I don't know," Peter said. "He's in for a surprise."

"But not more than once, child. Not more than once."

"The trouble with you," Visenta said flatly, "is that you're *trastornada, loca,* crazy." She pulled the woman's skirt down. "Just because there happen to be men here, don't think it's a party."

"She doesn't speak for us," José said promptly.

"Happy Hispanic New Year," Ernesto said. "Please celebrate as you will."

"Hush, you bastards," Visenta said, not unkindly. "Listen, Rosa, I'm going to make you so well you won't like it at all."

Rosa belched and sampled the bottle of rum again. She looked so precisely like Mona Lisa that I wondered if the wine had affected me or the rum her. Probably both, I con-

118

cluded. "I like everything," she said, turning on her inscrutable smile. "Pinch me here," she said to Peter, patting her left thigh.

"My government doesn't permit it," Peter said sadly.

"No government permits it," said Rosa sympathetically. "That's the trouble with governments. Down with governments."

"These days," Ernesto said philosophically, "they need no encouragement. They fall so freely it makes one humble."

"It doesn't make *me* humble," said the woman (feeling as I did about Rosa Linda, I found I preferred not to think of this one as a Rosa). "Only two things make me humble."

"What?" Peter asked innocently.

"Two men at once," said the woman, clapping her hands delightedly.

"Is it possible?" Ernesto asked wonderingly.

"It would seem to depend on the approach," said José.

"Yes, yes!" said the woman, blinking at José and Ernesto. "You two understand me."

"As long as they don't make you humble," said Visenta dryly. "If you don't stop your foolishness, I'm going to give you an enema. *That* usually takes the edge off romance."

"It does change the atmosphere," José said. "Even thinking about it changes the atmosphere."

"Then it shouldn't be necessary to give her one. I mean an enema." Visenta took a little green ball and a mirror crisscrossed with red lines from the leather pouch. "Swallow this, Rosa," she directed, offering the ball.

"What is it?" asked the woman.

"Goat puke," said Visenta. "Don't ask questions, just swallow."

The woman shrugged and swallowed. "*Carajo!*" she said. "It *is* goat puke."

"I've worse than that handy, if you don't settle down," Visenta warned. "Now look in the mirror."

"What am I supposed to see?"

119

"The truth about yourself," Visenta said.

The woman looked. "I see nothing remarkable," she said.

"That's the beginning of the truth," Visenta said.

"All those lines," said the woman, staring into the mirror. "They make me look old."

"You're not young," Visenta said.

The woman sat in a chair by the window, through which the moonlight caught her mirrored face. "The light makes it strange," she said slowly. "It's not what I want to be."

"It's not what you want to be," Visenta said softly. "No, it's not what you want to be." She drew a chair close to the woman and sat down. "What *do* you want to be, Rosa?"

The woman shuddered. "I . . . I always wanted to be a great lady, with a . . ." She glanced over her shoulder at the small moonlit opening. ". . . a big window in a big house in the city. Is there . . . there's more than one city, isn't there, Visenta?"

"Yes."

"The largest city, then. I'd sit in the window, sewing things that didn't have to be sewed, watching the other fine people pass." She looked back into the mirror. "I'd have servants to help keep me looking young and beautiful, and a husband to keep telling me I did. I'd have an *hacienda* in the country and . . ." She broke off, and held the mirror closer. "No, I can't say I really want all that any more. I can't believe in it. It isn't real."

"Isn't it, Rosa?"

"No. It's all . . . falling apart . . . like the face I can't pretend to see in here. There's a . . . rotting."

"Aren't there people who live that way, Rosa?"

"Are there? They aren't real. They only pretend they are."

"*You're* the one who's crazy, Rosa."

"No, I'm not. I don't hang onto what I don't really have."

"What do you hang onto, Rosa?"

"Nothing. That's why you're here."

"Yes, Rosa, that's why I'm here. I'm going to give you

something you can hang onto. Something nice. Something you can care about." Visenta took several small packets from the leather pouch. "If the men will please wait outside, I'll show you how to take these."

We were on the pueblo road again. "Why did you have us wait outside for *that*, and not the other?" Peter asked.

Visenta smiled at him. "There are some things for which I want no witnesses."

"Will it make her better?"

"No. It will make her worse. But it will make her *feel* better."

"How?"

"Every now and then she comes too close to reality—you saw the stirrings—and she can't face it. What I give her will help keep her from coming too close again."

"Can't you give her something to help her *face* it?"

"Why should I? What is there to face? She's happier the other way." Visenta chuckled. "I'm restoring her faith."

"In what?"

"In her dream. I'm keeping her in her dream. She can be a great lady there."

"But what . . . what are you giving her?"

"A little cocaine. Nothing I wouldn't give my grand-mother."

"That's the family spirit," Ernesto said.

"But . . . aren't you afraid of the law?" Peter asked.

"The law doesn't much care what we do to ourselves," Visenta said. "We are only animals, after all. Besides, if there were trouble, there would be no witnesses, child."

"Isn't it . . . expensive for you?"

"Oh, I expect to be paid, child. Remember, she likes parties."

The man was my age—in his middle thirties—and it was not wholly self-flattery that led me to think he looked twice as old. His name was Pablo Palma de Paula, and I was fonder of the name than the person. Not that I disliked him—I knew him only casually—but he was not very communicative, and the only intriguing thing I had ever learned from him was that he had once owned a monkey that could shave itself. The monkey had died (presumably clean-shaven), and with it, evidently, had gone much of Pablo's interest in life. He tended his small plot, drank two bottles of beer nightly in Alejandro's *cantina*, straggled in church processions, and seldom offered more than a silent nod to those he passed on the pueblo road. Now he lay on his bed, a meager pile of bones and blue flesh, whiskers sprouting every which way (Was he dreaming now of his monkey coming from heaven with its razor and little shaving cup to help him out?), unmoving.

With him was his mother, Doña Alicia, with whom he had not been on close terms for many years (she had never liked his monkey). Holding her soiled white wrapper around her like a nervous prizefighter confronted suddenly with the opponent of the night, she blinked warily at us. For the first time I became aware of the dark hair on her upper lip.

"Don't worry about them," Visenta told her. "They're just learning the business."

"For reference purposes only," Ernesto added.

"Hah?" croaked Doña Alicia at Ernesto, who blushed.

"He can't help the way he talks," Visenta said. "They let him out of school none too soon."

"Alas, I'm still in school," said Ernesto.

"Only to confuse the young," Visenta said. "It's a good thing children learn more outside school than in."

"Perhaps we ought to have you as our next guest lecturer," Ernesto said. "The *niños* would all love you. You could start out with a lesson on, say, the use of entrails in arousing sexual desire."

"How did you know about that?" Visenta asked suspiciously.

"Good Lord!" Ernesto said. "You mean you actually *use* them?"

"There's very little waste in my profession," Visenta said with dignity. She looked carefully at Pablo. *"Espantado,"* she said.

"I never thought I'd have a son who'd look so terrible," said Doña Alicia. Sweat dripped from the hair on her upper lip.

Visenta poked the body with her fingers. "A classic case," she said with some satisfaction. "I want my little Pedro to watch closely." She looked challengingly at Ernesto. "He's *my* pupil. I can teach him more than anyone else around here can."

"At least about entrails and such," Ernesto said mildly.

"More than that, schoolmaster, more than that." Visenta gave us all a look I could only interpret as castrating; yet her pelvis was so mobile (in a witchy sort of way—don't ask me to explain it) I felt that if my potency had somehow been victimized by a pair of garden shears or an overdose of Strontium Ninety, she would restore it with a vengeance at the moment of impact.

"It . . . It's kind of you, Doña Visenta," said Peter.

"Kind!" said Visenta derisively. "I'm many things, child, but not kind." She bent over Pablo. "Now observe, child. The man's been ghosted. You don't believe that, do you?"

"I . . . I'm not sure what it means."

"Look at him. He looks lifeless, doesn't he?"

"Yes." Peter glanced uneasily at Doña Alicia. (Say what you will about Philip Wylie, American boys are by and large sweet about mother figures).

"It's because the very core . . ." She looked triumphantly at Ernesto—he didn't know all the good words, did he? ". . . of his life—his essence, his spirit—is gone. Do you know where it is, child?"

"No, Señora."

"When I tell you, child, I want you to look at Doña Alicia and laugh as loudly as you can. Then look at Pablo and do it again." Visenta tapped the motionless chest. "Where's his life-shade? The evil spirits have it." She stared at Peter. "So why don't you laugh?"

"I don't feel like it, Señora."

"Neither does he, child, neither does he." Visenta lightly stroked Pablo's head, as if she were fond of him for being in a condition she especially liked to treat. I almost envied Pablo; I have tried to be conservative about Visenta's attractiveness, but I have often felt she could disastrously arouse anyone less than fully committed to vows. "*Espíritus malignos*," she said. "The evil spirits have taken what belongs in the body, and what does not belong in the body has entered it." She smiled at Peter. "Do you know what that is, *querido?*"

"No, Señora."

"The *mal viento;* the wind that freezes the blood and attacks the heart. Now let me hear how loudly you can call it nonsense."

"It . . . it seems to be a matter of custom, Señora."

"Custom, is it?" Visenta laughed sharply, stopped abruptly. "Yes, custom, very good. Now watch." She put her fingers on Pablo's wrist. "First we find the pulse, child. The farther up the arm we find it, the more serious the condition. In this case . . ." She moved her fingers deftly along the arm. ". . . serious enough. Serious enough, child. I've brought back some who were worse, and . . ." She looked blandly at Doña Alicia, who glared back. ". . . I've lost some who were better."

"She *is* a comfort," José said.

"Tend to your coffins, carpenter," Visenta said.

"Not here," José said. "I hope Doña Alicia doesn't think I've come to solicit business."

"Why not?" snapped Doña Alicia. "Why shouldn't you try to make a fool of me? I'm nothing. Old people don't count for anything anymore." She looked searchingly at Pablo, as if in doubt that this was really her son. "When he was a boy, there was more respect. Since we lost our lands . . ."

"We didn't lose our lands," José said. "We *gained* them. They gave us titles."

"I say we lost *our* lands," Doña Alicia said. "While we owned them together, they held us together. Titles! The whole countryside around here used to be ours. And now . . . little bits of land, worn to death and divided to death." She touched Pablo. "If only he were still a boy," she said almost accusingly, as if it were all his fault for daring to grow up.

Visenta took some small boxes from the leather pouch. "Stop your wailing," she said, "and bring me some *aguardiente.*"

"If there's any at all, it isn't much," Doña Alicia said tartly.

"I don't need much," Visenta said. "Just enough for a moistener."

Doña Alicia went grumbling into the kitchen. We heard sounds of pouring; then back she came with a glass. "I use it now and then for cooking," she said, looking sadly at the inch of *aguardiente* in the glass. "In the old days I never used it; things tasted better then."

"You had a taster that wasn't half dead then," Visenta said mildly. She took the glass and emptied two of the boxes into it. "*Altamisa* and *yerbabuena*," she said, swishing the preparation in the glass, then adding the contents of another box. "And K-85."

"K-85?" Peter said wonderingly.

"There's no room in the profession for backward *brujas*," Visenta said. "We too must keep up. I've seen your American magazines." She eyed the mixture with an expression of avid thirst that would have delighted Alejandro. "After all, where would witchery be without the mystery ingredient? It was our idea in the first place." She dipped an index finger into the mixture and moistened her lips. "Not dry enough," she muttered, as if commenting on a martini. She added more K-85 and moistened her lips again, not bothering with the finger this time. "Ah, that's it." She lifted Pablo's left hand. "Now watch, child. I'm going to draw out the *mal viento*. I start with the palms."

125

She sucked each palm three times, intoning Pablo's full name between sucks. Then she repeated the cycle at the small of the back, the crown of the head, and the pressure point in front of the ears, moistening her lips between cycles. Then she swallowed the rest of the mixture and closed her eyes.

After seconds of silence, she began to chant slowly, partly in Latin and partly in Spanish. It sounded like a distortion of a priest's chant—partly benediction, partly malediction. She named two spirits with which (even now I am strongly tempted to say with whom) she was said to have a special affinity: *El Guando* and *La Viuda*. *El Guando* (The Hearse) was a candle-lit cadaver on a moving bier that passed by the pueblo in the dead of night. Anyone caught in *El Guando*'s path was *espantado* (ghosted or seized by magical fright). *La Viuda* (The Widow) was a shrouded and veiled creature who accosted presentable males alone on the road at night. Those who succumbed to her advances were carried by her embrace to death, while anyone who untactfully rebuffed her was *espantado*. Visenta spoke sharply to *El Guando* and confidentially to *La Viuda* (one might have thought she was talking to her sister). Finally she stopped talking and remained silent with her eyes still closed for several minutes.

Then she opened her eyes and inspected Pablo's. She shook her head.

"Back to the drawing board," Peter whispered to me.

Visenta reached into the leather pouch and took out what appeared to be a twig. She turned it over in her hands meditatively.

"Wouldn't your friends help?" Ernesto asked.

"They disclaim all responsibility," Visenta said.

"They're a shifty lot," Ernesto said.

"Be careful, schoolmaster," Visenta warned.

"Is it true *El Guando*'s motorized these days?" Ernesto asked.

"Is it true teachers know less and less about more and more these days?" Visenta snapped back.

"You leave my friends out of it, and I'll leave your friends out of it," Ernesto said.

Visenta looked at him cryptically (Was she thinking that Ernesto, as a widower, would make fine bait for The Widow?), then shrugged. (When I began my report, I wondered if I ought to leave out some of the shrugs; I could picture the reader, if there ever was one, reacting to them all with one of his own. But I decided to leave them in; in certain respects, this was a pueblo of sighs and shrugs.) "More *aguardiente*," she said to Doña Alicia.

"More?" Doña Alicia said gruffly. "Is this a cure or a drinking bout?"

"There'll be no chance for either without the *aguardiente*," Visenta said. "Hurry."

Doña Alicia picked up the glass and shuffled into the kitchen. After a few moments of muttering and clinking, back she came with the glass partly full. Her face seemed less sallow than before, and I suspected she had sampled the source—perhaps anticipating that if she didn't, Visenta would get it all in time.

Visenta took the glass and held up what she had taken from the pouch. "A harmless sprig of rue," she said. "But potent, all the same." She plunged the sprig into the glass, then pulled it out and thrust it into a candle flame for a brief sputter and hiss. Then she began to beat Pablo's skin softly with it. "What do you think of this, little Pedro?"

"I don't really understand what good it can do, Señora," Peter said.

"It does no *good* at all," Visenta said. "That's hardly the principle."

Up and down the body moved the sprig, drumming against the skin in what might have been a caress or punishment, or both. Visenta's stained face bent close to the skin, as if she were studying a map. The candle by the bed flickered and

127

smoked from the *aguardiente* and the dampness of the air in the mud hut. Doña Alicia pulled the soiled white wrapper closer about her, grumbling to herself. Ernesto and José stood by the door, looking uncomfortable; José was trying to muffle a cough. Peter had come close to the bed; he was so wholly absorbed in the ritual I almost expected him to seize the sprig at any moment and say, "No, *this* way, *this* way." The drumming continued.

Suddenly Pablo shivered, moaned, and—so violently Doña Alicia wailed in terror—sat up.

We watched intently, waiting for his first words.

"*Carajo!*" he said. "That thing tickled."

"Of course it tickled," Visenta said, as we walked back toward her hut. "But it wasn't the tickling that brought him back. If he hadn't been brought back, he wouldn't have felt the tickling." She held Peter's arm, keeping him close to her. Peter seemed dazed; he walked as if he had little control over his legs, like an old man. Visenta, on the other hand, walked with a lightness and litheness that made her seem startlingly like a young girl—it was almost as if she were tapping his youth. "So what do you think of all you saw, my little Pedro?"

Peter shook his head. "I'll have to sort it out," he said. "I . . . I *do* want to thank you, though, for . . ."

"Hush," Visenta said, drawing him closer. "Gratitude means nothing to me. Are you hungry?"

"No, Señora. Just tired, I guess."

"Do you want to stay with me tonight, child?"

"I . . . I guess I'd better stay with my friends, Señora."

"My poor little Pedro. When I was younger, I preferred weak enemies to strong friends. Now I've learned to prefer strong enemies to weak friends." Visenta sighed and looked back at us, as if hoping we were no longer there. "And tomorrow, child? Will you fix your bridge then?"

"Bridge? I . . . I'd almost forgotten about the bridge,

Señora." Peter seemed to be having difficulty keeping his chin from his chest. "So strange to be talking about a bridge . . . so little to do with what really . . ." He coughed; the pre-dawn mist was heavy and cold. "Almost . . . like a game," he finished.

"Don't worry, child," Visenta said reassuringly. "After all, games were *meant* for children."

VII

After three days of doubts and dysentery ("They go together very well," he told me ruefully), Peter decided to fix the bridge ("Not because it's the most I can do, but because I can do no less, really.") and go on from there. Where from there he didn't know, but he hoped the bridge would suggest something, if only through the criticism it might draw.

José, Ernesto, and Romelio helped him organize a community work party which—thanks largely to Romelio's zest for form—came to have so many officers and committees that there was much disappointment when the job was finished. Some, who were in the pueblo discussing strategy at the time, were so depressed at news of the end that they were all for tearing the bridge down and starting over. Doña Victoria, who had had her rocking chair brought to a crest overlooking the bridge, and had been enjoying herself thoroughly puffing away (she sent up so much smoke that from a distance the project appeared to depend on her for power) and hurling down encouragement or imprecations (it was often difficult to tell which) on the workers, sulked for days afterwards. Sebastian, who had come regularly to picket with a large poster inscribed "Down with Yankee Imperialism Canal Robbers" and bearing a sketch of the Henry Hudson Bridge, was also put out; his sketch was really very good, and had brought many admiring comments.

Most people, however, appeared to be quite proud of the

whole business, and while they might have liked it to continue a while longer, they now liked settling back and talking about it. Moreover, Romelio resolved some of the disappointment by suggesting that the work committees be converted to use committees; for several days the committees took turns using the bridge—"testing" it by going back and forth across it or resting their collective weight on it for sustained periods.

The bridge itself was very attractive; essentially simple in design, the wood and metal structure had a hand rail so well suited in height and firmness to those who liked to lean and fish or lean and just watch the water that the committees became more and more sedentary in their testing. Eventually the whole arrangement broke down, as one committee member after another brought food and family to spend the entire day on the bridge. "A day on the bridge" became such a popular recreational pattern for a time that traffic across it was virtually precluded.

Not that this seemed to bother people; at first those who had to cross the river would go far out of their way just to be able to go across on the new bridge, with the result that commerce was greatly slowed. Later, when "a day on the bridge" became popular, those whose course of travel would ordinarily have led them across the bridge either went out of their way to find a less congested crossing or spent a lot of time visiting their way across the bridge, with the result that commerce was again slowed. But the few who complained about such conditions were said to be "enemies of progress"; after all, anyone could see how modern the bridge was.

Various incidents and minor crises enlivened the early life of the renovated bridge (Procopio called it the "resurrected" bridge). A cow wandered onto it for several mornings running and defecated rather freely, so that the first arrivals from the pueblo complained of the slipperiness and bad manners. The cow was traded for a *guarapo* press and a constipated goat. Two children fell off the bridge, and there was such excitement in rescuing them that in the next four days eleven other children jumped off. (They picked a spot less than three feet deep.) Young lovers began to meet on the bridge at night; the practice was abruptly ended when Visenta, on appeal from a number of parents, put a sterility curse on the bridge. Sebastian surreptitiously put up the flag of the USSR on the bridge one night, but when nobody recognized it (Some of the children tore off strips for toilet paper.) he took it down disgustedly. At high noon a young man named Eusebio Justicia Constancia de Rodillo tried to assault an eighty-year-old lady named Felicia Alegría, who calmly threw him into the river. Eusebio apologized so elaborately they became good friends. A stud horse—hopelessly unsuccessful to date—on his way to market suddenly began to copulate with his companion mare just after he had stepped on a guava sandwich on the crowded bridge, and was saved from horseburger by the cheers of an engrossed audience. One of the fishermen actually caught a rather stubborn fish, which caused some of the other fishermen to put away their poles. "There are enough distractions already," one of them said. A man on crutches announced halfway across the bridge that he was cured, threw away his crutches, and landed violently on his behind.

These, however, were only ripples in the general tranquillity (I speak only of the kind of tranquillity a time and motion study would show) of pueblo life—a tranquillity into which the bridge was increasingly assimilated. "Nothing's really changed," Peter told me one afternoon, as we walked toward the plaza to help Ernesto repair some of the school benches. "But at least I found out what I'm going to do next."

"What?"

"Well," he said slowly, "it seems to me the chief reason for anyone like myself—a foreigner—to fool around with things like bridges and fences is that they're the *safest* things to work on. Not that the work can't be useful, and not

132

that people can't get excited or upset over a bridge and fence. But by and large they're externals. They're not really close to the mainspring—not around here anyway—so while you're not as apt to get hit by the recoil, you're also not as apt to touch anything fundamental." He wiped his face—thinner and more intense than before—with his handkerchief. "Maybe that's the whole idea, of course. Maybe you're not *supposed* to touch anything fundamental. Maybe the people who let you in the country in the first place don't really want the boat rocked. How far can you go? Is it fair to give the impression you're working toward the heart of a problem when you know you're only permitted to putter around the edges?"

"I see you still have a few questions left," I said. "But maybe you have to start with the edges or you won't start at all."

"Maybe. As long as you don't fool yourself the edges are more than edges. Where you start, sometimes you stay. It's easiest, and you can work out all kinds of reasons why it's the best place to be. And all the while the people who keep the mainspring tightly wound can go about the way they always have, and if anyone asks questions, they can show pictures of *you*. So you wonder if you're being used. Maybe it's a *caballeros'* agreement. They let you in to scratch as long as you don't really dig." He paused and wiped his face again. The road was dry, and the afternoon wind kept the dust in the air.

"You're just a young pup," I said. "Who are you to decide where the scratching ends and the digging begins?"

"How old do you have to be to know something's wrong?" he said angrily. "It's the young people who are going to have to change it. Look at all the student protests and demonstrations—all over the world."

"Maybe that's just part of being a student," I said. "Maybe you outgrow it."

"Well, you shouldn't," he said.

"Maybe you take yourself too seriously," I said. "Like the young hopefuls just starting to write: everywhere they look they see misery and injustice. Pathos is their meat."

"Well, there's enough of it."

"It's not your discovery. You and your little sense of wonder are a dime a dozen."

"So you think I'm wrong."

"Wrong about what? You're so quick to put things on a right-wrong basis. Right-wrong, black-white, good-bad, for-against. Sheesh!"

He gave me a hurt look. "I thought you were on my side."

"There you go again," I said. "On your side. For you, against him. Either-or." I took a pack of *El Sol* cigarettes from my khaki jacket, shook one out and lit it. "That doesn't mean I'm *for* straddling, or *against* taking a stand. It means I want to look a little before I judge. And even then I might find both sides guilty. Or partly guilty. Then, too, there's an old saying to remind me maybe I shouldn't judge at all." I offered him a cigarette; he shook his head. Ahead of us, on the near edge of the plaza, there was a group of children playing with hand-carved wooden tops. An old man sat on a log watching them and laughing with them as the tops made the dust spurt. Beyond them I could see María cleaning the church steps. "Are people really so badly off here, Pete?"

"It's not so much what they are," he said. "It's what they could be."

"Maybe that's true of us, too."

"You goddamn anthropologists!" he said with an exasperated smile. "Everything's relative, is that it?"

"Not everything," I said. "We're as much interested in the universal as the relative. After all, if everything were relative, the truth of relativity itself would be only relative, and the whole relativity doctrine would break down. The very basis for what's relative is what's universal. That's something like saying that without standards you can't note variations. What I'm suggesting is that individuals and

134

groups are all too apt to mistake their own relative truths for universal truths, and history's full of people who slaughtered other people—or reformed them to death—in the name of truth." I stopped; I was beginning to sound too much like the person I thought I had left. "You never did tell me what your next move's going to be, Pete."

Ernesto came from the *Escuela de Varones* and waved to us.

"I'll tell you a little later," Peter said. "It's nothing spectacular. It's just a step closer to the mainspring."

We had moved all the school benches into the plaza—"to have proper working room," as Ernesto put it, though at the moment we seemed to be testing them for comfort. José had joined us, however, and there was a definite expectation that he would soon rise, look them over, and give us a professional diagnosis. It seemed only fair to wait.

"They fit rather poorly," José observed.

"There seems to be a certain shrinkage," Ernesto said. "Every year they grow smaller. When I was a boy, benches were more dependable."

"It's true, it's true," José said, sighing. "They just don't make benches the way they used to. Or anything else. Take coffins. Where's the pride these days? The way things are now, it's the coffin that falls apart around the body. Have I told you about my cousin Eusebio recently?"

"Not recently," Ernesto said. "But fairly often."

"Congratulations," José said. "Still, I've never told young Pedro." He paused. "Are you listening, Pedrito?"

"Eagerly, Don José."

"You see, Pedrito, my cousin Eusebio is a used-coffin dealer in the city, and . . ."

"A *what?*"

"A used-coffin dealer. Now, the interesting thing is . . ."

"Excuse me, Don José," Peter broke in again. "How could there be a *used*-coffin dealer? I mean, where would anyone get *used* coffins to sell?"

"Oh, that. It's very simple, Pedrito. What with the hospital in the city, and the medical school for the little slicers, there's a good market—not seasonal at all—for bodies to practice on. So whenever the supply gets low, enough graves are opened to build it up again. Oh, they're not pigs about it, but all the same they don't like to be caught short. So that leaves empty coffins here and there. And as long as they aren't being occupied, my cousin—he hates to see things go to waste —figures he might as well offer them to someone else. So he revarnishes and resells them; at a very reasonable price, I might say."

"But . . . but how does he know about these empty coffins?"

"Oh, he and the doctors have a sort of understanding about the whole business. But I haven't told you the only part of interest yet: Eusebio swears the old coffins are best."

"That's the interesting part?"

"I knew you'd be fascinated. It's what I've said all along, Pedrito: they don't make them the way they used to. *Pues,* Eusebio has about twenty of what he likes to call his old faithfuls. He's been selling them over and over for more than forty years, and they're as good now as the first time he sold them. What with all that digging up and dropping, you have to figure on a certain amount of wear and tear, but he swears they haven't really suffered at all."

"He keeps on reselling the same ones? Over and over again?"

"Only the old faithfuls. Some of the others—the newer ones—aren't made too well, and he draws the line at one or two resales of *those.* It's a matter of ethics, he says. Then, too, some of the reburials are in hard-to-get-at places. But he won't part with an old faithful unless he knows exactly where it's going, and it's not in some God-forsaken out-of-the-way place all covered with those heavy monuments. The best plots are the ones for transients."

"Transients?"

"The people who die while passing through. No local ties.

Little people like us, but without a community like this for company. There are advantages in the city, you see; at least for Eusebio. With transients, you can use the same plots time and again, and there's nobody to care. If you've ever tried opening a grave, you'll know it isn't easy; and the first time's the hardest, you can ask anyone. But these pre-opened graves are a real boon to science. The dirt and sod, what there are of them, come right up, and you don't even have to pack them down again; in fact, it's better if you don't."

"But how does Eusebio collect for . . . from . . . for the transients?"

"Oh, that's no problem, Pedrito. He has a talent for finding a relative somewhere to send money. Then, too, he can always manage to get something from the public agencies. And the doctors contribute a little. Finally, the transient may be carrying a thing or two of value. No, it's no problem."

"But don't you think it's *wrong*, what he's doing?"

"Wrong, Pedrito? *Pues*, now that you mention it, I've often thought there was something about it that wasn't quite right. But I've never been able to say just what. After all, science is served, Eusebio is served, and the customers themselves get a very good and very reasonable—if somewhat temporary—service."

"That's just it, it's *temporary*."

"Dead things aren't meant to last forever," José said imperturbably. "What good does it do to hang onto what's dead? This way, even transients get a chance to serve science."

"Then you approve?"

"I? Approve? I have nothing to do with approval." José yawned and stretched. "Come, Pedrito, let's start on the benches."

"You sound so callous."

"I have never claimed otherwise. Whatever that fine word you used means."

"Sometime you must tell him about your cousin Rafael," Ernesto said.

"Ah, yes, the one with Christ tattooed on his chest. He lives in the valley, you see, where it is so hot the image of our Lord sweats almost constantly; the agony seems always there. And when he bears down on a woman, the woman is apt to cry that her Savior is . . ."

"On second thought," Ernesto interrupted, "perhaps you shouldn't tell him about Rafael. The story repels me. Yet, just as I feel most repelled, I find myself laughing. It traps me into sacrilege."

"But why?" José said, picking thoughtfully at a patch on his workpants. "It is not a story about the Lord. It is only a story about my cousin Rafael. What he has on his chest is only an image, a thing of holes and ink. Is it possible to desecrate a thing of holes and ink? The priest himself said we shouldn't confuse the image with the deity. Didn't he? Didn't he?"

"Yes, of course," Ernesto said. "But the association . . ."

"Association, is it? If I were not a mild man, I would spit on your association. If I thank the Lord for the healthy state of my pig, there'll be someone to say I insulted the Lord by associating Him with my pig. *Carajo!* And that doesn't mean I just swore at the Lord. *I* know the difference between my Lord and my pig, and between my Lord and a thing of holes and ink. I never laugh at my Lord. I only laugh at people, and at their confusion." The patch on his workpants came off in his hand, and he looked at it almost tenderly, then dropped it in the dust. "And at my confusion."

The wind was rising, and as I looked across the plaza the sight and sound of the priest's robe cracking like a whip came to me. There, I thought, was certainty. And then the sight of the priest toppled by a Peter with a fool's head, an animal's head, came also . . .

José stood up. "I regret to say it, but I am ready to work. Is my assistant ready? Pedrito?"

"I am ready, Don José," Peter said.

"Is the schoolmaster ready?"

"I'm afraid so, carpenter," Ernesto said.

"Are you ready, Don Guillermo?"

"Yes, Don José," I said.

"Then there is nothing we cannot do," José said, his voice gentle. "We have myself to take measurements. We have Pedrito to ask questions. We have Don Guillermo to listen. And we have Don Ernesto to figure out everything, and to keep the answers from falling into the wrong hands."

"I do the last part very well," Ernesto said sadly. "I haven't let out an answer in years."

"I feel humbly grateful to be included among those who have been denied your answers," José said. "But such a talent shouldn't be wasted on so limited a collection of little people. Why don't you go into politics, where you can reach the whole country?"

"If I do, you can have the coffin concession for my first revolution."

"It would put new life into the business. I thank you, Don Ernesto." José bowed stiffly.

"That's what friends are for," Ernesto said, returning the bow from his bench.

Within ten minutes after the diagnosis had been made ("A progressive deterioration of a general nature," José had announced. Ernesto had commented that he was very pleased to hear the condition was progressive, since there was very little else that progressed in the pueblo.) the wind brought a burst of rain that—unfortunately, we all agreed—prevented us from repairing the benches. "At least they'll be cleaner," Ernesto said as we ran for cover. "When the mud's wiped off."

"The shape may be improved by the warping," José said.

"If the wood isn't washed away entirely. Lately even the trees haven't been what they used to be."

Peter and I paused under the overhang of a thatch roof so steeply pitched the rest of the hut seemed like an afterthought. This was the dwelling of Francisco Medina, a brother of the muscular Faustino Medina who had sliced wicks so assiduously on the night of the fiesta of the *Sagrado Corazón*. Francisco, his wife Alegría, and their six children had gone to visit Francisco's godfather in a nearby pueblo.

José and Ernesto, who were either faster or thirstier than we, had gone ahead in the general direction of Alejandro's *cantina*. The rain was coming down very hard now, and up the road a toddler, who had been sent out naked for a quick shower, was being summoned by his mother to hurry into the warm blanket she held outstretched in the doorway. Here and there along the road, women were placing out clay pots to catch the rain.

"So what's your next move, Pete?" I asked.

"It's nothing the Peace Corps hasn't thought of," he said. "But it seems closer to what really counts than working on bridges and fences. It means trying to do something about the whole basis of the economy here: the way the land's used. If I can help people get more out of their land without wearing it out, there'll be all kinds of dividends. Nutrition and health, for example—I could show them how to improve their diet. And with more of a surplus to sell, they could buy better clothes and other things they can't afford now; they wouldn't have to live so close to the margin."

"It has a logical ring to it," I said. "If I say it won't be easy, I'm sure I won't be saying anything you haven't realized by now."

He shrugged; the gesture might have come from a native of the pueblo. In fact, he seemed to have taken on more and more of the little characteristics—as subtle but distinctive as the sound of a footstep instantly recognized—of his hosts.

140

His tendency to walk slightly stooped over had at first seemed part of the ungainliness of a boy who has not yet learned to straighten up properly; it now seemed closer to the way of those who plodded along the pueblo road with heavy burdens on their backs, to the way of those who had learned to lean into the wind, to the way of the partly defeated who had learned nevertheless to endure. The redness that came so quickly to his face had at first seemed a residue of adolescence, a sign of naïveté; it now seemed closer to the weather-beaten look of those whose faces were tempered by sun and wind and dust and cold. The way he touched the elbow of the one he walked with, the way he often averted his eyes as if looking beyond the one he talked with, the way he sat silently—as if he might never move or speak again—when there seemed to be nothing to do or say: such ways were of the pueblo, and when I saw him coming from a distance, bent into the wind, his straw hat pulled over his eyes to shield them from the dust, his faded trousers flapping around his slowly moving legs, I sometimes thought I ought to ask him if he had seen Peter.

"I won't be doing it by myself," he said.

"You mean you'll have José and Ernesto and the rest of our little Rat Pack to help."

"More than that."

"You mean you'll be working with the whole pueblo."

"More than that."

"You mean you'll feel you have the support of your country."

"More than that."

His face seemed to be burning, and it occurred to me for the first time that he might be seriously ill. "You aren't sick, are you?"

"I'm sick of being helpless. I'm beginning to understand what Visenta does: she's fighting what's wrong with what's wrong. Sebastian is, too. I'm going to try another cure."

"Who's the patient? The pueblo or yourself?"

"Both. And maybe more."

"You're pretty gutsy today, Pete. I just hope you last."

"I'll last. I hope it won't upset your study if things change around here."

"Shucks, no," I said. "I could make it a study of directed culture change, as we ethnologists are wont to say."

"Is that what you'd call it?"

"Sure. What would *you* call it?"

"I don't know," he said, looking out at the rain. "I just don't know."

"Don't brood," I said. "What's in a name? Directed culture change by any other name would . . ."

"Oh, stop it," he said, grinning. "How would you write it all up, anyway?"

"I think I'll turn it into a novel," I said. "I'll be able to tell the truth that way."

VIII

The next few weeks, I may say fairly, were hard on us all. Even Sebastian, who had so enjoyed picketing the bridge project, and who now followed in Peter's wake trying to undo whatever was done, threatened to stop protesting if Peter didn't slow down. (Later Sebastian apologized. "I was selfish," he said. "I had to miss some fine riots in the city. Oh, riots are tiring, too, but the hours are shorter.")

Sebastian actually had very little to undo. People listened politely to Peter, offered him coffee and bread, and went on doing things the way they had always done. "But our rows have always run up and down the slope, Señor," a man would say. "They *expect* to run up and down the slope."

"Yes," Peter would say patiently, "but you lose topsoil that way. Every time it rains the runoff carries some away. And that's another thing; you lose the water that way."

"It is the way of our fathers, Señor."

"I appreciate that," Peter would say. "But the land is no longer what it was when your fathers used it that way."

"True," the man would say, nodding.

"You see," Peter would say hopefully, "it quickens erosion."

"Ah," the man would say. "So that is what it quickens. Imagine."

Peter would explain about erosion, and crop rotation, and

143

proper fertilization, and the man would listen and nod, and promise to think about it, and in the end would make no changes.

"I know all the arguments," Peter told me, "but no one really argues. If anyone ever *does* plant a row across a slope instead of up and down it, it won't be because of anything I've said."

"Exactly," I said.

"What do you mean?"

"Talking's great fun, but if you really want to make your point you're going to have to *show* you understand what you're talking about. Why not rent a piece of land and plant your own rows?"

"I know, I know," Peter said. "I guess I was looking for a short cut. But people listened so well, I thought I was making headway."

"Good old passive resistance," I said. "They've had a few centuries of practice. They know how to wait the man out: listen politely and nod every now and then, and soon enough he'll look for someone else to bother."

So Peter rented part of Alejandro's land and became even more like a *campesino*. From his little store of checks from home—he usually tucked them carelessly among his shirts in José's unfinished coffin, and when he took out a shirt, two or three checks were apt to flutter back in, as if in payment to the other world—he cashed enough to buy the simple hand tools and basic supplies he needed. Then he began to work so hard—clearing, plowing, planting—that he seemed close to a physical breakdown.

"Look, Pete," I told him, "it's not going to help your cause much if you produce more by working twice as hard as the others. They'll say it's not your methods, it's all that sweat. After all, the glory of know-how is that it gives you *more* leisure time, not less."

"I suppose so," he said. "But I worry when I leave it. I keep wondering what would happen if I *don't* produce more. What if my crops are the only ones that fail?"

144

"Hell, Pete, you'd probably make more friends than you ever dreamed of," I said.

Though he slowed up afterwards, he still seemed so close to exhaustion that José and I took turns spelling him. The time of the big September "dry planting" was at hand— the earlier "wet planting" of potatoes in the low swampy areas was considered only a warmup—and as I made little clods out of big ones and scattered my seed like a stud cabbage, I appreciated as never before the role of observer. Ah, fellow anthropologists, I thought, now I know why we stress observation; by and large, we're anti-work. Of course, we have our Participant Observation, where we take part in what we observe the better to enhance, as the saying goes, understanding, but we mostly save that for such activities as games, feasts, and fertility rites. I had learned in graduate school to make a distinction between the early "armchair anthropologists" and their successors who went Into the Field, but now I was of the opinion that what the successors managed to do very well was to take the armchair with them. And now I had been uprooted (you can see the horticultural influence) from mine.

I marveled at José: he seemed to get his work done without moving. Whenever I came to relieve him he looked as cool, unruffled, and unhurried as always. "It is nothing," he told me modestly. "One pokes a little hole periodically." Yet he always got his quota done.

María teased me gently. "You mumbled in your sleep again last night," she said, smiling her beautiful smile.

"In Spanish or English?"

"Both, lover. At least I supposed the gibberish was English. Why don't the *Yanquis* speak Spanish like the rest of us?"

"They haven't caught on yet, María. What did I say apart from the English gibberish?"

"The only words I caught were, 'Why do there have to be *five* kinds of beans?'"

"Well, why *do* there?" I asked defensively. "They all

taste about the same. Why don't you just grow one kind?"

"Why don't we just raise one kind of child?" she countered softly. "After all, children are children."

Sebastian came only once to the plot. "I see no point in picketing where there's only you to watch me," he told us stiffly, as if he were delivering a formal apology. "I thought I ought to inform you, so you wouldn't wonder why I stayed away."

"As long as it's nothing personal," I said.

He looked vaguely at me. His brooding eyes were bloodshot, and his round little face was puffed with fatigue. "The truth is, I'm in a little trouble."

"Congratulations," José said. "Welcome to the rest of the world."

Sebastian glared at José, then turned back to me. "It concerns my posters. The regional committee has accused me of sneaking capitalists into them. Our heroes seem to have the faces of our enemies."

"Amazing," I said.

"Those magazines of yours . . ."

"Not mine," I said. "Yours. I gave them to you freely and absolutely. To do what you would with them. It appears that you've done it."

"Our peasants, our guerrillas, our leaders—all with the faces of our enemies. It's as if the rich and powerful reactionaries were invading our ranks. I . . . I'm accused of subversion." He blinked. "Imagine! I'm said to be subversive."

"Stand tall when anyone calls you that," I said. "Aren't you *supposed* to be subversive?"

"But not against my own," he said plaintively. "I've been loyal. You know I've been loyal."

"We'll vouch for you, Don Sebastian," said José. "You've never given us anything but trouble." He patted Sebastian on the shoulder. "I'd be willing to put that in writing, if I could write."

"Thank you, Don José," Sebastian said gratefully. "If I were permitted to accept help from you, I'd accept it."

"Why don't you tell them it was all a kind of joke, Don Sebastian?" I suggested. "You could all have a good laugh over it. If it's permitted, that is."

"I tried to tell them something like that," Sebastian said gloomily. "But I am not very good at explaining jokes in the first place, and in the second place the committee does not enjoy having jokes played on it." He shivered.

"Our secret weapon," I said.

He looked at me uncomprehendingly. "It was horrible," he muttered. "A life's work turned into something else."

"It happens all the time in the good old USSR," I said. "Remember, the cause is always more important than the individual. Especially the other individual."

"I must straighten it out somehow," he said. He nodded absently at Peter, who nodded as absently in return. Here they were, I thought, the two enemies, each preoccupied with his own problems, not really seeing each other.

Rain, mud, sun, dust—the days passed in a damp-dry blur of grime. I never quite dried out or got wet enough to feel clean. The midday burning never quite dissipated the chill of rising at dawn; I had never before shivered and sweated at the same time, but I did so now. Beans, corn, yuca, cabbage, and arracacha—these were my litany, my little band from a stuck record: BEANS, corn, YUCA, cabbage, and ARRRRRA-CACHA. Reason was numbed; caring was curbed. My skin was roughened and my hair became a nest. I had always approved of the role of exercise in keeping trim, but the gambolings of the tennis player had nothing in common with this drudgery. While the tennis player was keeping trim, the farmer was growing old before his time.

Five kinds of banana tree to transplant and look after: the "common" banana (God bless the common banana), *platano*, *geneo*, *jardinero*, and *taiti*. Another litany, another band from a stuck record. And then there were coffee trees . . .

147

Little flags tied on stakes. Strings between stakes. Mosquitoes and flies. Saltpeter and excrement; Peter was a fertilizer man's fertilizer man (Ah, that rich, rich muck!). That, I thought, was the real key: nothing would dare stay down in that stuff.

One day Rosa Linda stopped me on my way back to María's. "You look interesting," she said. "So dark."

"A million-peso tan," I said.

"You smell interesting too." She wrinkled her pretty nose.

"It's my natural odor," I said. "I've been concealing it from you."

She kissed me quickly on the chin and ran off. The parts of me that could still move wanted to lunge after her, but there were too many parts that could only creak and sigh.

My own labors, unaccustomed as they were, were as nothing compared to Peter's. When he was not in his plot, he was making the rounds, talking to his fellow *agricultores* about the weather, pests, past crops, markets—not trying to convert now, but trying to learn. "The book doesn't help me when it comes to what's right under my nose," he told me. Local conditions, local variations—the book doesn't tell me about those. But the people can. It's not just a matter of facts; it's a matter of feeling. In the middle of a hot, dry day, I swear they can feel rain coming, or a cold spell. I don't know if I'll be able to help them, but they've sure as hell helped me."

And they had. They'd told him when to cover plants, and when to store up all the water he could—they'd even loaned him cloth and barrels. There were countless little courtesies, little touches—a jug of hot coffee brought to the field, a plate of freshly baked rolls waiting for him in his room, a guinea pig presented to him by a child. (It had been her pet, he discovered, and she asked him gravely please not to eat it for awhile. He promised not to, and made her joyful by asking her to take care of it for him.) Most of all, they gave him a sense of being a farmer. He looked over his field as if the land held everything a man might want, and he drew

148

breath as if he were testing the air for what it might bring tomorrow.

His khakis wore out, and he bought the cheapest work-pants and workshirts, and when his belt broke he used a rope in its place. His shoes gave way to sandals, and broken fibers in his straw hat poked out here and there. He was not consciously going native; it was an osmosis, a suffusion from the soil, his personal harvest.

I took out my notebook again, and tried to keep track of what was happening to him, but he kept walking right off the page—gaunt, bent, plodding past my pencil point. He always seemed to be moving, moving slowly, and this, I thought, was the hardest kind of motion to follow. It was the way the pueblo itself moved; and in an age of blinding speed, I thought, it could be easily mistaken for no movement at all. But there was a force to it, perhaps, that might some day shatter the things that moved with blinding speed . . .

Tired as he was, he had trouble sleeping. Sometimes he moaned in the deep of night, and José would rush in, and talk quietly to him until his eyes and lips closed again. "I'm not easily unnerved," José told me, "but I've lived so long without company that it's difficult for me to hear calmly the sound of moaning from the room where I used to keep my coffins." Once, on a stormy night, when José was on an over-night market trip to the city, and Peter tossed and turned feverishly, Visenta came, almost as if she had been called, and gave him an alcohol (*aguardiente*) rub that led him into a sleep more restful than any he had had for weeks. "It was like a caress, really," he told me, blushing. "A long caress. And she kept murmuring, 'Sleep, my child, sleep.' At first, you know, I was nervous, but she didn't try any magic on me. It was just . . ." He stopped and looked at me thought-fully. "Hell," he said finally, "it *was* magic."

He seemed much more serious than before, but he had his moments. One afternoon, when I met him on the road, he was grinning so foolishly I was worried. "Guess what I heard from Carlos Sandía," he said gleefully.

149

"He's pregnant?" I suggested.

"It was just as surprising," he said. "He's always been very reserved with me, very cold. On his guard, you know. Well, he just told me the filthiest joke I've ever heard."

"No!"

"Absolutely from the bottom of the well. Oh, it was awful! Terrible! Just grand!"

"Aren't you going to tell it to me?"

"The joke?" He scratched his battered straw hat. "It was about bestiality, but I don't quite remember how it went . . . what counts is, he *told* it to me. Three months ago he wouldn't have come *near* me with a joke like that."

"You're in," I said.

Another time I saw him coming out of Doña Victoria's hut, hand pressed over mouth, full of wild rumbles. He beckoned to me with his other hand, and after we had walked up the road a little way he freed his mouth and let out the laughter. He was so thin he looked as if he were going to shake himself to pieces.

"Don't tell me *she* told you a filthy joke," I said.

"No . . . no," he gasped. "Oh Lord, I shouldn't laugh at all. It was just . . ." The laughter came out again with a whoosh, and it took him a while to calm down.

"This is the second time I've caught you laughing lately," I said. "What do you think life is, one long haha?"

"I . . . I just dropped in to see how she was, you know, and I had some tobacco to give her, and . . ." He stopped and wiped his eyes on a handkerchief that had been to the rocks once too often. (Detergents were unnecessary here. Preferred washing directions were: (1) dunk garments in stream (2) beat dirt out with rocks.) "Anyway, she said she'd dreamt that Wally Frank had jumped her, and forced her at pipe point to . . ."

"Pipe point?"

"Like gunpoint, you know. Or knife point. Only with a calabash."

150

"Of course, of course."

"Anyhow, he forced her at pipe point to take off her legs, and . . ."

"You *did* say, take off her legs?"

"Yes, she unscrewed them, you see, like pipestems—her legs *are* a bit like pipestems, you know—and then he pulled out a long pipe cleaner . . ."

"Now I know why I never took up pipe smoking," I said. "Too many phallic symbols."

"Then he cleaned out her legs, you see, because they were all clogged with stale blood . . ."

"Naturally. Whose wouldn't be?"

"I'm just telling you what she told me, so don't . . ." He used his handkerchief again. "Anyway, I haven't got to the funny part yet."

"You'll tell me?"

"Yes, I'll tell you. So after he cleaned out the stale blood, he screwed her legs back on . . ."

"Trick of the year."

"Quiet, please. Then he said, 'Where's your bowl? I'm going to fill it.' And she said, 'You can't. Sebastian's sitting in it.' "

"Taking a bath, no doubt."

He looked at me reproachfully. "That would be silly."

"Forgive me," I said. "He *wasn't* taking a bath. He was sitting there not taking a bath."

"I don't know *what* he was doing. Or not doing. She didn't say."

"I should think not."

"But that's where the posters came in, you see."

"The posters. It must have been a big bowl."

"They weren't *in* the bowl," he said, exasperated. "Now be quiet. I'm coming to the funny part."

"You'd better hurry," I said. "I feel less like laughing all the time."

"So she woke up and started yelling at Sebastian. 'It's all *your* fault he wouldn't fill my bowl,' she told him. Well, he hadn't slept any too well, with that committee business bothering him, and he didn't know what she was talking about anyway—for all he knew she'd gone berserk—so when she grabbed one of his poster sticks and started swinging at him, he clipped her but good. He hit her right in the gut."

"Sebastian did?"

"Sebastian himself. Oh, she was proud as could be. To hear her tell it, it was the first manly thing he'd ever done. She showed me the poster stick and went through all the motions—the way she'd swung it, and the way he'd ducked under it and nailed her."

"Is that the funny part?"

"No, not yet. So the poster stick led to the posters, and she showed me some of the last ones he'd done before the committee put the freeze on, and . . ."

"The freeze?"

"I guess he's more or less in cold storage until they decide what to do with him. He's not to make posters or march or take part in anything they do. Anyway, I was looking at the ones he had there, and I can see why the committee got excited."

"Tell me more, cried the first mate breathlessly."

"Well, there was one with Maggie—you know, Maggie, Jiggs, the comic strip bit—and she was squatting in the dust, and fields were burning in the background—there always seem to be fields burning in the background; he does that very well—and she was suckling a . . . a . . . ."

"For God's sake, what was she suckling?"

"A baby, of course."

"A baby what?"

"A baby girl, I think. A little creole—I couldn't remember that word—girl, though it could be a boy, I suppose. Is it important?"

"No," I said, "it's not important."

"And then there was Sir Cedric Hardwicke eating from a trough . . ."

152

"In front of Maggie?"

"It was a different poster."

"Then we must be sure to keep them separated."

"I'll do my part," he said, getting into the spirit.

"Stout fellow. Pray continue with your tale."

"Thank you. So there he was, eating from a trough, dressed in rags."

"The pathos of it! A trough dressed in rags."

"So it struck me. Anyway, his hut was falling apart, and the fields were burning in the background, and there was this caption, 'How Long Will You Be Kept an Animal?' Somebody had scribbled under it, 'Bow wow.' "

"A brave answer."

"Yes." A turkey buzzard swooped low over the pueblo road and landed on the back of a sleeping burro. A small boy started throwing chunks of dirt at the buzzard, hitting only the burro, making it shudder violently without waking it. "Then there was one with a monastery in it, and all these well-fed monks playing little children's games, and you could see the fields burning in the background, of course, and there was one monk at the gate, getting ready to leave—he was pretty obviously fed up with the others, and was about to throw in his robe; he had it half off already." He stepped over a dirt castle some children had been making in the road. One of the towers had been broken off, and he bent to restore it before moving on. "So Bond . . ."

"James Bond?" I interrupted. "How did *he* get into the monastery?"

"He was the good monk, the one who was so devout he couldn't stand all that hypocrisy, you know, and with one hand on the gate and the other pulling off his robe, he was saying—the caption was: 'It Is Time for the Pure in Heart to Show the Way.' "

"It's good to know he's going out into the world," I said. "He'll learn a thing or two about life."

"Exactly what I . . ." He stopped. Visenta was cross-

153

ing the road ahead of us, and Peter's face seemed to tighten. He partly closed his eyes, as if he were trying to keep something out and something in.

"You *will* tell me when we get to the funny part?" I said finally.

"The . . . the funny part?" he said vaguely. "Oh . . ." Visenta went into a hut. "I . . . I think we passed it."

For Peter, more than the funny part had passed. When he had seen Visenta, something of his youth seemed to have gone. More and more, in fact, what he saw seemed to cost him something of what he had been. It was as if lines I could not quite detect were settling in his face, just below the skin, ready to come out tomorrow. A child with stumps of teeth, a potato doll in the dust, an old woman mending an older market basket, a pretty girl trying to cut away a growth on her face with a dirty knife, a drunken man jamming mud into his mouth, patched walls and pots and ponchos ("That's what we are," José told me once. "Patches.")—such sights seemed to make him a stranger to the boy who had come. Exhausting as his work in the field was, he turned back to it as if it were only there he could be, for a while, unhurt.

José and I were on our way to the bridge. He carried a basket filled with rolls and white cheese, contributed by María. He had on a new old suit; that is, he had bought it from an old-clothes merchant on his last trip to the city. "I feel obligated to buy from him," he explained to me. "He has a connection with my cousin Eusebio." Whether Eusebio —the used-coffin dealer—supplied him or he supplied Eusebio, José did not say, and I did not ask. Looking at the rumpled brown suit with the buttonless coat, I found I preferred not to know where and by whom it had last been worn.

"Have you ever thought of moving to the city, Don José? You might do more business there."

He shrugged. "It is not so easy to move. And those who move do not often escape from the bottom of things. The truth is, it is too late for me."

"Surely you're not too old?"

"I was too old the day I was born," he said. "For some this has not been true, but for most of us—I speak of the rich as well as the poor—our place in life has been set from the time we first drew breath. For myself, I prefer it that way; it excuses my failure. Or so I can comfort myself. The fact is, one can learn to enjoy failure; one develops a taste for it, until nothing else satisfies quite as well. I feel I can count on it; it is my friend, it expects nothing of me, it never pesters me to be more than I am or want more than I can get. It lets me sleep. Did I ever tell you about my father?"

"No, Don José."

"He was nothing, as men are judged by most. But he was so dedicated to not amounting to anything that I thought of him first as a dedicated man, and only secondly as a man who amounted to nothing. He was a carpenter, like his own father and like me, but it was not a fact he expected anyone to notice." A wasp began to buzz around José's head, and he watched it with mild interest and no animosity. "He had eight children, but only three of us lived beyond the third year. My mother never quite understood this, and I was often called by one of my dead brothers' names. I never regarded her as demented then—her way was just her way—but now I think perhaps she was. The only one in my family who was considered crazy then was my aunt Felicia: she used to walk around with shoes on. They're all dead now except my brother Antonio; he went to live in the Valle when they broke up the reservation. I don't complain, and I have no talent for grieving—some do, though; death is the most common thing we have, and some make the most of it—still, I find I think of my father a lot these days."

"Do you feel you're like him?"

"I don't know. But he always seemed a happy man to me; content in a way I favor. He never shouted, never flung himself about, never intruded. He was full of respect for things as they were, and was careful not to disturb them."

"What makes you believe he was happy?"

155

"He laughed so seldom I was convinced of it. I speak only of him, you understand, not of others. It seemed to me that it was only when he was troubled that he felt he had to laugh. Again, I do not speak of others. Why, just down the road from us there was a man who laughed almost all the time, and believe it or not, I think he was happy."

"How did you feel when they broke up the reservation?"

"It meant nothing to me. I was only about ten years old, and we stayed right where we were; the only difference was, we had a paper saying our land was our land, but I'd always thought it was. None of us could read the paper anyway. For some, though, a little paper like that was a wonderful thing—the end of some kind of slavery, I suppose. For others it was a terrible thing—the beginning of another kind of slavery, they said; we weren't protected any more. *Pues,* I'd never known we were protected, and we were still at the bottom of things, so I couldn't make too much sense out of what was said. All I knew was that the old people wanted to keep the reservation and the young people wanted to end it, and now that the young people are the old people, *they're* the ones who don't like change. But change is a strange business here. You break up a reservation, and you might think that means a big change, that nothing's going to be the same any more, but things go on about the way they were, most people do as they did, and you say to yourself, 'It's all the same, it's all the same.' And you're partly right: it's much the same. But then, when the years go by and nothing stands out the way the reservation breakup did, you start thinking there's never going to be any change, and then you start noticing how things *have* changed, how they've been changing all along. It's not just a matter of more brick and less adobe, more tile and less straw; of new buildings here and there and new faces everywhere. It's a matter of asking questions that weren't asked before, and listening to voices that weren't heard before—voices like Sebastian's, voices like Pedrito's. And you start thinking, there's a pressure building up, and one of these days there's going to be an explosion; and then, remembering what went before, you suspect *that* won't make as much difference as a lot of people figure." He tucked the ends of his buttonless coat in his trousers to keep them from flapping in the wind. "*Carajo!* I seldom run on this way, but the thought of my father sometimes draws out what should probably be left in."

"I thank you for letting it be drawn out in my presence," I said.

"I thank you for thanking me so formally," he said. "But I still plan to eat most of the sandwiches. My father taught me that; the pueblo fathers taught the pueblo that: eat what you can when you can—it's a gift of perpetual hunger. I could offer one of these sandwiches to a man who was at that very moment throwing up from overeating, and he would somehow try to stuff it down—no one ever declines a gift of food."

"There aren't very many fat people here."

"Food doesn't stop long in the *campesino*—it's poor stuff to begin with, and it refuses to stay in such miserable surroundings. A *campesino*'s stomach is a home only for worms."

"My God!" Peter said. "Look at the little bastards come up!"

The green rows rustled in the cool light breeze, and the smell of leaf and stalk came up the rows to meet us. Below us was Alejandro's *cantina*, smokeless and lifeless in the early morning, a tilerouged and limepowdered celebrant sleeping it off. Peter looked like a scarecrow, and his arms flapped as if blown. "Peter's Little Acre," I said. "Don't you feel a bit supernatural?"

"I don't know how I feel, except . . ." He stooped, sniffed, plucked, and came up chewing a leaf. "Except everything I see gives me a kind of excitement, and I'm too tired . . ." Pieces of the leaf came dribbling out as he talked. ". . . too tired to control it." He stooped and sniffed again.

"Maybe you ought to have Visenta give you another alcohol rub?"

He stood up and gave me a strange, distracted look. "Maybe I should," he said slowly. "Maybe I should."

"Just remember, pal, you reap what you sow."

He looked back at the green rows. "I hope so."

IX

"It's going to be a good harvest," Doña Victoria said, rocking at half speed and puffing on a calabash—Sherlock Holmes ready to leap out of disguise on a forward rock. "Or so the fools tell me."

"What fools?" I asked.

"Those who tell me," she said, waving the calabash in a vicious sweep that indicted the whole pueblo. "Anyone who bothers talking to an old lady is a fool nowadays. You're as guilty as the others. Oh, I know I'm enchanting, but . . ." She spat in the corner. "I won't sell my body no matter how you beg." She leered fiercely at me and wiped the calabash stem on the musty blue blanket draped around her wrestler's shoulders. "Oh, I can see you're ready to leap on me," she went on. "Your little haunches are quivering. The others are as guilty as you. They all want me. And why not? I dare you to tell me why not?"

"Why not?"

"I didn't dare you to *ask* me, I dared you to *tell* me. That's the real problem." She spat again. "Tell me why or tell me why not, either one, one's as big a problem as the other."

"Because women like you are so scarce," I suggested.

"Scarce! They're mostly dead and buried twenty years or more. Scarce is right! But does that answer the why or the why not?"

"Either one, perhaps."

"*Dios!* Either one, indeed! You remind me of a husband I had once. He dipped me in a pot of understanding at the moment he shattered the clay. "Did I ever tell you about him?"

"No, Doña Victoria."

"Good. What women my age do best is repeat themselves. They might as well be put away; they've already said what they had to say. But that husband I had—I hope I never repeat myself about him; he doesn't bear repeating." She squinted at the window. "Some days I see him more clearly than others. That miserable face of his. Ah, it was beautiful! If he brought it in here right now I'd squeeze it to my breast. So he'd drop dead of disgust. Agghh!" She blew smoke toward the window. The aromatic tobacco Peter had been giving her smelled like peppermint. She had kicked off her sandals, and flexed her toes as she rocked. The veins on her throat throbbed as if fuel were being pumped through to keep the chair moving. "I was an Indian at the time . . ."

"You were an . . . oh, you mean before they broke up the reservation?"

She nodded and chuckled. "It's not everyone who can change from an Indian to a non-Indian without knowing it. I was sick while it was all being arranged, and when I came around it was done. Oh, it was a gradual thing really, but when it was finally official no one dared call anyone else an Indian. I remember just after I opened my eyes, a cousin of mine was in the room, and I said to him, 'Who put all these blankets on me, you stupid Indian?'—and he looked as if he wanted to smother me under them. 'I'm *not* an Indian,' he told me very proudly. '*Pues*, you're not the Lord Jesus,' I said to him. 'It's too hot for heaven, and not enough for hell.' So he explained what had happened, and I got out of bed and headed for the door. 'And where do you think you're going?' he asked me. 'I'm going to find some Indians to spit on,' I said." She blew smoke dreamily toward the window. "If the ones who stayed Indians could see us now, they'd spit right back."

"Did your husband live on the reservation?"

"He didn't live anywhere, not even after we were married. As far as I know, he married someone every place he went. Vile! He had a way, though, a crawling crazy way, with his little jigglings, and his beautiful face sucking every No out of a woman—ah, vile that he was, I loved him." She patted her hair in a startlingly feminine gesture; her hair, as often as not hidden under her musty blanket or a shawl, was actually rather lovely—richly gray and abundant—but it did not seem a thing that might be called lovely while she was rocking under a full head of belligerent smoke (she often loosed her potent clouds as if she were launching a mustard-gas attack); it seemed part of her arsenal, to be wadded up and used as a club at the next provocation. "He sold *azabaches* . . ." These were the small jet amulets worn by children to protect them from the evil eye. "Some said he had the evil eye himself, and parents who heard this were afraid not to buy from him, but I think he spread the story himself, wherever he went, to help his trade along. His evil was not in his eye. *I* know." She rolled her yellow eyes. "He sold love charms too, and played up so well to every woman who bought one she thought it was working already. *I* know. He sold one to me, and that was his mistake and my mistake too. Ah, Guillermo, he had me going, but he went too far himself. I knew how to get to a man then, and I still do, only it doesn't please me any more. But then—ah, how it pleased me!" She was rocking now as if in the rhythm of love-making. "Before he knew it his charms were scattered all over the floor—for years afterwards the cats came from miles around to make love on that floor—and I had him, ah, I had him. Vile! Beautiful!" She spoke both words with the same fervor. "I even got him to marry me, it was nothing to him, he knew all the words by heart. Ah, and then! And then!" She puffed vigorously for a minute; then the rocker slowed and the calabash drooped. She sighed and put the pipe on the small wooden table beside her. "Sebastian tells me it lasted over a year, but I remember only the first three weeks. He was gone soon enough, and a few missing months don't matter to me now—I lose whole years, five or ten in a row, and I let them go, I don't need them now. But those three weeks . . . ah, those I'll keep."

The dead smoke curled slowly in the window light, and the smell of peppermint dulled to a stale suggestion. Doña Victoria closed her eyes, but it was impossible to tell how close to sleep she was—daydreams and night dreams, sleeping dreams and waking dreams seemed much the same with her, and neither sound nor silence was a sign of either. She could cry out as readily from a nightmare as from one of the little pockets of fancy and fantasy into which she slipped so often by day. Each, moreover, could pass into the other—Sebastian once told me she often woke to visions, and ate breakfast as if with her ghost lovers of the night, cursing them and him equally for the hardness of the bread.

"I've just come from your aunt."

"My aunt . . . yes." Sebastian blinked at me. I had caught him coming out of the church, and he seemed as embarrassed as a preacher caught leaving a burlesque show. His small round face was a week into stubble, worn now, it seemed, not as a mark of oneness with the unshaven poor but as a protective coating, a shield thrown out from the flesh— he tugged at it nervously, as if he would coax out more of it to stand between him and the world. Yet it would not be fair to say that he seemed defeated; he seemed confused and uncomfortable—a witness for the prosecution who had suddenly been plumped into the defendant's chair. His blue and gray *ruana*, always tentlike, now billowed at the elbows as if to cover a withdrawal of the body, so that it might be snatched off like a magician's cape to reveal nothing except, perhaps, a small creature of fur or clipped wings.

"How goes the purging?" I asked in my most irritatingly friendly way.

"There is no question of purging," he said angrily. "The committee is doing only what ought to be done when there is

162

a . . . problem. That is its function, and I'm pleased to do whatever I can to help it."

"Yes, I can see you're practically hilarious about it," I said.

He blinked at me again, then said coldly, "You see me and you think that is all there is. 'Sebastian is only a little fool,' you say to yourself. 'What can a little fool do?' Well, *gringo*, if you do not see what is coming, you are more of a fool than I. It is what I serve and not what I am that you ought to be watching."

"I have tried not to underestimate either," I said.

He looked at me suspiciously. "You *gringos* look at us and see devils and fools. What you still do not understand is that too many people have been kept too long under the fat white thumbs of those who are most like you. You know only them—the ones who meet you at the airport and show you only what they want you to see and tell you only what they want you to know—but you do not know our country. Those you deal with are only five out of a hundred, they are not our country."

"Nor are you," I said. "Nor is the committee. We are coming to understand more than you think."

"We'll see," he said. "We'll see."

"Sooner or later," I said, "I believe we'll all see."

Inside the church Romelio was sitting on a front bench making out a report. He looked up and nodded. "I sometimes come in here to work in peace," he said. "When the wife is sour, when the children are noisy. Almost no one intrudes; perhaps the saints *do* protect me here. I don't mean that, of course, though anything's possible. Still . . ." He efficiently flicked a beetle from his knee. "Unless this place is giving me visions, I saw Sebastian here a few minutes ago."

"If you caught him in an act of contrition, I hope you won't hold it against him," I said. "Anyone can slip. On the other hand, he might be trying to organize a cell of angels. Or perhaps we ought to listen for ticking."

"What?" He started to reach for his cap, then stopped and looked critically at his fingernails. "Oh, I see, you did a joke, no? Ha."

"Don't let it overcome you," I said. "There's nothing more disturbing than a hysterical man in church."

"Mm." He looked at me impassively. "You remind me of the last man I saw before a firing squad, Don Guillermo. He started to tell a joke, but his head was torn off before he finished the . . . how you say . . . ?"

"Punch line."

"Yes, punch line. A pity, because it was a very bad joke, but to this day I wonder what the punch line was."

"A little bit of revenge," I said. "And perhaps immortality."

"Mm. His head was much like yours. A so-so thing, not unpleasant. Disorderly hair and a child's eyes. I have never much liked to shoot heads."

"This was when you were in the army?"

"*Sí.* We were having border trouble, and I thought it was right to fight for my country. I would still fight for my country, but since then I have learned that we are always having border trouble. No one whose mind I respect seriously thinks there will ever be a United States of South America. We do not trust our neighbors, they do not trust us, and they do not trust their other neighbors. But it is more than a matter of trust. We *feel* different from the others, as they do from us, and from one another—we are really different peoples, and when you lump us all together you seem blind to us." He put his unfinished report on the bench beside his hat, and with thumb and forefinger began to sharpen the trouser crease on his blue uniform; he did it as automatically as a woman might knit as she talked. "Have you been in the army, Don Guillermo?"

"Navy," I said. "Not for very long."

He nodded. "Our navy is a joke, but no one dares tell the admirals that. So much of what we have and are is pride only, and a ragged pride at that. The officers have most of the pride—they come from the best families, after all—but what they lead is very ragged. It is good to be a general or admiral—one may control the government some day—but a real war? Ah, there is nothing to fight such a war with, it is really beside the point, it distracts from the business of being a general or admiral. Oh, a few skirmishes, real or imagined, can always be managed at the border; just enough to give one a respectable number of medals. Our best families all have their glorious heroes; it is what best families must do. I don't sound bitter, do I?"

"Not exactly."

"I'm not. What else is there to do with an army here? To make heroes, to change the government every now and then —it is less harmful than driving other countries into the sea, even if one could. But I did not understand this then, I had expected to drive our neighbor into the sea. Nothing of the sort was required, of course; only a show of honor, as in a duel entered with the idea that scratches rather than death would end it. That is why our little wars seem like games to some; but we do not think of them as games, we take them very seriously. There is not a final death, but there are little deaths. There is always a bloodletting, it is part of our history. Our museums must have their bloodstained weapons, our churches go in for gore—have you seen the murals in the city churches? We keep the hearts of our heroes in jars, and our best homes have properly bloodstained rugs or chairs. Yet you *gringos*, who have such a horror of bloodletting—I have seen your tourists pale at the sight of a squashed cockroach—may end up killing half the world. No offense, Don Guillermo, but I think we settle more with our bloodletting than you do with yours."

"As you say, Don Romelio, anything's possible."

"When I was in the army, I was made a corporal, then a sergeant. I had a talent; that is why I like this uniform. The fighting itself was very confused. Magnificent orders were given—for frontal attacks, charges up mountain sides, daring raids. But they were only to put in the paper, they were kept in a separate box and not to be given to us under any circumstances. But an orderly knocked over the box one day, and some of the orders really got to us. My lieutenant looked at the one that would have us going up a mountain and got sick. 'This will not do, no, no, it is impossible, out of the question,' he kept saying. He showed me the order. 'A day's climb at least,' he told me, 'and for all we know, there may be somebody up there.' 'It's not likely,' I reassured him. 'Why would anyone want to go up there? There's nothing to do up there.' 'I don't know,' he said, 'if *we* can get orders like this, *they* can too.' 'Well, sir,' I told him, 'why don't we pick out a mountain we're sure is unoccupied, and go up that?' He liked that idea. 'I'll pick out a small one,' he said. 'There's one a few kilometers behind our lines that ought to do very well.' So we went up that one. At least, *I* went up it, with about thirty men; the lieutenant decided to stay behind and make out the battle report; he knew just what he wanted to put in it, and wanted to get everything down while he was fresh. I didn't mind; it meant I wouldn't have to go all the way up—out of sight would be far enough. But while we were looking for a place to have lunch, we met a platoon of the enemy having theirs. We were all very embarrassed. We explained to them that it was our mountain, well behind our lines. They hadn't known that, they'd just stopped to rest, and they promised to leave right after lunch, and would we please tell them where the lines were. So we told them where we thought they were, and after lunch they left. We traded some things, so we could each bring back some booty, but on the way down I decided to bury our share; I didn't want to upset the lieutenant, or his report."

"I thought you were ready to drive the enemy into the sea," I said.

"Oh, this was after I began to understand. But part of me still wanted to; it was just that it was the wrong time. After all, they were eating lunch, and we were preparing to eat ours. Less than a week later we were in a battle that turned out to be very bloody, very messy, the rudeness alone was astonishing. The lieutenant himself killed three men, but after it was all over he was unable to make out a report. 'I'm too tired,' he told me, 'and besides, it was all mixed up, I would never have planned it that way.' He had a sense of form and style, the lieutenant. He's well placed in our economic recovery program now; I saw one of the bulletins he wrote—we're making fantastic progress. He had a real sense of order: there was a question of successive rape—the girl was alone, after all—but she was taken in complete accord with rank, from top to bottom, and he was so pleased at that he took no action against any of . . . them."

"Them? You weren't going to say 'us,' were you?"

He shook his head. "Only a *gringo* would boast of a little thing like rape. I have heard that your women live much like men, and like to sit on them from time to time, so for a *gringo* it is perhaps an achievement to succeed in rape, like winning a wrestling match. But our women are not deluded; when caught alone, they submit, like good sports. Not that we need rape; we do it only with profuse apologies. After all, there is more than enough for us all. The red light district in the city is one of the glories of our democracy. I ought to know, it was one of my assignments, I was ordered to find out if the girls in one of the cities were diseased. There were so many of us who put in for the assignment it took four months to pick a winner, and even then I had to share honors with two others. Of course, we found no disease, but for many months the question was in the balance, we had to be sure. It was only fair, no? To be frank, the very old and the very young girls worried me, but with one understanding came another, and I learned the value of tolerance. I came out in favor of it even before the United Nations did. Are you surprised I know so much about politics?"

"Politics? Were you talking about politics?"

"I put them in every now and then. Democracy, United Nations; you see? I only have to mention such things to impress people. To tell the truth, I have a directive with a little list of words—some words are changed every month or so—and I know just what to do if any important *gringos* are brought here for an official visit. I can say anything I like, as long as I stop every little while for a Viva: Viva the United Nations, Viva the Alliance for Progress, Viva the Next Word on the List; you see? The schoolchildren can make banners with Vivas too. But even so, I take an interest in these things, and others here do too; more interest, perhaps, than our own leaders give us credit for—some, I am sure, would be alarmed. It is more than a matter of the word of the month. Something is happening, we all feel it, even those who don't want to feel it. And we are seeing a different kind of *gringo* these days. You, who come to listen, and Pedro, who comes to help." Romelio shook his head. "There are those here who think you are trying to fool us, and there are those who think you are trying to fool yourselves; but there are also those—and I am one—who think you are not trying to fool anybody."

"Thank you," I said.

"*De nada.* But I wish Pedro had more meat to go with his bones. Every week I think he can get no thinner, but thinner he gets. His spine can no longer hold his chin up; when I see him on the road, he puts me in mind of a sickle cutting through the wind. If I had a jail, I might put him in it just to make him rest."

"What would you charge him with?"

"Disturbing the peace, I think. Yes, disturbing the peace."

"Has he really disturbed it?"

He studied his trouser crease. "Anything different disturbs the peace. But it is too soon to say how seriously he has disturbed ours. Most of all I think he has disturbed his own."

"Is that bad?"

"Who knows? If he exhausts himself and fails to move us, what can be said of it? Perhaps it ought to be enough for him to have tried."

"Do you think it would be?"

"No," Romelio said promptly. "I do not think it would be."

"Yes, yes," said Ernesto, as he looked dubiously at the plate of scrambled eggs he had produced in his small smoke-filled kitchen. "You have just come from church, where you talked with the police inspector, who was making out a report at the time, interrupted only by the devotions of Sebastian, and I suppose all the images were dancing the mambo, and Saint Peter was selling lottery tickets, and . . ." He tasted the eggs and winced. "The next time I ask you where you've been, please say nothing."

"Or I can come right back at you and ask where *you've* been," I said.

"Since you ask," he said, putting the plate on a table that had been pieced together from a broken school bench, "I'll tell you. It all began . . ." He slid two chairs to the table, sat in one and waved me into the other. Then he picked at the eggs with a fork that could have been used to dig through the walls at San Quentin and appeared to be considering his beginnings and the eggs simultaneously. "Or did it?" he said finally. "Yes, I'm certain it all began. Would you care for a portion of these eggs?"

"No thanks."

"I was afraid you wouldn't." He took a bite, chewed, chewed, chewed, and swallowed. "They resist to the end," he said. "Every year more things seem to resist me. What was easy has become hard, Don Guillermo—there is no appreciation."

"You don't expect appreciation from your eggs, do you?"

"Why not? I was kind to them, I gave them all the grease an egg could want, and I did not beat them long. But I was not criticizing my eggs just then; my thoughts had gone beyond them—hatched from them, so to say. I was thinking, for example, of my pupils. More and more I feel I count for less and less with them. I no longer fool them, or believe I fool them. I am a bad teacher, a fraud, I offer them a drop

169

and want them to believe it is the ocean, but they know, they see through me, and I wish it were not so. When I was younger, it was easier for me to pretend. A young teacher can be a lion, and an old teacher can be beloved, but there is something distinctively ridiculous about a middle-aged teacher. Here I am, full of education, at least by the standards of my neighbors, and my daily company is children who laugh at me and discount what I say before I say it. Why shouldn't they? What can I give them that matters to them? It will all be the same for them after their two years in school. Where can they go? Do I open anything for them that isn't closed to them when they get back to their fields? Do I tell them on the last day, 'Well, children, it's all over, that's all you get, and you may as well get used to the idea of being poor farmers the rest of your lives'? Or do I tell them, 'Well, children, take your two years of schooling and leave this place. You'll find many opportunities for those who have finished the second grade'? Fortunately for me, I don't have to tell them anything. They know how useful books are around here. They know I am not a practical man. Everybody knows it. Even the eggs know it; they refuse to amount to anything for all my pains."

"Your family wasn't rich, was it?"

"Mine? Hardly. My father was a janitor in the Office of Public Works."

"Yet you managed to get a good education."

"The worst possible example for my pupils. Of course, we lived in the city, where I could get more schooling. Though even there most drop out early. Still, I'll admit, I took pride in going all the way through. But what was open to *me* then? Most of us—persons with my sort of background —were steered into minor white collar jobs. The upper rungs of the ladder were out of sight—reserved for feet that had always worn not only shoes but socks as well. I wasn't a rebel; as I say, the upper rungs were out of sight. And teaching seemed just the right place for me; in a way, I was a dispenser of luxuries. From the standpoint of those

170

who gave me a license and sent me here, I was the poor being returned to the poor. And now? Can I say to my pupils, 'If you leave your family and study hard for years and years, you can be like me?' No. Why should they want to be like me? I myself would not want them to be like me."

"Do you always feel this way when your eggs go wrong?"

He smiled. "Always. Last week they turned out very well —one of my pupils fixed them for me—and while I ate them I felt quite in love with myself and my job. It does not happen very often, but when it does all seems well with me—a reasonably secure and peaceful life, as lives go; a certain status; a lack of temptations and complications. If I do not contribute enough, at least I contribute a little—perhaps as much as most men do—and it is right that children should laugh, even if at my expense. Children should not be in terror of their teacher, should they? Besides, I tell myself, I am probably oversensitive—and so on, and so on. Should eggs have so much power over me? I don't mean just eggs, and I don't mean just me. I sometimes wonder how many of the villains we see are traceable to indigestion, to a lack of regularity, to an undisciplined gland or two. History must have heard squeaks like mine a billion times or more—little belches, a letting of air, that's all they amount to—nothing new discovered, just the same old record repeating itself here and there, squawking the same thing over and over again until it's jiggled on toward the next squawking, like the records in Alejandro's *cantina*. How tiresome! There is nothing I really need, nothing at all, that I can't find here. And even to say that is tiresome; I should not have to say it."

He ate his eggs quickly, not stopping to speak again. A piece of egg dropped on his black suit, and another on the frayed open collar of his white shirt, but he did not pause to brush them off. His long fingers kept the fork moving in sharp dips and scoops between the cracked black plate and the mouth that worked reluctantly but well a foot away. The black plate was one of a dozen José had given him for Christmas. José in turn had received the black plates as a birthday present from his cousin Eusebio, the used-coffin dealer, who claimed they were ideal for serving refreshments for wakes. (I was not to meet Eusebio—a large, jolly man with a tattooed black armband—until shortly before my return to the States, at which time he gave me a rabbit's foot with a tiny death's head, which I still have, though I do not know what its effect is supposed to be.)

Ernesto finished the eggs with a flourish of the fork, then pushed the plate away and tilted back in his chair. "Now that I have defeated my enemy of the moment," he said, "I must release my victory cry." He belched grandly. "That's my contribution to philosophy. Shall we talk about sex now?"

"Why not?"

"I'll tell you about my great temptation. It was just before I came here, in a little *vereda* the other side of the city. I won't tell you the name; I wouldn't want it in your notebook. The girls' teacher was sick—the poor thing weighed less than eighty pounds stripped, if she ever was, and had an acute and very dramatic attack of dysentery in the middle of a geography lesson—and I took her classes for two weeks. Of course, it wouldn't do to have the boys and girls together, so we operated as an *escuela alternada*, with the girls coming one day and the boys the next. The girl who cleaned the erasers for me was a little overage; her father had died, and she'd stayed home helping her mother for a number of years until her mother remarried. There's apt to be a considerable age range in classes here in the country; school is something to be managed when a child can be spared from the fields or the kitchen, if it can be managed at all. It's supposed to be compulsory, but there's not much enforcement. Anyway, she was a nice girl as far as I knew, never talked unless she was called on, but she used to stare at me constantly. She never laughed at anything I said, or nodded, or shook her head; just stared. She was barely a centimeter into puberty, but it was a centimeter that almost ruined my life. Have you ever been stared at constantly?"

"Not by anyone a centimeter into puberty."

"I'd always been more or less proud of my features, but with her staring at me they began to feel lopsided and misplaced; she made me want to rush to a mirror to see what had happened to my nose. At the same time, I felt partly flattered; I was vain enough to believe she wouldn't pick out something wholly distasteful to stare at. Esmeralda del Campo, that was her name, and at first I thought it was a beautiful name, but now—it's the sort of name that keeps popping into my head, like a stray line from a song too nauseating to be forgotten readily. Esmeralda del Campo, Esmeralda del Campo, Esmeralda del Campo—it brings a shudder. Yet Esmeralda herself was not the kind to bring a shudder. She was quite pretty, with a child's prettiness, an unformed prettiness that suggests much more to come. Of course, for some it never comes, but for her—with that centimeter—it was a certainty; one could almost see it approaching, as in a flower after watering. She always wore a white dress, too short and too thin. When she cleaned the erasers in the sunlight through the window, I trembled to look at her. Whenever I did, of course, she knew it; what was in her eyes, as she stared at me then, I did not know, but I felt sure she noted my trembling as well as my look. I cannot even say she was aware of what the sunlight did to her; she did not seem to be concerned with what she did with herself, or might be done to her. I do not think of myself as an excitable person, but I am surely no stoic, and while I struggled to reduce the frequency of my trembling by trying to look at anything but her—I once studied an inkwell for at least five minutes—the intensity of the trembling grew when I *did* look at her. For I *had* to look at her sometimes. I remember groping for the erasers as she held them out to me one day; I felt so ridiculous I finally looked almost savagely at her, and then, meeting her stare, feeling its force, shattered by the shock of it, I knocked them right out of her hands. I remember the girls laughing—the laughter of girls is more musical, more magical than the laughter of boys, but it is less bearable somehow, it does not wear as well—but she did not laugh, and I did not laugh. She picked up one eraser, I picked up the other and, pointlessly, we handed them to each other.

"What is most astonishing to me now is that it all happened in a few days. Perhaps if the class had been mine for the full term, with the sense of novelty gone we would have settled into a reasonably normal teacher-pupil routine with nothing more potent than boredom or exasperation on either side, and I would have forgotten her by now. As it is, I feel as if we were together for years—the moments seem to be held endlessly for me; I keep picking up the eraser and handing it to her.

"There were no living quarters in the boys' school there, but a hut was provided rent-free—it had been built by the government for a post-office that was never established there —and one evening, as I lay on my bed correcting papers, there was a very soft knock at the door. I thought it might be the *maestra;* she was due to take over her classes again in two days, and I expected her to ask for a progress report. Since she would not, of course, come in, I went to the door without bothering to straighten up the room or bed. Just before opening the door, I realized it was probably too late for her to be out, even if accompanied. I was right, and my first thought on seeing Esmeralda was, 'There, you see, it *was* too late,' not yet realizing that what I saw was a far more serious breach of the very custom I had just pronounced unscratched. For it was inadmissible to me then that it should be Esmeralda. I stood there dumbly, looking at her, meeting that same—as it appeared to me; I was not yet aware of the great fright in it—stare of hers.

"She wore her school dress, and I did not notice at first that it was torn, badly torn; she was virtually holding it on. Curiously enough, what suggested to me that something was

wrong was that the white ribbon in her hair was untied; this
small fact I could accept, and it led me, slowly, to the ac-
ceptance of other facts: her presence, her torn dress, her
fright.

"Finally she spoke; she had never spoken to me first before. 'Please,' she said, 'may I come in?'

"I let her in. The chairs in the room were covered with
papers and clothes, and she sat on the edge of the bed, holding her dress together, for all the world as if she were sitting
in class; I almost began to talk to her about her writing—
she printed her 3's backwards—and then she let her dress go,
clapped her hands over her face, and cried out to me.

"It was to *me* she cried out; I must always remember that.
I sat beside her, and held her, hoping she would understand
—and trying myself to believe—that what I was doing was
solicitous rather than solicitation. I took off her dress, with
the notion—was I deluding myself?—that if it were to be
sewn together, it ought to be removed before it was ripped
further by her small movements. She shivered and sobbed,
but did not try to escape—did I think of it as escape? Poor
girl, to seek help from a man whose purposes were so confused . . . I did not even think to close the shutters, or put
out the candles; anyone might have looked in. What little
she wore under the dress was also torn, and came off so
readily in my hands that now, looking back, it seems that
they at least were not confused. I almost feel like calling
back to them over the years and explaining to them that it
was not that sort of thing at all. As it was, they moved easily
from cloth to flesh, from comfort to a caress, while the rest
of me, like a drunken chaperone, sat there numbly.

"Yet even now I cannot admit that it was lust impure and
simple behind the caress. It seems to me that, most of all,
there was a need to hold and touch what had become, in those
moments, a beloved person to me. There is so much that goes
into affection . . . I cannot deny that sex was there—isn't
it always?—but at the same time that I was holding an un-
dressed female I was holding a hurt child, a pupil who

printed her 3's backwards, a potential—by age and feeling —daughter. I say feeling; I believe it was her feeling as well as my own, and I also believe she felt more than that: what was mixed up for me may have been just as mixed up for her. Not that I would or could attribute lust to her; but she had in her the beginnings of womanhood, and I suspect those beginnings found a place in her response.

"Minutes passed and, pressed tightly against me, she became very quiet. Then she told me—at first, almost as if she were reciting in class, then in a wild, whispered outpouring —how she had been hurt.

"As I told you, her mother had remarried. Esmeralda had never spoken of her stepfather before, and even now she spoke of him as if she owed him silence. That day, when she had come home from school, her mother and stepfather were quarreling. They had quarreled before, but not this violently—at least not in her presence—and she tried to go to her room. Her stepfather ordered her to stay, and her mother told her not to, and—partly because she was used to obeying her mother, and partly because she could not stand to be there—she hurried to her room.

"The quarreling grew louder outside her door. She threw herself on her bed and buried her head in the blanket, trying to shut out the noise, trying to think of other things— she told me she tried to imagine herself back in school, to pretend the muffled sounds were the classroom hum, the voices of friends.

"She did not remember dozing off; she remembered only the terror of waking: her stepfather, very drunk, had burst into the room and, pulling her from the bed, began to shake her and curse her. He accused her of being disobedient, ungrateful, disrespectful; of turning her mother against him —she tried to put her hands over her ears, and this made him even more furious. He tore her clothes, saying he had provided them and, since she appreciated nothing, he would take them from her. Then, suddenly, he pulled her close to him and, in detail, in blunt and grotesque detail, he told her

176

exactly what he was going to do to her. She did not understand all of it, but from what she told me I understood more than I wanted to; it was shocking, and I do not repeat it even to myself any more. Whether he meant it or not—or, even if he meant it at the time, whether he would have done it —there is, perhaps fortunately, no way of knowing. Terrified, she broke away, ran outside and hid in a field until long after dark. Then she came to me.

"Whatever else I felt when she finished her story, I was ashamed. Was I really any better than her stepfather? At least he had not masqueraded as her friend. Was my justification—that I was consoling and comforting a frightened child—less deceiving, less dangerous than his—that he was punishing a disobedient child? Mine, perhaps, was more dangerous, since it seemed, as I held her, that soon . . . I will not say it. I no longer trust my memory: not that it is blurred; it is too vivid to trust. It is too crowded with what I need to believe about myself. I must believe both that I *would* have done something, for the sake of virility—my image of her as a child may after all be exaggerated to excuse my failure—and that I would *not* have done something, for the sake of conscience.

"Her story, however, gave an edge to conscience, and I withdrew . . . I am not in a position to disagree that it would have been unnatural morally to persist, but I *know* how unnatural it felt to withdraw. I covered her up, tucked her in, and fixed her some hot chocolate. By the time the chocolate was ready, she was asleep.

"Before, I had had one kind of problem; now I had another. What could I do with her? Could I let it be known that she spent the night in my bed? Would people believe in my—and her—innocence? What if her stepfather, or someone else, found her there? Yet, would it be right to send her home? I paced the floor for more than an hour, trying to decide what to do.

"Finally I went to see the *maestra;* she was, after all, Esmeralda's regular teacher—by rights, I thought perversely, Esmeralda ought to be in *her* bed, not the substitute's. The *maestra* was horrified to see me at that hour—did she imagine I was coming to seduce her? When I told her what had happened, she was even more horrified. At first she wanted to turn me out and let me face it myself, but when I suggested that a public scandal would affect her as well as myself—people would wonder what the *maestra* was teaching the girls these days, and why the *maestra* was *really* staying out of school for two weeks—she became more cooperative. She warned me to say nothing to anyone else—a warning I scarcely needed—and promised to go see Esmeralda's mother the first thing in the morning. I was to stay with Esmeralda until I heard from her.

"My little narrative is no longer so little, but it is really over. The *maestra* found that the stepfather had gone, supposedly for good, and helped me spirit Esmeralda back home the following night."

"You stayed with Esmeralda that day?"

"I taught that day. Esmeralda stayed alone in my hut; she missed only the one day of school. While I was in class, of course, I kept worrying that someone might find her, but she told me after school that no one had been around, and that she had stayed in the back room as I had asked—so the shutters could be left open. We still had to wait until dark, but it seemed to me the danger was already over; certainly the sense of excitement was gone, perhaps with the passing of the sense of danger, and I found her company tedious, almost unbearable. The glory of the night before was now part of a hangover, to be endured until it left. We said inane things to each other—she told me at great length how to get erasers especially clean, and how much she liked to sew (she had fixed her dress)—and by the time the *maestra* arrived I felt as if I had grown old in the company of this child, and was fit only to dodder off to bed . . . which I did."

"No one found out?"

"No one *found* out, but in places like that, and this, nothing's so open that people get it quite straight, or so hidden that people miss it entirely. So there was talk—there had, it seemed, been talk about those stares all along—and I could never be certain it wouldn't all come out, perhaps embellished fantastically, so at the end of the term I took a routine transfer."

"And that was the end of your temptation."

"In a way . . . though it had really ended long before then. Just now—perhaps because I have had to go through it all in the telling, or perhaps because of indigestion—I regard it with distaste. I shudder when I think of myself there with her, and am thankful to be out of it. Other times, I feast on the thought of myself there with her, and wish something more had come of it—I mean love. I might even have come to marry her; it is not impossible; in the very best families of the city men marry girls much younger than themselves, and in the country . . . but enough. It was only a temptation. My great temptation, to be carried around with me . . ." Ernesto shook his head. "Somehow it makes me think of your friend Peter."

"Why?"

"Perhaps this is his great temptation . . . the Peace Corps kind of thing: young, virginal—save the world from a horrible fate and so forth, with the possibility always there of some illicit excitement for yourself. Oh, it's all confused and mixed up, just as I was confused and mixed up, but . . ."

"But what?"

"Just as I felt I grew old with her," Ernesto said thoughtfully, "he may grow old with us."

X

It was not that Peter was deliberately growing a beard; it was simply that he no longer bothered to shave. When I asked him if he were planning to organize a *Sing Along with the Peace Corps* group to go with his Mitch Miller tufts, he rubbed them with an expression of vague surprise, as if someone had put them there when he was not looking. He was busy with the harvest now, and paid no attention to his appearance; if he had met himself, I could picture him nodding abstractedly as he passed, without recognition. He had taken to chewing coca leaves—as people of the area had done for centuries with the hope of easing fatigue—and when he smiled, which was not very often, he showed so much green one might have thought it was harvest time in his mouth as well as in his field. One day Visenta, who had come to give him an *aguardiente* rub, cleaned his teeth also. I asked her why she hadn't shaved him too, and she said, "Beards appeal to me. Green teeth do not."

His harvest was not exceptional, but it was good. People came to see it, and praised it. "Very abundant," they would say, or "Your children turned out well," or simply *"Carajo!"* There had been a certain amount of betting for and against the *gringo,* so there was a light flow of pesos and a heavier flow of drinks.

José and I helped Peter bring in the harvest, but we did not help very much. He told us he wanted to do all he could by himself. "I suppose it's a sort of example," he said. "If the *campesino* can become more self-reliant as an individual, the community can become more self-reliant too. There's been too much dependence—centuries of it—too much putting off. The only kind of independence they've been able to develop here is pretty much a defensive thing, a thing of suspicion. It keeps them from working effectively with each other, but it doesn't give them any confidence in themselves as individuals. The change that's needed has to start with the individual *campesino:* the more he can do for himself, the more he can do for others, and the less he has to fear from others. So far they've mostly worked together to hold each other back." Almost angrily he added, "Why do I bother saying it? Why do I think I'm an example? You might think I expect confetti from the second balcony. Back in Peace Corps training, we kept getting cornered by reporters who asked us why we joined the Peace Corps, what we expected to accomplish. Apart from the early shock of being put on the spot, I felt that it was really impossible to say that if I were the sort who could come right out with an answer I wouldn't be in the Peace Corps. What we mostly did was throw out platitudes—we'd even say, 'I know this sounds trite, but . . .' and so forth—but even while I was throwing out my quota I knew that, underneath the words, there was a *groping* toward an answer I would not be able to give until the work was done . . . if then. And now, when I'm in the field, alone, I feel I'm drawing closer to it, but it still isn't ready to be said. So what do I do? I keep trying to say it, or part of it, knowing it isn't finished, knowing the words aren't right yet."

"At least it lets us know what you're going through, what your thoughts are like," I said.

"What does that matter?" he said bitterly. "I'm nothing to be glorified. I'm not wise, I'm not strong, and I'm not confident."

"You produced a pretty good crop."

"*I* didn't. The fertilizer did it. That's my contribution to a higher standard of living for one and all: crud."

"It wasn't just that."

"Don't jolly me along," he said impatiently, and went back to work.

He took much better care of his harvest than he did of himself. He sorted and packed his vegetables as neatly as if they were going on exhibition. When they were ready to take to the city market, he seemed almost unhappy to part with them. "When I was a boy," he told me—rubbing his beard, talking to me as he might to a grandson—"I used to feel sorry for things that had to be sold. Especially in the small shops that always seemed about to go out of business. Little toys, little games, little knickknacks, to be dusted off and offered hopefully day after day. I feel something of it now."

José went with him to the market, to fill him in on procedures and help out on details. I had planned to go also, but Alejandro had asked me to help him replaster his *cantina*, and I had been so surprised by the request I had given the wrong answer: yes. When I had told Peter I could always do a study of culture change, I had not expected to be one of its targets. After all, I was the observer, detached from it all, recording what happened to others. But people were learning from Peter that *gringos* could really be quite helpful, and I began to find myself involved in all kinds of jobs —from looking after children to relocating outhouses— that would never have reached me before Peter had come. Time and again I tried to explain patiently that there were doers and non-doers, and that I was a non-doer, but it seemed that I was impaled on Peter's precedent, and my neighbors, expressing great admiration for my explanations, as patiently involved me anyway. In this case, I rationalized that I owed the *cantina* a new coat of cow dung in return for past evenings of fuzzy pleasure there. But as I worked, I realized that it was one thing to be immersed in a culture empathically, and another thing to be immersed in cow dung (though certainly part of the culture) physically.

"Ever since I was a child," Alejandro told me as we

chucked (splat! I hear it yet) and smoothed, "I have made a study of liquids. You make your little studies also"—mine, his tone indicated, were of no consequence—"so you will understand. Liquids!" His great dry lips trembled. "When a man is thirsty enough, he will push aside the most beautiful woman in the world and the largest bag of gold for a small glass of water. Man comes into the world thirsting, and everything follows from that."

"It does?"

"*Absolutamente.* Your friend Pedro comes here because he thinks we are a poor thirsting people, but you *gringos* are really the thirstiest people of all. That is why you make such a big thing of a woman's breast. Ah, you make it a truly gigantic thing; it could crush a man. I have seen your movies and magazines in the city."

"What about the Italian actresses?"

"Ah, it is the *gringos* who buy their breasts. They pay enormous sums for enormous breasts, but they get nothing out of them. A baby would howl in terror to see them bearing down on his little face. But they are only pumped up with air, and when you turn them loose they do nothing but flop to the knees. Your gold and your women do not make you happy, because they do not bring you your small glass of water. You see, I know all about *gringos*." He winked at me, and wiped a blob of dung from his huge moustache.

"What about *campesinos?*"

"Ah, we are more complicated. But it is really about the same everywhere. It is thirst that moves men. When men settle anywhere, the first thing they look for is a source of water. Everything is built around that. The children know where the source is, but sometimes the grandchildren do not. In your country, I think, they have forgotten where the source is."

"And here?"

"Here they stay too close to the source. They are afraid to go too far from it. So they remain, generation after generation, in the same place."

183

"Are you still talking about water?"

"As I said, Don Guillermo, we start with thirst and water, and everything else follows. There are those who think of my profession and my *cantina* as embellishments, as little extras that serve no useful purpose. But I say there is nothing more basic than what I do. I cater to thirst. I am no child: I know it is more than the parched tongue kind of thirst that brings men to me. But it is thirst, all the same. Man needs his *cantina*."

"You don't think it may hurt him?"

"Of course it may! Drink can save, drink can ruin. It gives, it takes away. But man needs his *cantina*, whether it hurts him or not. Man also needs love, whether it hurts him or not. My profession, in fact, is as old as the profession of love. It is no accident that every whorehouse worthy of its name offers strong drink as well as weak women, and the man who goes there takes a drink before he takes a woman. Women grow old and repulsive, but while an aging woman is becoming useless, an aging brew is becoming better. There is more variety in drink than in women, moreover, and . . ."

A beetle thunked into the fresh plaster, and Alejandro paused to pry it out. The day was hot, and I longed to be able to wipe my face, but there was nothing uncaked or unspattered to do it with, and I let my sweat drop into the mix, thinking that I could at least say my sweat had gone into the pueblo. Alejandro's bristly head was soaked, and the water ran down his face and dripped from his moustache as if from a fountain that rose with the bristles to shower the face. From bristles to bare feet, only his lips were dry, although—so well did they mark for me his persistent, abiding thirst—I suspect I could see them no other way. I could almost picture him swimming underwater, his lips still dry, still searching for liquid.

"You see, I know women also," he was saying. "My wife does not realize this; I have never told her. But it is true, I know women, I understand them; one has only to watch a drunken woman or two to find them all out. Of course, the

women who come into my *cantina* come not so much to drink
as to be drunk, some to be sipped and some to be swallowed.
They come here to be served up with the *aguardiente,* but
most of them are taken only in doses that leave a man empty
or make him sick. What they really want is not to indulge
but to be indulged. I know them, I know them. I have heard
that drink is a substitute for women, but I say that women
are a substitute for drink. The baby who sucks is not really
after his mother, he is after his drink, and everything else
follows *Entiende?*"

"You put it very clearly," I said. "I'm not sure I agree,
but then my studies have been in another area . . ."

"There is really no other *serious* area," he said kindly.
"There is nothing that cannot be traced to thirst. The
campesino is denied many things, but he is not denied his
drink. And so he drinks. There is nothing truer of him than
this." Alejandro unbuttoned his sopping shirt and let out a
few folds of fat. "I would try to take you off, *viejo,*" he said
to his shirt, "but you would tear. You shouldn't drink so
much on such a hot day."

Peter returned from the city so dejected I thought at first
he had not been able to sell his harvest. But he had. "So what
do I do now?" he asked, showing me the small bundle of
pesos. "Buy a yacht?"

"Isn't it what you expected?"

"I don't know what I expected. But *I* don't need these. I
can't very well give them away, and about the only thing to
spend them on around here is liquor."

"Hell," I said, "go buy yourself some more fertilizer."

"I don't need *that* much fertilizer," he said.

"You can build a silo for the surplus," I said. "Start a
fertilizer bank."

He looked at me speculatively, as if he could not decide
whether or not I was joking; if I had known, I would have
told him.

"No," he said finally, "the whole thing's too limited. I

185

realized that in market today. About all I did was depress prices, and I didn't get that much more money out of it. These"—he waved the pesos—"are tickets to nowhere. If I were really a *campesino*, they'd tie me a little more firmly to my land, without ever amounting to enough for a break-through, for a boost that mattered. There just isn't enough to be squeezed out of these plots. What I'm actually doing is telling people, 'Make the most of a bad situation' without trying to do anything fundamental about the situation. I'm really helping preserve an arrangement that keeps clipped —and grounded—the very wings I'm trying to draw out. They may look better, those wings, but they're no good for flying."

"So why fly?"

"So why live?" he said angrily. "It's a matter of . . . well, justice."

"Listen, Grandpa Moses," I said, "stop trying to settle everything for all time. You've been working hard, your crops are gone, and you feel let down. Give yourself a few days before you make a philosophy out of it. See if you've made any converts before you knock conversion."

"I'm not really knocking it," he said. "There's good to be had from it, I suppose—from the bridge sort of thing, from the better crops sort of thing—but sooner or later it leads you to a wall, and you feel the way you're going there's no way over. I know, I haven't even got to the wall yet, but I can see it. Does it have to be shattered, blown up? That's what Sebastian would do. But I have this feeling there's a way to put doors in it. What I'm looking for is right in front of me, I've been touching it as I've gone along, but I can't seem to hold it. I . . . I'm tired, I'm blind."

"Get some rest, Pete."

He looked away from me, up the pueblo road. His face was a mess—disordered whiskers, circles under his eyes, sunburned nose. He was so bent he seemed almost a hunch-back. Yet his eyes were so fierce with power one might have thought it took the rest of his body to feed strength to his eyes; they strained to see . . . what? He finally closed his eyes. "I'm tired," he said. "I'm so tired."

Peter tried to sleep, but it was so hot he seemed only to pass from work exhaustion to heat exhaustion. I saw him stumbling toward the river like a scarecrow headed for Oz. Later I met Rosa Linda, who told me she had seen him there; he had dropped into the water, clothes and all, then had crawled onto the bank to dry. When I saw him again, I knew he must be cleaner, but he was so grass-stained and rumpled it scarcely appeared to be an improvement.

We walked to the edge of the pueblo, where the bus from the city was taking on produce. Three middle-aged ladies, obviously American tourists, sniffed with manifest displeasure at the *chontaduro*, the odor of which I had not liked at first either. Their crisp walking clothes had clearly not been walked in, and their skin was so pale compared to the weathered look Peter and I wore that I suspected they would take it as a racial difference. They now, in fact, caught sight of Peter, and from the look they gave him I gathered they were quite satisfied he was one of the grubby natives. I had seen that look of disdain so many times that I wondered how many *compesinos* thought tourists' faces just naturally came that way. Peter, for his part, was staring open-mouthed at the ladies, as if at a different form of life, and I could imagine the ladies clucking to their home town bridge club about the poor half-starved native who had gawked at them so pathetically ("He probably wanted a crust of bread," one of them would say.) "Wave to your fellow countrymen, Pete," I said. He did not hear me; he just stared. He was still staring after the bus had gone.

Peter's empty sacks were soon refilled, and his first market trip was followed by others. He seemed almost surprised that this should be so—the sort of surprise one might have to see a baseball player keep circling and recircling the bases after first touching home plate. "I'm caught in the crop cycle," he told me. "Beans and cabbages, then *choclo*"—this was the early green corn used in soup, and from which *envueltos de choclo* (something like unfilled tamales) were made—"then arracacha, then the ripe corn, and by the time the goddamn yuca's ready there'll be more beans and cabbages and . . ." He groaned. "I should be planting those beans and cabbages right now, but after all those stragglers I don't care if I never see another bean or cabbage again. Maybe this is the time to start ending it. No wonder the *campesino* gets trapped! There's always something to be looked after, and everything you do means there'll be something else to do later on, and there's never enough money so you feel you can break off at any one point, and round and round you go . . . it's a merry-go-round with no ring to catch. Staying on doesn't get you anywhere, but it's dangerous to try to get off. Except for me; I can jump off any time and go home, and they know it. Where can *they* go? What would they do? Francisco Medina said something to me last week, and I'm just beginning to understand it. He said, 'It's different for you. You're the stranger who comes to pat the baby on the head. Does the baby cry? You can make it smile. But when you leave, the baby cries again.' I must have looked pretty confused and discouraged, because he added, very kindly, 'But when the baby grows up, it may remember who made it smile.' I want to do more than make a baby smile for a little bit, even if it does remember me later on. Or maybe I still misunderstand what he said. Maybe I misunderstand everything."

We were standing in the pueblo road. A family group passed us, on their way to the *cabecera* market, a smaller but more sociable affair than the city market. The man rode the burro; the wife and three children walked behind. After a kilometer or so they would probably trade places; women were acquiring equal burro rights these days. Dress-up items were concentrated toward the top, farthest from the dust: all wore fairly clean straw hats, all were barefoot.

Ruanas hung down like dust-catchers, with the colors fading toward the waist into caked edges. We all nodded at one another, and Peter made a mock grab at the cheap beads worn by the little girl, who squealed in delight.

Peter watched them go, his eyes full of affection (I remembered the way he had looked at the tourists), and reached for his pipe. It was not the handsome pipe he had arrived with; he had given that to Doña Victoria, who had given him this in return. It was a crude but efficient corncob she had made herself ("A terrible pipe," she had told him), and he was never without it. Sometimes, as now, he took it out only to hold, not filling it or, if he filled it, not lighting it or, if he lit it, letting it go out almost at once; he seemed almost surprised to find it in his hand—yet, if he put it away, he soon reached for it again. "You spoke of converts," he said slowly. "Why should there be any converts? It's one thing to do well with beans and cabbages; but then one must wait to see what the arracacha is like, and then the corn, and then the yuca—and the next crop of beans and cabbages, and so on . . . for how long? How long? Proving something to myself doesn't mean it's proved to them, and maybe proof is something that's important only to people like me. I don't think there's any real doubt here that the rest of my crops will turn out well, but the thing to do is to wait and see. Wait and see. It's bad enough to feel that what you have to offer isn't enough; it's even worse to feel that even the little you have to offer won't be taken." He groaned. "What do I really have to show for this?"

"A hell of a lot of beans," I said.

"Yes, beans," he said. "I contribute crud, and get back beans. I ought to get a medal for it: The Grand Order of the Bean."

"Give it time, Pete boy. Stick with it, and give it time. You haven't learned much patience from your neighbors."

"Maybe they've learned too much patience," he said grimly.

189

"Maybe," I said. "And maybe you could do worse yourself than wait and see."

Peter stayed with it, settling into a routine which, while demanding less in the way of energy than had the job of getting started, demanded more in the way of constancy. "I'm going to ride the cycle," he had told me as he set out to plant more cabbages. As the days and weeks passed, I began to wonder if and how he would ever get off it; as he had said, one thing done meant another to do later, and the effect on him seemed largely to be a dulling one. Ernesto observed, "Before, he protested too much; now, I think, he protests too little." Sometimes, when I saw him, he appeared to have forgotten why he had come: he fretted only about the things of the day—broken row markers, bugs, weeds. Once I asked him how the wall looked to him. "Wall?" he said blankly. "What wall?"

He started dropping into Alejandro's *cantina* in the evenings for a few drinks and some light conversation before going off to bed. Sometimes he drank a little too much and had to be helped back to his room. Yet he slept much better than before, and no longer drove himself by day. One evening, when he had downed his fourth shot of *aguardiente*, he told me, "You know, I was all wrong about these people. They don't have such a bad life. They know the score. They can work their fields with one hand and relax with the other. Why should they do more? Sure, they've got troubles, but so has everybody else, and they've got fewer worries than we do. You don't see anybody in a stew about fallout shelters, do you? What have I been trying to do here, give them ulcers? Live and let live, don't bother anybody, that's the way. Why fight dragons? The only thing I'm worried about right now is thinning out a couple of rows tomorrow, and if I don't get it all done tomorrow, so what? I never had such satisfactory worries before." He refilled his glass and smiled contentedly. "If it weren't so much trouble, I'd like to see a few of the people here go to the States as a Peace Corps.

Hell, *they've* got peace. *We're* the ones who don't have peace."

"So you'd just go on and on?"

"Why not? Even the Bible says you ought to be content with your place. What comes, comes; there's nothing like a little dose of fatalism. Visenta's coming over tonight to give me another rub. I'm about to reach an understanding with her."

"Is that fatalism?"

"Maybe. What was meant to be was meant to be. Ride with the tide, drift with the current, put yourself in harmony with nature, and so forth. Say what you will, professor, it sure as hell beats trying to keep up with the Joneses. You know what I've discovered? There are no Joneses. They're a mythical beast. Or beasts. Let Sammy run, I say. Let AT&T jump around like a kangaroo. It's not for me." He started to empty his glass, then put it down again. "The Peace Corps was right not to want me. I don't sound very dedicated, do I?"

"Are you?"

He looked at me blearily; more than anything else I saw pain in his eyes. "I can't tell about myself. But I know I love my country, and maybe it's true you always hurt what you love, sooner or later. Am I hurting my country by being here?"

"Not as far as I know. You're liked; you've been helpful . . ."

"I haven't really been very helpful," he said, "and I can't be sure I'm liked. But putting that aside, this whole business of being liked and being helpful bothers me. We set such great store by being liked, and being a big benefactor. Maybe that's really why I came here; not because I *cared* about these people but because I wanted to be a success in that way. Well, I've learned to care very much for these people, regardless of what they think of me, and whether or not I'm seen as any kind of benefactor. I don't want to give them my worries; I want to understand theirs. I've stopped

191

my pushing and tugging; I just want to fit in, if they'll let me—and if they don't let me, that's their business." He pulled out the pipe Doña Victoria had given him, and turned it over and over in his hands. "I'm not crusading any more."

"You're just going to keep going along?"

"Yes."

"For how long?"

"How long?" He smiled. "That's what I used to ask. How long, how long? That's another thing we think too much about: time. Tick tock, synchronize, an hour for this and an hour for that. Well, I don't know for how long. Maybe if my crops keep coming out well, some people will change, but that's their business." He took out his tobacco pouch. "And all I'm going to do right now is put that in my pipe and smoke it."

Peter became almost invisible. He came and went so unobtrusively he was virtually lost among the *ruanas* and sombreros that shuttled through the morning mist and afternoon dust. Even in Alejandro's *cantina*, in the evenings, it was difficult to pick him out right away; he was just another figure bent over a table in the smoke. It was as if he were being swallowed up by the pueblo, to be absorbed eventually without a trace. I had started to write my report, and did not go out of my way to keep track of him. There were times when, pulling my notes together and coming across references to him, I realized with a little shock that I had not noticed him for days. Even those who spoke with him seemed to find him sliding out of focus behind a light cover of words. Procopio, the bell-ringer, told me abashedly, "They'll have to put me away soon. I'm getting too old to keep. I was talking with that young friend of yours, and it slipped my mind completely who he was. It was just a familiar face, I'd seen it here and there, or one like it, and I didn't worry about it. In the back of my mind I took him as one of José's cousins.

So we talked about this and that for a few moments, nothing very exciting, and I asked him whatever happened to the young *gringo*. *Pues*, he smiled, and it came to me then who he was. I started to say it was a joke, but I'm too old to fool anybody, so I just apologized, and said he'd changed so much I hadn't quite been able to recognize him. It didn't seem to bother him, not even a little. 'Yes,' he said to me, 'I'm the one who's changed.' I wasn't certain just what I was supposed to get out of that, but if it was all right with him, it was all right with me."

Sebastian was greatly puzzled by Peter's behavior. One morning he brought me a pail of only slightly soured milk, and lingered to put some questions. "It is a *gringo* trick, perhaps?" he said, watching me very closely, as if to warn me he knew well the quivers and flushes that betrayed the liar.

"I don't know," I said. "My best opinion is that it is not a trick. Of course, that's only a *gringo* opinion."

To my surprise, he laughed. It was a brittle laugh, but it was a laugh. "Before you come to your senses," I said, "let me tell you the one about the traveling salesman who stopped at a *finca*."

"Tell it, tell it," he said expansively. "There's nothing wrong with humor. I enjoy it. Even yours, feeble as it is."

I began to understand. "So the committee's decided about the posters?"

He nodded. "Yes," he said, obviously pleased at the chance to announce it (I almost expected him to pluck a cigar from his *ruana* and offer it to me). "The committee has decided the, um, episode was, ah, funny." He beamed at me, as if to indicate the whole world was now free to laugh.

"Congratulations," I said. "It was a wise decision."

"Naturally." He held up a smile for a moment, then dropped it. His round little face was suddenly troubled. "As long as a higher committee does not decide it is not funny, I am safe."

193

"Now you're joking."

"Joking," he said flatly. "Yes, I must be joking." He flicked his smile on and off. "That Pedro," he resumed, as if he had never mentioned the committee, "what is he up to now?"

"More or less what everybody else is up to, as far as I can tell."

"That's just it," Sebastian said. "Why would he want to do what the others do? I ask myself, 'Is he winning or losing?' It is useless to keep track of him; there is nothing to protest. I don't trust a man like that."

"It does seem like a pretty shady way to operate," I said.

"Even so," he said, "it will not help him. There is only one way to throw off shackles. I thought he was looking for another way; instead he works into them. Why would he want to wear them?"

"Maybe to find out what they feel like."

"It is unnecessary," Sebastian said. "He brought his own shackles. Just as you brought yours. It does not help to take on another's shackles. At least it will not help *him;* already he is bent almost into the soil . . . he was not made to carry such a load."

"He says it feels lighter now."

"A strange young man," Sebastian said. "A few years ago no one would have thought there could be such a *gringo.*" He shook his head wonderingly. "A curious business, I think. One side draws on malcontents and misfits, and the other side counters with children. And the struggle may decide everything! It seems like madness. And yet it is only reasonable. After all, it takes those who are not content with the way things are, and those who do not fit in, to work most earnestly for something new. And your country sends those who are not so likely to show its corruption. It bundles up its innocents and scatters them abroad, saying, 'Look, everyone, their innocence is mine!' The lion hiding behind the lambs!'"

"The Peace Corps sends out older as well as younger people," I reminded him.

"Yes, but mostly younger. And those who are older in years are still children; it is no accident that there are so few of these. It is not easy to escape corruption in your country. *I* know what goes on! *Gringo* money! To buy bodies, to buy souls! And you deliver up your children, your lambs, to protect your bags of money." He spat into the dust. "But your lambs will not save you. And some day, because they are less corrupted, they may learn the truth, and return to pull the teeth of the lion."

"It's amazing how many people are so certain they know just what my country is like," I said. "Of course, no other country works as hard at criticizing itself . . . or at improving itself. No other country gives the world as much—CARE packages along with the hula hoops, *Alianza* aid along with jazz, schools and roads and hospitals along with hot dogs, hamburgers, and the Twist. No other country has been a homeland to so much of the world. You spoke of escape—the fact is that all over the world people are escaping, or trying to escape, from your way to our way. We don't have to wall our people in. We're not afraid of criticism; our system was built to stand it, and to be bettered through it—yours would crumble if the people living under it were free to speak out. As they will be some day."

"Ah, Guillermo," he said indulgently. "You are a pawn after all."

"Unlike yourself."

He shook his head. "Not so, not so. Naturally I am a pawn. You and I are both pawns. The difference is that those of us who work for a new order know that we are pawns, and are willing to sacrifice ourselves to win the game; in your country the people want to be kings, and feel that they cannot afford to sacrifice themselves, because if they did the game would be over from their standpoint."

"It is interesting," I said, "that throughout our history

our enemies have not believed we would make the necessary sacrifices—a delusion that has led them to one disastrous commitment after another."

"You people need a war to wake you up," he said complacently. "But what if your enemies do not offer you war, at least not the kind you understand? We know the game we are playing. We are making our sacrifices now; when are you going to begin yours? When New York is bombed? Yes, do wait." With a calloused toe he made a little hole in the dusty road, and covered it over. "Yes," he repeated softly, "do wait."

Christmas came and passed quietly, marked by night candles, morning prayers, and afternoon visiting. The church was open but the priest was not expected. The Fiesta of the Christ Child (*Niño Dios*) was by custom held the following month when the priest could arrange to come. Sometimes it was held in conjunction with the observance of Epiphany (*El Día de los Reyes*). This time it was deferred twice and then called off, because of the illness of the priest. After the second deferral Procopio the bell-ringer grumbled, "If he delays much longer we will be celebrating the birth, crucifixion, and resurrection all on the same day. It will seem like a very short life, shorter than that of a flea. That priest! Bless him, bless him, a good man, but still . . ."

Peter had received two Christmas presents that greatly moved him. The first was a plate of small cookies brought to him in the field on Christmas morning by Rosa Linda. "I . . . I didn't know it was Christmas," he said to me. "I mean, I'd heard people talking about it, and wondering when the priest would come, but it always seemed as if they were talking about something farther away, and I lost track of the days, and . . . well, when she brought me the cookies, I just looked at them stupidly, and then she told me it was Christmas, and smiled at me in such a beautiful way. Suddenly I felt very strange, being there in that field on Christmas morning, with cookies and a smile being offered to me

196

. . . I felt very lonely, and yet good somehow, and I . . . I kissed her." He blushed. "Only a kiss, but it shook me so much I could hardly stand. It was so . . . *right*. Lately I've had the same dream over and over. I'm in the plaza, and the whole pueblo is there, and I'm right in the midst of the people, but their backs are to me. I try to pretend I'm one of them, but I feel so desperately alone. I press against them, but there's no response. Their voices go on and on—as if they were chanting for the dead—and their *ruanas* give way before my touch. Then I see a few hands, reaching toward me between the backs, and I strain to grasp them, but I can't. I wake up full of longing, feeling cold and cut off, a million miles from nowhere, with no hope of release. And then, on Christmas morning, a hand reaches me . . . a plate of cookies, a warm smile, someone as young and fresh as the morning to hold for a moment. Oh, I know, there've been kindnesses all along, but this one came at a time when I needed it most. Need . . ." He looked at me apologetically. "I shouldn't even talk about what *I* need . . . I'm supposed to be serving needs, not showing my own. I wish I were stronger . . ."

"You and a few million others."

The second present was a visit in the afternoon by three men who, after many small shiftings and shufflings, announced that they intended to use Peter's methods in their fields, and would he please advise them? "So," Peter told me wonderingly, "I have converts after all . . ."

Christmas had not been so rewarding for José. His cousin Eusebio had given him a weeping madonna, framed in ebony, with a rubber bulb and flow regulator in back. Eusebio had tried unsuccessfully to get the archbishop to bless it, and had finally settled for a priest's blessing on a shroud which concealed it. José had reluctantly hung it on a wall in his hut. "It is not a good likeness," he told me. "It looks too fierce, as if it wanted to chew up the infant." Something had gone wrong with the flow regulator, and at unexpected moments jets of water would spurt halfway across the room, dousing anyone over four feet tall. "Perhaps it is a judgment," José said. "One never knows when it will strike." After three days, however, he had evidently had enough judgments, and did not refill it. Shortly afterwards, he caught some children trying to refill it with horse urine, and sent it back to Eusebio. "I am not one of those who see sacrilege in everything, but when I see it, I see it," he said. "Things like this make me realize that at heart I am a religious man. A bad one, yes, but not without faith. I am not criticizing Eusebio, you understand, but I have decided not to let him have Manuelito."

Manuelito was a coffin José had finished. It was a beautiful piece of work, and Eusebio had been trying to get José to let him handle it. José told me later, "He was greatly offended. I said to him, 'I prefer not to part with it at all: it is too attractive to be buried. I may keep it as a storage box. But if I ever do let someone have it, you will not be the one. The thought of it bobbing up and down through the years is distressing to me. You understand?' No, he did not understand; he was already angry because I returned the madonna, and now he started shouting at me. I felt almost pious, being shouted at by such a man. I remembered how, as a boy, I had been led a meter or two toward the priesthood by a great-uncle who had visions when drunk. Of course, there had been no chance for that, but as I listened to Eusebio I could all but hear the call. I told myself that at least I would try harder to seek goodness. What I sought when he was finished, however, was the red light district: my dip into holiness lasted only as long as he was there as my standard. And now that I have lost my cousin—he told me he would have nothing more to do with me—who knows when my next dip will be? It is hard, Guillermo. One tries, one tries, but one ends as one began. There are moments when I am drenched with goodness, as from my fierce madonna, but even that, perhaps, is more like a joke than anything else—a pinched tube, a passing pressure, nothing more. But I don't complain, Guillermo. God does what He does, and I do what I do, and things will turn out as they turn out. Would you like to buy a storage box for your papers?"

A week of heavy rain in January turned the pueblo road into a river of mud. *Campesinos* and burros struggled through it, looking like fugitives from a Mauldin sketchbook. Everything one touched seemed to have been touched first by the mud. Once I saw Peter, who was slogging along under a large sack of fertilizer, slip and fall. I tried to help him up, and fell myself. He looked at me, and at the fertilizer oozing through a tear into the mud, wiped mucky hands on mucky trousers and said, "There's no such thing as cleanliness. It's just an illusion I used to have. I can't even remember what it felt like." There was literally no way to be clean, unless one stayed in one of the streams below the pueblo, and by the middle of the week even the streams were muddy. "It is what we deserve," José said glumly. "We are pigs meant to wallow." Alejandro fell four times trying to carry a barrel of rum to his *cantina*; so liberally did he refresh himself from the barrel after each fall that he arrived, rolling the barrel, in an extravagantly generous mood, and offered the rest of the barrel to his customers free of charge —the rum was by then so gritty that, when I entered the *cantina*, there was as much chewing and spitting as drinking, and the floor was a mess. "No matter," Alejandro kept saying. "No matter."

The mud held up ("It lives," Procopio said.) through two weeks of cool, cloudy days and nights of heavy dew. Pueblo activities were dominated by it. In the plaza, below the church steps, there was a mud pit in which the children played. They leaped from the steps into it, trying to see who could leap the farthest and sink the deepest. From time to time mothers came to retrieve their own; it was not easy to tell whose were whose. Ernesto cut the school day in half. "It's bad enough when they get here," he told me, "but after they dry out, they smell rather badly." Romelio prepared a detailed report on the mud for his superiors, but since there was no way to send it to the *cabecera* (bus, hoof, and foot traffic to points outside the pueblo simply stopped), it was filed away to be sent during a dry spell. As the statue of the *Sagrado Corazón* was moved in its rounds from household altar to household altar, despite the greatest care it became muddier and muddier. No one, however, presumed to clean it: "It is a sign of the closeness of the deity to us," a woman told me. "Who would remove what the saints choose to wear?" Later, when it was caught in a downburst, the mud was largely washed off, and it was dried clean with the assurance that "It is the pleasure of heaven."

With access to markets cut off, meals became more limited than ever: a bowl of muddied *sancocho* was typical. Well water was brown, and consumption of *aguardiente* was spurred. Visenta was busier than she had been for months, attending to a variety of chills both natural and supernatural. Three old men, two old women, and four infants died. José stayed up late whacking together simple coffins, and Alejandro volunteered on behalf of his regular customers to spend two days digging graves. Alejandro supplied the sustenance, while his customers supplied the labor. One morning Doña Victoria was found sitting in the mud in her nightclothes, cursing the world. She had evidently stumbled out and toppled in during a nightmare, though at first she denied it. "I came here to have fun!" she yelled at those who found her. "Can't you see I'm having fun?" It was feared that she would come down with pneumonia and follow the others to the grave, but she contracted only a mild case of sniffles.

Fields were left largely untended, and while some of the men took up small household tasks, there were many who simply stopped doing things. Several of these were tapped for the grave-digging detail, but the rest continued to, as Ernesto put it, "just be." One could see them slumped in doorways, against walls, wherever there was a fairly dry spot. It was as if the pueblo had, for the most part, run down.

I was reminded of a tableau in which, superimposed on a scene of frozen waiting, there was a flickering of children playing, people dying, and graves being readied.

Peter was affected by the prevailing inactivity, and in time joined the slumpers. It was curious to see him sitting in the doorway of José's hut, for all the world as if he would never rise again, his bearded face gaunt and impassive— a boy seemingly drained not only of youth but of life itself. I remembered a phrase in a U. S. TV commercial: "the lively crowd"; this was emphatically the unlively crowd. And Peter had become a zombie in good standing.

On the day the four infants were buried, Peter was sitting in the doorway when the small coffins passed. He watched them dully; then, as the last went by, listlessly joined the stragglers. It was a gloomy, overcast day, with fog close to the ground: coffins and heads seemed at times to be floating. Yet the way was hard: mingled with the mumbling of prayers were the sounds of squishing and sucking as feet fought through the muck and ooze. The cemetery was on a small rise west of the pueblo, and as we moved up the rise the heels of those before spattered those behind. My camera was tucked inside my khaki jacket, but I would probably not use it; when I had first settled in the pueblo, I had turned my lens to the living and dead alike, and if it troubled me to photograph the newly dead child with grass in her nostrils or the woman who had come dead from labor with only a puzzled look in her eyes to show for it, I reminded myself that I was after all a scientist and that professional detachment was the order of the day. But with time I found the appeal to science less and less reassuring, and more and more often as I raised the little black machine adjusted for depth and light and focus and everything except emotion, I felt as if I were intruding, intruding on death itself, impaling its truth instead of capturing it. The woman had her puzzled look and I had my fossil stills, and we had both lost too much. So now, trudging up the rise, I wore my camera as a talisman, my *azabache* against the spirits of scholasticism.

Perhaps they would note that I carried it, and leave me alone.

Peter moved up to walk by my side. His eyes were on the floating heads and coffins before us; they seemed to be filling with pain, the pain of one waking to his wounds. His bared head was wet with sweat and mist, his hair and beard were wildly matted and fused together like a sling worn by a man with a toothache, and the hand that gripped his battered straw hat was raw from yesterday's soil and today's cold. He looked like a hermit on a pilgrimage. "I . . . I've been here forever," he whispered. I knew just how he felt.

"So many," the woman ahead of us was saying to her husband. "So many to go without last rites. What will their souls do?" Her husband shrugged. "It is not the priest's fault," he said. "He comes when he can. But the roads . . . and his sickness . . . and they all went so quickly . . ." "If only we had our own priest," the woman said. "If only the moon would drop pesos on us," the man said wearily. "Yes, but I worry about their souls," the woman said. "It's not for you to worry," the man said. "The Church will work it out somehow; their souls will not be damned." "I don't know what we'd do without the Church," the woman said, sighing.

The gate to the cemetery always stood open. Not that its closing would keep anyone out, since there was no fence, just a gate. José's father had built it to mark the entrance. Inside, wooden crosses were scattered over the rise and part way down the opposite slope. Many were all but hidden by high grass and weeds. The markings on the older crosses had been largely weathered away. The four newly dug graves were partly filled with water.

We stood in the mud, waiting for the small coffins to be lowered. The wind was growing, and *ruanas* flapped in the cold wet gusts. Procopio moved slowly to one of the graves; with the sexton still ill in the city, Procopio would say a few words. At the edge of the grave, he turned and looked at those who waited. Tears rolled down his dark, pinched face; one of the infants to be buried was a grandson. He had once told me it was the lot of women to cry, and that a man who did so was a fool. Still, he cried. Romelio stood near him, trying to appear at attention in a uniform that was very much out of attention. When I had seen him earlier, he had been pressing the uniform with an ancient iron heated by charcoal. I had asked him why he bothered, since the iron was no match for a trip to the cemetery. "The thing for me," he had said, "is to start out well." José was standing by the first box to be lowered. He had helped carry it to the cemetery. "I always try to carry my own coffins," he had once explained to me. "What I put together, almost anything may put asunder. A few years ago, when I was laid up with jaundice, a *compadre* of mine was carried to the cemetery. He was a very heavy man, the pallbearers stumbled and my coffin was dropped. It shattered at once, and there was great embarrassment. It was a good thing for me I had jaundice. I claimed I had built part of the coffin from my sick bed. I lied, but it was only proper to lie." His frozen face was turned on the box as if willing it to hold together. On the other side of the grave Ernesto shifted from foot to foot in obvious discomfort; death seemed to make him very uneasy. I remembered how he had acted at the burial of one of his pupils: "Paulo, Paulo," he had burst out, "you don't have to do your arithmetic now." It was as if death had somehow slipped among the assignments he had given in class, and he was trying to take them all back.

Standing a few paces apart from the others was Sebastian, a little fuss of a man who had drawn his oversize *ruana* around himself as if it were Napoleon's cape. He stabbed at us all with his chin, as if to say, "You see? You see what happens when you don't listen to me?" Yet there could be no doubt that the grief on his face was genuine.

Peter, by my side, was looking at Procopio. Their eyes met, and it seemed that the eyes of the one were no less old than the eyes of the other. Procopio nodded vaguely, as to a contemporary dimly remembered; I could almost hear him saying, "We're next, aren't we? Any day now . . ." Peter nodded in return, acknowledging the gift of years. He worked his lips, cracked and blue with cold, silently, as if rubbing them together to keep them warm.

Procopio started to speak, but the wind carried his words away. He tried again, but there was only the rising moan of the wind to hear. He took out his bell, which was stuffed with moss, and with trembling hands began to pluck out pieces and drop them into the grave. A dog howled, challenging the wind. A sudden, sharp rain came to us. Yet we waited. I had once thought of waiting as something done when there was nothing else to do; here I had come to think of waiting as an act of constancy, of perseverance; as a way of dealing with a strength that could only defeat those who ran either way. We waited.

There, in the mud, with the icy rain on us, Peter began slowly to straighten. So long had he been bent that he seemed to be turning into a giant. He lifted his head to the rain and held his shoulders high. Those near him looked at him in wonder. The height he had brought with him seemed now increased. His face was set not against the rain but into it. A child behind him began to cry as his *ruana* blotted out the sky for her. He turned and reached out to her, and she smiled. He put his hat on her head and lifted her to his shoulders; a young man and a child, towering above the others.

XI

The sun came, the mud firmed and began to flake into dust, and there were two more births than there had been deaths. Visenta, helped by Rosa Linda, presided at six of the deliveries; the others were do-it-yourself affairs. Two of the boys were named Pedro.

Romelio spent several days at the bridge Peter had renovated, counting the crossings, and reported to the *cabecera* that on the average 12.4 persons used the bridge daily, an increase of 3.1 persons since the last report. "This," he concluded, "is a satisfactory result." He noted that a market route to and from San Isidro had been developing across the bridge, and that "another increase can be expected." His wife had advised him to be more cautious in his conclusion by amending it to read, "This is a satisfactory result for that type of bridge," but he had decided that, since no one really knew what a satisfactory result was, what he called satisfactory in the area under his authority was officially satisfactory; besides, he did not want to have to worry about one of his superiors asking him what "that type of bridge" was.

There were four more converts to Peter's farming methods, and Peter was able—by serving as guarantor—to secure new tools and supplies for them on credit. He worked out a balanced diet, calling for a higher intake of protein

205

(fish, eggs, and cheese would be the principal local sources), and, when he failed at first to make any headway with it among pueblo households, he got Visenta to prescribe it for her patients. Those she put on it stayed on it—the prospect of supernatural retaliation for failure to do so was not one to be ignored—and many came to feel so much better Visenta's stock rose considerably. "I'm working real magic now," she told me banteringly, but there was no mistaking the new pride in her voice and manner. Since sooner or later she would come to virtually every household in the pueblo, there was little doubt that the diet would be adopted generally in time.

Instead of giving himself to the routine of the crop cycle, Peter now made it work for him. "It finally dawned on me that, with all the practice I've been getting, and knowing just what has to be done well in advance, I can plan all kinds of things and set aside the time to do them." He showed me a list of projects already planned: they included an aqueduct, a drainage system, and a hard surface for the pueblo road. "I don't see these as striking at the core, really," he told me, "but they all need to be done. I've been moving away from the idea I had a while back, that what you did was shuck off projects like the layers of an onion till you got to the center. But I see now that you don't have to stick your finger directly into the mainspring; you can stop the watch that way. Everything sort of fits together, so if you do something here, something happens there, and even if you press at what seem to be the peripheries, you can get a chain reaction that can reach to the core. Of course, now that I've *felt*—and that's been the most important part for me—now that I've felt what mud and dust can do, the projects I work on are going to have a lot more meaning for all of us than they would have otherwise. Even so . . ." His face was troubled; he was like someone who, having just announced that he holds a winning ticket, begins to wonder about one of the digits.

"Is there something wrong with the way you've worked it out?"

"Not as far as it goes, maybe, but . . . I've got to go beyond it, and the key's been dangling in front of me all along. I . . ." He looked at me intently. "There was something at the cemetery, something I did . . ."

"All I remember you doing was holding up a child."

"A child!" He began to tremble with excitement. "Of course! A child, a child . . ."

We went to see Ernesto. He was munching on a roll in his quarters. His bed was unmade, there was a coat of dust so general it seemed to extend to the roll (one almost expected to see him blow before biting), and composition papers littered the floor. His black suit was soaked under the armpits, and his frayed white shirt was open and tie-less. "Excuse our condition," he said, referring to the room and himself with an apologetic sweep of the hand. "I hate correcting papers, and every now and then I let them accumulate to a frightening height. Then I have to tell myself I'm not permitted to clean anything until I clean up the papers." He looked reproachfully at the floor. "The only effect that seems to have at first is to reduce my quarters to a sty. But in time I'm shamed into action." He leaned back in his chair and smiled at us. "You've caught me at the peak of my shame."

"Would you like some help?" Peter asked.

Ernesto looked at us thoughtfully, drumming the table with the roll. "The papers are my responsibility," he said. "If you were planning to rescue me from my shame, the answer is no."

"I didn't mean the papers," Peter said. He spoke very slowly and carefully. "I'd like to help you build something. Education's the key, and the doors we can open with it can make all the difference in the world. I'm not talking about brain-washing; I'm talking about brain-freeing. It's the greatest power there is. What you have here are the people who are going to decide about the future, if they're able to decide. It's not for me, or for Sebastian either, to decide for them. What I want to do is help equip them to decide for themselves. Does that sound phony?"

"No," Ernesto said. "It's worth believing in. But with only two years to work with them . . ."

"We can offer more than two years. If we work hard, there's no limit to what we can offer. Let's start something growing! This is the planting that counts most."

"Calm down, *joven*," Ernesto said, not unkindly. "You are rushing off like the *vaca loca* again. Perhaps not so blindly now, but still . . ." He ran a hand wearily through his long black hair. "Don't you think I have had such visions?" he said softly. "Don't you think it hurts to have a light cut off at a glimmer? But even the two of us . . ."

"Others will help," Peter said confidently. "José, Romelio . . . there will be enough to do enough. We can help teach some to help teach many. The program we set up will reach the whole pueblo. We'll make it a model program. I've got seven families already who can expect more from their fields. The children won't be tied to the fields so much, and neither will the adults; there'll be more opportunity for more learning. There'll be more and more families like that. Freedom *from* something can lead to freedom *for* something. I used to feel I was drawing close to a wall, the kind of wall people like Sebastian would blow to bits. A better approach, Don Ernesto, is to hold up a child to see over it."

"Hold up a child to see over it . . ." Ernesto mused.

"It's going to be his wall," Peter said. "He's going to inherit it. If he doesn't want it, if he prefers what he sees beyond it, he'll be able—if he's helped, if he's equipped—to say what doors and windows will be put in, what bricks will be replaced, and what parts of it will go into a new foundation. I repeat, it's not for me to say. If I help give him a stronger voice, and a basis for judging for himself, he's free to say he doesn't like my notions. He's free to say what's best for *him*." Peter smiled apologetically. "I'm really wound up, aren't I? But I mean all of it, all of it. I've heard so much of it said so often before, pieces here and pieces there, but it's never fit together for me like this before."

"What you have in your mind is, after all, only what you have in your mind," Ernesto said. "In principle, the Ministry of Education certainly favors more education, and the *Departamento* does what it can with the facilities and staff it can muster, but there just hasn't been enough to go around where it's needed. And there are so many other priorities and clearances and commitments and red tape that any kind of real program change is a complicated business. I'm just an employee, and not a very important one. You can't expect me to set aside the regular program simply because you're enthusiastic."

"Not to set it aside," Peter said. "To build it up. What we do we'll do on our own, unofficially, after hours, without any question of pay or outside support. If it catches on, the support may follow. But meanwhile let's go ahead, and I'll take all the blame. In any case, you'll still have the regular program. But that's going to be the minimum, the base. I have a little extra money from my crops; it's not enough to buy myself a big *finca* and *hacienda*, but I can buy pencils and paper with it. I used to think that what could be got out of these small plots wasn't enough for a breakthrough, but it is, not if it's invested in oneself but if it's invested in one's children. It's so!"

Ernesto smiled. "A young man I can barely recognize as myself once talked like that," he said. "It is good to have such a young man back again. With what I know now and what you do not know we might be able to do something. But if there is any blame to be taken, I accept my share in advance." He stood up and held out his hand.

Peter shook it so vigorously Ernesto protested. "You'll disable me before we begin. And remember, I promise only to try. And if the *maestra* does not agree, we are in trouble immediately: I take it you wish to help girls as well as boys."

"Yes! Yes!" Peter said excitedly. "All of them! Everybody!"

Ernesto winked at me. "He is a puppy again," he said.

The *maestra* was a drab woman in her late forties who seemed always in shadows, as if she sought them out to cover her comings and goings outside the classroom. In my notes I referred to her as the kind of person who manages to pass people when they're thinking of something else; awareness that she's there comes only when it's too late to say hello. My notes contain only two other references to her. One goes: "Almost bumped into *maestra* today. Didn't see her coming. Apologized. She seemed surprised at being found." The other states: "Found out *maestra* widowed seventeen years ago. Three children, two died malaria (V insists smallpox), other drives bus between San Marino and El Hondo. *Maestra* has nickname: '*Tiza*,' chalk. Liked, but no one says why." I had thought there were other references, but evidently hers was a drabness too drab to keep noting. I had twice dropped in on her classes. The first time the children were working by themselves—copying letters and numbers from the blackboard, drawing and coloring pictures, even doing embroidery—while she slipped almost invisibly from row to row. The second time was during a visit by the zonal school inspector, who—possibly mistaking me for someone important—took charge of class activities with an air so grand he might have been conducting the New York Philharmonic in a command performance. So that now, as I walked with Ernesto and Peter to her school, I had not yet really seen her in action, and my best impression of her as a teacher would have been that she was probably colorless, dry, and perfunctorily adequate.

I was wrong. Within five minutes after we entered her class I could see that her drabness was essentially leftovers: she gave what she truly was to her pupils, saving nothing warm and vital to show anyone else. She introduced us to the class as if we hadn't really come, seated us on a bench in back, not listening to Peters' overtures, and went on teaching. Her range of knowledge was clearly quite limited—dates escaped her and almost any fact that contained a number was beyond her—but within that range she taught with fire and love, striding into a subject with a blend of purpose and wonder that suggested she was exploring new and exciting woods with old friends; and outside that range she said simply, "I don't know," and promised to try to find out with the help of those who had led her there.

Eventually she sent her pupils out to play and, so listlessly one might have thought the pupils had carried away all her energy, came back to us. She looked at us without interest, and sat down as we rose. "So," she said. "You tower above me like bullies. Have you invaded my class to overpower me?"

"Brutally, if necessary," Ernesto said with a gracious bow.

She glanced up at him and sniffed. "You've disposed of your pupils already, I see."

"They asked too many questions," Ernesto said. He had put them to work in the school garden. "There is only one way for you to save yourself. You must submit to our proposition."

"I never submit," she said. "I either take or reject." She scratched idly at a dab of paste on her blue cotton dress; I had never seen her in any other dress. "What is it?"

Ernesto nudged Peter, who began to explain. As Peter talked, the *maestra* gave no sign that she was even listening. Her mulatto face was set as if for sleep. Somehow it upset me to observe that to her we were not quite real. I felt like protesting to her, "No, no, it's *you* who haven't been real to *me;* you've got it backwards," but I realized she would pay no more notice to me than I had to her. With her indifference added to the audience, Peter's phrases sounded trite, tiresome, and unconvincing; I began to understand the need for taped applause. Cut the crap, Peter, I thought;

but on he went, doggedly, naively, still full of an enthusiasm that now seemed only foolish. His ragged beard, starved face and tattered clothes would make him appear ludicrous to her: who was he to be talking of such things? I felt partly embarrassed for him, partly protective toward him, but mostly irritated at him. Shut up, Peter, shut up; can't you see it's nothing to her? "Will you?" Peter was saying. "Will you?"

You poor kid, I thought as she finally looked up at him.

"Of course," she said mildly. "It is what I have wanted for years."

The two pueblo schools, plaza neighbors, were tile-roofed adobe structures with cement floors, wooden doors, and open windows fitted with wooden bars and shutters. Each contained an antechamber, a classroom, and kitchen-bedroom living quarters for the teacher. They were mirror partners, identical in dimensions and reversed in arrangements. They were lime-coated, with the white of the boys' school relieved by a patch of green at one end, where José had begun a trim he decided he disliked. The patch was never covered up, since parents found it handy to refer to "the green school" when sending their pre-school children there on errands. Ernesto once complained that he could never take a nap with any certainty that he would not be waked by a persistent knock to accept an egg or onion. "The worst time is shortly after dawn on weekends, holidays, and the days after holidays," he said. "My inclination on such days is to sleep forever, but the hand of hospitality keeps slapping me awake. The smaller they are, the more stubbornly they knock. When I finally manage to drag myself to the door and open it, and see that small hand holding up the egg, I partly want to kneel and kiss the little head, and I partly want to smash the egg on it." Another time he grumbled, "All it takes is an egg or onion to check up on the teacher. The egg can be stale and the onion dry, but the teacher had better be there when it comes! If children were allowed out at night, I wouldn't be. As it is, the later I stay in Alejandro's *cantina* at night, the earlier I can expect a morning knock."

Behind each school were three outhouses, nicknamed "study rooms." Each classroom was furnished with a national flag, a picture of Jesus, portraits of national heroes, a wall map of the country and another of the *Departamento*, a wall calendar, a blackboard, an abacus, work tables and benches. One work table served as the teacher's desk: the *maestra's* was virtually free of materials, a clearing in the woods she explored; the *maestro's* was a jungle, and Ernesto stayed away from it as much as possible. Between the classroom door and the outhouses were the school gardens and play areas. The gardens were maintained by the pupils, and the produce was prepared and consumed on the school premises as an informal and highly variable school lunch and snack program. Ernesto dreaded the times when his pupils took over the kitchen. "I go outside," he said. "I don't want to know what they're doing. The strange thing is that they usually come out with something worth eating. Have you ever had coffee with corn in it? Or cheese flattened and fried until the outside's crisp and the inside's chewy as meat? It's terrible, terrible, but good all the same."

Señora Margarita Calderón de Riasco, the *maestra*, was going over the school records for the past several years. The new candle and half-pencil with which she had begun were down to stubs. Sweat, like brown sugar beads, dotted her face; they seemed oddly dry, as if there were no underlying pressure or energy to make them plump out and fall. The smell of sweetness they seemed to send to us came from an ointment she rubbed into her face every Saturday night, while the men were carousing in the *cantinas*. Peter had told me this that afternoon, before we had come to the green school with the *maestra* and Ernesto to make plans. Visenta, who supplied the ointment, had told him. I had been shocked, not realizing why, to hear it. Now I understood my shock: Visenta had touched what I had not thought could be

213

touched. Reason *versus* superstition—the one did not necessarily fight the other. In fact, remembering how the *maestra* had manifestly doubted my reality, I was uncomfortably aware that these were my categories, hardly binding on anyone else. Perhaps, I thought, the *maestra* owed at least part of her classroom force to Visenta; perhaps without Visenta the *maestra* was a drab perfunctory creature after all. I did not believe it, but I was no longer impressed by what I did or did not believe. The only time I sensed I knew the truth was when I was drunk, and the only articulation of that truth I had ever managed was, "I love the bastards," an articulation that made me shudder when, sober, I confronted myself with it.

While the *maestra* went over the records, Ernesto corrected papers with a determinedly nauseated expression, and Peter studied the *maestra*'s knee as if surprised that she had one. Knees were not often seen in the pueblo—sex was easier to find than nudity—and the way the *maestra* had hitched up her skirt attested that she either was or was not emphatically a woman. I could not have said which, and evidently Peter was as undecided as I. I can still see him hunched forward on that bench, studying that knee, his beard barely a yard away (reminding me of a pointer just before the quarry is flushed), his eyes grave. He might have been studying a novel chess problem.

The *maestra* pushed away the records and sighed. "It is difficult," she said. "There are enough bright ones to begin with, but they are all different ages, and the number of years they have been out of school varies so from one to another . . . Some are married, some would not be interested, some are not well . . . It will not be easy at all."

"We could always start with the ones we have," Ernesto said. "We could set up a third year for those who are about to finish the second, and next year set up a fourth year for those who finish the third, and every year add a year."

The *maestra* nodded. "We can work on that as we go

along," she said. "But there are some who've already left school I don't want to lose. I think we'll just have to take them up one by one, start them off at the third level and let them find their own place with our help. Those we can't group we'll just have to work with individually." She shook her head wearily. "I feel so helpless, Don Ernesto. You and I are going to have to work hard on ourselves along with everything else. I'm afraid you'll have to give up some of your *cantina* evenings."

Ernesto groaned. "Why did I ever say yes? Why did *you* ever say yes?"

The *maestra* looked at him steadily. "You know why we said yes."

Ernesto hesitated, then looked as steadily back. "Yes," he said quietly, "I know why."

Peter and I were perched on a work table in the rear of Ernesto's classroom. The table, he had advised us correctly, would be more comfortable than a bench. The school day had just begun with the collective recital of the catechism. "They couldn't get away with that in New York State," I whispered to Peter.

"You don't say?" Peter whispered innocently. "And all the time I've been thinking everything here was just as it is in New York State."

Ernesto began checking the attendance. "Where's Jorge?" he asked.

"Sick," someone said.

"But he brought me an egg early this morning," Ernesto said.

"Maybe he ate one just as old for breakfast," someone suggested. Laughter exploded as soon as Ernesto smiled.

"Whatever the reason," Ernesto said, "he was supposed to make a presentation today."

"That's the reason," someone said. Another smile and explosion.

"Ah, my little clowns," Ernesto murmured. He finished with the attendance, then put the first grade to work copying sentences from the blackboard (A sentence that especially intrigued me was, "Never eat the same thing twice." It baffled me until I learned that it was an expression made famous by the patriot general who had taken and held the nearby city during the revolution. It had been his way of saying that he would never submit to the old rule again.) while the second grade was started on oral drills.

Ernesto fired questions, and the second-grade pupils virtually shouted back the answers in unison. "A good school," Procopio had assured me soon after my arrival in Melita, "sounds like a beehive." It was certainly true that the almost constant classroom din left no doubt outside the school that education was going on inside. Prolonged silences were regarded with suspicion that the teacher was not on the job. "I try to keep the school humming," Ernesto had once told me. "But people make no allowances for headaches, and every so often I have everyone work quietly. Sometimes I stand by the window then, and watch the people creep into the plaza, straining to hear, wondering what's wrong in the classroom."

Now, however, the school was humming.

Ernesto: "What is six times four?"

Pupils: "Twenty-four!"

Ernesto (craftily): "What is four times six?"

Pupils (triumphantly): "Twenty-four!"

Ernesto: "What is eight times three?"

Pupils: "Twenty-four!"

Ernesto: "What is four times eight?" He smiled expectantly.

Some of the pupils shouted "Twenty-four!" Others howled "Thirty-two!" The rest floundered in a miscellany of half-voiced wrong answers. Those who had come up with the right answer thundered it out again and again, a few of them leaping to their feet and shaking their fists at the

216

others, and gradually the Thirty-twos overwhelmed the Twenty-fours and those who muttered and mouthed indecisively.

Ernesto: "We're all agreed now on thirty-two? Antonio, you've joined us at last?"

Antonio (grinning): "*Sí, Maestro.*"

Ernesto: "That was a good battle you put up for twenty-four."

Antonio (modestly): "It was right before. It won for me three times."

Ernesto: "So it did. Carlos, you win the prize for giving the most answers to the question. I didn't catch them all, you were jumping around too fast for me, but I did hear twelve, twenty-four, forty and forty-eight, didn't I?"

Carlos (defensively): "They're all good numbers."

Ernesto: "True, true. Their only fault is that they didn't answer the question."

Carlos: "I didn't hear the question."

The second-grade drills were interrupted only once, when a first-grader wet his workbook. "Ah, Ricardo," Ernesto said, "you've soaked the pages on Manners."

"It's a good thing he wasn't sitting on his catechism," someone said. There was an eruption of shocked laughter.

Ernesto whanged the workbook down on his desk, and the drills were resumed. When Ernesto had finished with the second-graders, he set them to work writing out the multiplication tables while he drilled the first graders.

I had once asked Ernesto how many subjects were taught. "How many? *Pues,* there's mathematics—since you asked for a count, we might as well start with the subject that shows us how to make it—then there's language, including speech; and social studies—that's history and geography—music, art, crafts, religion, and physical education. How many does that make? Two, really. What we're basically concerned with are literacy and marketplace arithmetic. About all we can do in the time we have is to make the contractual side of farming less strange to them. Most of what we have them do in class is varied practice in that direction. Of course, what they practice with is supposed to help them become more moral and patriotic. When Simón Bolívar is compared with your *Jorge* Washington, for example, we try to give Don Jorge his due, but there's no mistaking our favorite."

The first-graders seemed to be trying to outdo the second-graders in volume. It always amazed me how the pupils assigned to silent lessons could work so imperturbably in the uproar from the others.

Ernesto: *"Un momento!* Rafael, you move your mouth very well, it's a beautiful sight, but what are you saying?"

Rafael: "I don't know, *Maestro.*"

Ernesto: "You don't know? Why not?"

Rafael: "I can't hear myself, *Maestro.*"

When the tumult of the drills gave way to a recess roar outside, Ernesto closed the door and came over to us.

"Do you feel uplifted?" I asked him.

"Downtrodden," he said, wiping his forehead with an already soggy handkerchief. "Flattened out. Sometimes I think the best way for me to get through the school day is howling drunk."

"How can you tell who's saying something and who isn't?" Peter asked.

"One learns. A man who listens year after year to the sea can tell how the waves are breaking." He brushed chalk streaks from his black suit.

"How long does recess last?" Peter asked.

"As long as it takes for me to pull myself together," Ernesto said. "The first part of the term I showed them what they could do out there, and now I let them do it. Oh, sometimes I'm called out to explain a soccer rule or get a basketball game started or stop a fight, but mostly they play well enough by themselves, and I hide in here." He stretched out on a bench. "The only real trouble I've ever had was when some of the second-graders talked three of the first-graders into taking off their clothes and running into the girls' school. There was so much screaming half the pueblo came charging into the plaza with machetes and buckets of water. People thought it was a terrible thing, a great lack of respect, but funny too, and some of them had so much fun throwing water on the *maestra* I believe they half hoped it would happen again soon."

"But why did they throw water on the *maestra?*" Peter asked.

"There was such a commotion at first that all kinds of rumors got started. Someone suggested that she'd gone crazy, and by the time the crowd reached the school she was so hysterical they thought it was true, and they doused her and tied her down. That was the *maestra* we had before Doña Margarita came, and she was such a nervous woman it wasn't surprising people thought what they did. She was little, but she had an enormous head, and people never could decide whether it meant she was very smart or a freak or both. She always seemed jumpy about things in general, and later on, after she left here, she really did go crazy, *trastornada*. She went around saying God was a woman."

"Did that mean she was crazy?" Peter asked.

"Not all by itself, no," Ernesto said. "That was just the part that made people notice. I heard she did all sorts of foolish things in class. She'd call on the same girl five times in a row, and burst out crying in the middle of a lesson, and answer her own questions before anyone else had a chance, and have her pupils copy backwards words she'd written backwards on the blackboard—that would make them come out right, you see—and so on. It's not easy to tell the difference between an odd teacher and a crazy teacher, but when she went around saying God was a woman, people realized she was crazy and sent her away."

"What happened to her?" Peter asked.

Ernesto chuckled. "Oh, she's up in the capital now, working for the government; it's a good job she has, *maravilloso*. Some say it's because she got better, and some say it's because she didn't. Sometimes I think there's no better place for crazy teachers."

"But why would she be hired if she had beliefs that weren't acceptable?"

"*Quién sabe?* Perhaps she learned to lie about her beliefs."

Peter shaved. In one sense, it took years from him; in another sense, it added years. Before, old as his beard made him seem, it was possible to imagine that beneath the beard was the boy Peter. Now it was no longer possible; the beard was gone, and no boy was found. What was found was the face of an almost cadaverous young man who might have appeared in a Buchenwald photograph. There were new hollows in the cheeks and new lines around the mouth, and the skin had lost its collegiate freshness. Yet it was a stronger, sharper face, with the attractiveness of a Montgomery Clift or a Sinatra; it was far more compelling than the one he had brought.

He had shaved because the *maestra,* whose head came barely to his chest, had looked up into the burning eyes of this gaunt giant and told him to. "If you're going to be coming into *my* class," she said, "you're going to have to do something about yourself. You look like a bear. A slovenly bear." She had him turn over his clothes to her class for cleaning and mending. "They're disgraceful," she told him. "Disgraceful. If my girls can fix those, they can fix anything." Whatever she felt was too far gone she threw away, and at her insistence he bought a cheap cotton suit in the city. "It's your teaching suit," she said to him. "If I'm going to help you, you're going to help me. You can start by telling my girls some things about that peculiar country of yours."

His first class presentation left him so excited José and I took him on a long walk to calm him down. "I said absolutely nothing important," he told us boisterously, "and yet it was all important. I don't even remember most of what I *did* say, but it wasn't a hard sell or soft sell or any kind of sell, it was just, you know, *being* with them, sharing things with them, learning about them while they were learning about me. Sounds like *The King and I*, doesn't it?"

"You have a king?" José asked, surprised. "And you know him?"

"It's just a play, Don José, with a lot of music, and one of the pieces is called 'Getting To Know You,' which is the way I felt, you see, and . . . and . . ." Peter smacked his hands together. "It was so *good!* When I started out, I thought there were certain things I'd have to cover, to make it all neat and tidy, but I forgot all about that, I just let them lead me wherever they wanted to, and told them about the things *they* wanted to hear about. Some were things we—we *gringos*, Don José—we're proud of, and some were things we're not so proud of, but the longer I talked with them the more certain I was that I couldn't expect them to be honest with me—at that time or when they grew up—if I wasn't honest with them. So . . . I'm going to do the same tomorrow with Ernesto's class."

José took off his straw hat and fanned his frozen face. He was puffing a little from the pace of the walk. "I'm only being honest with you," he said, "when I say you walk too fast."

"I'm sorry, Don José." Peter slowed down.

"I don't mean just you, Pedrito. You only do it now when you're excited. I mean *gringos* in general. You walk so fast what we say doesn't catch up to you."

"It's going to be different, Don José. We'll listen, and we'll hear. I promise."

"How can you promise, Pedrito? You're only one *gringo*, and for all I know if you were home they'd just brush you aside."

"I don't know how I can promise," Peter said. "But all the same, I promise."

A Saturday morning knock brought Ernesto not an egg or onion but a letter from the Departmental capital, granting the permission he and the *maestra* had requested "to supplement the existing program on a voluntary basis, without cost or obligation to the Department, subject to (1) local approval (2) continued compliance with Departmental directives and regulations and (3) periodic review and approval by the zonal inspector." He let out a whoop and rushed part way down the road to show Peter and the *maestra* before he realized that he still had his pajamas on. He owned the only pair of pajamas in the pueblo, and it was said that children liked to bring the early eggs and onions not only to wake him up but in hopes of seeing his pajamas. The bearer of the letter, a six-year old named Emilio Salcedo, was almost overcome with delight, and spent the rest of the day going from door to door describing the pajamas in detail as vivid as his vocabulary would permit. It was such a strain on him (the pajamas were blue with an intricate red trim) that he was put to bed well before dark with a slight fever.

Over the weekend Ernesto, Doña Margarita and Peter agreed to canvass the pueblo, beginning Monday after school, with the joint purpose of securing local approval ("Whatever that is," Ernesto commented. "If people say, 'Go ahead for all I care,' is that local approval?") and identifying prospects for the expanded program ("The first old man who says he wants to study nuclear physics gets my arm down his throat," Ernesto said).

The first visit on Monday was to the Inspector. Romelio looked at me curiously. "You too, Guillermo? I thought you did nothing."

"I haven't stopped," I said. "I'm just an observer."

"He's supposed to be summarizing public reaction," Peter explained.

"*Puta madre!* You call that nothing?"

"The way I do it, it will be nothing," I said modestly.

The *maestra*, who had been standing inconspicuously by the door, said sharply, "Don Romelio, did I hear you curse?"

222

Romelio flushed. "A thousand pardons, Doña Margarita. I almost never have women in my office."

"I should hope you didn't," said the *maestra*. "Your daughter is in my class, you know. I wouldn't want to send her home to a man who keeps women in his office."

Romelio looked at her nervously. "How . . . how is she doing in school, Doña Margarita?"

"So well, Don Romelio, it pains me to think that after this year there may be nothing more I can give her." The drab face flared into a reproachful beauty that shocked me. That morning I had gone over my notes for the last time before my return to the States, and their pedantic dullness had so disturbed me I had pinched María to make certain, as I told her, that people were still alive, and after I had been assured that they were (not by her leap for life but by her answering slap), we had drunk *aguardiente* together until she began to talk about her dead husband ("He always seemed wet") and I began to mumble about my notes ("Do you realize I've got over three thousand pages?" I said. "I don't think he ever wiped himself," she said). It came to me then that there was at least one great truth in my notes, though I didn't know exactly where, and that was that social science would be a lot better off without people, at least the social science I had been taught. I had already pigeonholed the *maestra*, and there was no place for that flash of beauty, just as there had been no place for her classroom transformation. She was plain, and however animated she became in class she had nothing to do with sex; yet now I knew she did. She could have been saying to Romelio that it was to him she longed to give herself, and in that moment she seemed supremely worth the taking.

"I . . . um . . . you say she does well?" Romelio said, twisting his cap as if it were a schoolboy's.

The *maestra* nodded, almost sensuously, as if she were acceding to a proposition.

"Is that . . . is *that* the sort of thing you want to do?"

Romelio asked. He might have been asking her if she *really* wanted to offer herself to him.

"Yes."

"Then . . . then you certainly have *my* permission," Romelio said, finishing crisply and authoritatively. It occurred to me, now that the first mission had succeeded so quickly, that perhaps the *maestra* really *would* offer herself wholly for her pupils—and perhaps for nothing else.

"What, no forms?" I asked.

Romelio smiled coldly. "If I find that any forms are necessary, I'll fill them out myself. You people never do it right."

Subsequent visits met with comparable success, due largely to the presence of the *maestra*. Ernesto was liked; the *maestra* was trusted. There were only a few misunderstandings. An old woman thought we were back about the bridge. "Fix it, fix it," she kept saying. "It's about time something was done." Procopio thought we had come to put him in charge of the whole program. Ernesto started to correct him, but the *maestra* interposed, and with a few gentle phrases (such as, "There would be no drinking, of course") got him both to decline and to give assurances that he would support the program in every *other* way he could. Three persons thought we had come with grievances about the schoolwork of their children, and were so relieved to find out we had not they at once assented. The most intriguing interpretation of our visit was by Doña Victoria, who thought we had discovered she had cheated on a spelling test three-quarters of a century ago. "It wasn't even a regular school," she said defensively, "and the teacher didn't like teaching Indians. He thought we couldn't learn and wouldn't learn. So I cheated every way I could to show him how wrong he was."

"If you cheated all you could," Peter said, "why are you worried only about the one test?"

"How did you know about that?" she said accusingly.

"You told us when we came in," Peter said.

"It was plain enough you already knew," she said. "People don't walk around with teachers for *pleasure*, do they? I tell you, young man, there's no respect any more, I've known for years they'd pry until they found out. And what of it? I only cheated once; they don't hang people for that any more."

"You mean you didn't cheat other times?" Peter asked.

"Of course I did!" she snapped. "But there was only once that it counted. The teacher was away, and the priest tried to teach us. Poor man! I almost lost my religion, he was so helpless. But I shouldn't have cheated on the test he gave us. I meant to confess it, but the longer I waited the harder it seemed to mention a thing like that. But I knew," she finished triumphantly, "I knew it would all come out some day."

After getting her permission to build up the school program so that other children would be able to learn without cheating, we left.

Sebastian wriggled. "*Gringo* propaganda," he scoffed.

"Then you're against more education?" Peter asked.

"I didn't say that. Russia has the best educational system in the world." (I learned later that Sebastian was regularly given sentences by the Committee to memorize, and that he had had so much difficulty that the process was simplified for him by building the sentences around two basic forms, "Russia has the best —— in the world" and "Everyone knows the *gringos* are to blame for ——," with a list of key words and phrases to insert where appropriate. Once he got into serious trouble when, during a city demonstration lubricated liberally by *aguardiente*, he mixed up the two sets of words and shouted, among other things, that Russia had the best racial prejudice in the world.)

"At least the Russians know how important it is," Peter said. "So do the Chinese. Too bad they're not taught to think for themselves. It's a kind of gray sludge they get."

"Lies, lies," Sebastian said. "They learn enough to make you *gringos* unhappy, no?"

"That's not much to brag about," Peter said. "But I'm all

for them getting all the education they can. Even when people try to use it to chain minds instead of free them, it's likely to work the other way in the long run."

"The long run!" Sebastian said sarcastically. "Who are you to talk about the long run?"

"I can see as far as you can, Don Sebastian," Peter said firmly. "And I don't see the same thing at all."

"So how do we stand, Don Guillermo?" Ernesto asked.

"I would say, Don Ernesto, that you have local approval, weather permitting."

"Weather permitting?"

"The best conclusions always have conditions attached, Don Ernesto. That one seemed as good as any other I could think of . . . not very precise, perhaps, but at least we're all agreed on what weather is, aren't we?"

Ernesto bowed formally. "Thank you for your contribution, Don Guillermo. I'm not sure we could agree on what it was, but I have a small feeling there was one."

"The small feelings are often the very best, Don Ernesto," I said graciously. "Weather permitting."

"Exactly," Ernesto said.

"You two," said the *maestra*, "are crazy."

"Of course we're crazy," Ernesto said cheerfully. "We're crazy to be doing this, and everybody else is crazy to let us." He put his hands on her shoulders and kissed her solemnly on the forehead. "So, Doña Margarita? Aren't you going to slap me?"

She turned her drab face away, trying to hide the moisture in her eyes. "I suppose," she said, "I suppose I'm crazy too."

The School Council was an irregularly functioning organization that now began to function regularly. The first problem it had to solve was who was on it? Not that no one was certain about the membership; several persons were certain, but their convictions did not coincide. Procopio

226

claimed that he was a member because he had been one years ago and nobody had ever told him to stop being one. José claimed that he was not a member, and that he was widely regarded as one only because Council meetings had in years past been held in his house (drinking on school premises was forbidden, and José had an extra room and no family to be disturbed by Council deliberations). Romelio claimed that he was *ex officio* a member, but had to write to *cabecera* headquarters to determine whether that meant he really was or wasn't a member (he never received an answer). Finally the *maestro*, the *maestra*, and Romelio held a public meeting to which "interested fathers of schoolchildren" were invited, and Council members were formally elected. These included Procopio, José, Alejandro ("It will ruin the Council," someone had said when his name was proposed. "No," Alejandro had answered glumly, "it will ruin *me*." He was promptly voted in.), Tomás Medina (a one-time barber and a cousin of the muscular Faustino Medina), Jorge Sandía (who had had more children—thirteen—in school over the years than anyone else in the pueblo), and Juan Vegas (who had spent more time in school than any other pueblo native, having repeated the second year three times). Romelio was again named as an *ex officio* member, but whether he was entitled to take part in Council meetings or not no one could say, until it was pointed out that he was the only one who could write well enough to make a record of what was decided. Someone else pointed out that the *maestro* would be invited to the meetings as an advisor, and that *he* could keep the record. As confusion mounted Ernesto said that he would be happy to attend meetings when invited but that he thought it would be more proper for Romelio to keep the record. José then stood up and suggested that everyone go home. He was at once elected President of the Council, and his first official pronouncement was that Romelio was to be Secretary-Treasurer and that the proceedings of the evening were over. On his way out he told Ernesto he was on his way to begin thinking about educational matters in the company of, and on the property of, his fellow member Alejandro. Ernesto said it was only fitting that he go along too, as advisor.

Peter and I escorted the *maestra* to her quarters. She was very quiet, and Peter asked her if she was discouraged. She shrugged. "They will get drunk," she said tonelessly. "Our new President, our schoolmaster. But I don't care; let them wallow in their *aguardiente*. The world's what it is, and I don't tamper with it, I don't even want to see it, and I don't want it to see me. It's only my girls I care about." Her voice suddenly sharpened. "It was sickening back there! People bobbing up and down, acting like fools, baboons, clowns . . . they can't even begin to save themselves without trying to take along what's ridiculous. I've heard that when homes are on fire people are all too likely to save the trivial things, little things. That's how these people act . . . too often, too often."

"Still," Peter said, "what really counted was getting the Council organized, and they did it. Was it wrong for them to have fun doing it?"

"You call it fun? I don't. You might as well say my husband had fun drinking himself to death. Sometimes I think *campesinos* are better kept in *tristeza*; they don't really know how to escape from sadness, up or down. They know only how to betray themselves. Perhaps fun begins when one learns how to betray others; there is no real fun in betraying oneself."

"But you're doing what you can to help . . ."

"Not to help *campesinos!*" she interrupted. "I don't help *campesinos*. I don't like *campesinos*. Even *campesinos* don't like *campesinos*. Don't I know? I'm one myself, though I deny it as often as I can."

"But people like you, Doña Margarita."

"You can like a *campesino* without liking *campesinos*," she said. "When I was young, my parents sent me to the city to live as an *hija de la casa* in the home of a merchant. An *hija de la casa* is said to be more than a servant, almost a member of the family, but all it's likely to mean is that she isn't paid. My parents told me there would be advantages for me, and they were right, there were advantages. Both the merchant and his son liked me, and I was sent through school . . . for a price. Oh, it was a price I had to pay anyway, I couldn't stop their . . . visits. And, for them, for what they were, they were kind. I always thought it was dangerous for them to send me to school, but I suppose they looked on it as an investment. They told me it made me more interesting, and sometimes they even made me recite while they . . ." She looked at us angrily, as if we had no right to be with her while she was talking this way. "Later on, they had me help them with letters and accounts. I was a secretary, housekeeper, mistress . . . and all but dead inside. When I finished school, I left. I think it surprised them that I left, especially since I had no money; they had never given me any. But I found a teaching job; there was a great shortage of teachers in the rural areas, and the pay was not high enough to attract much competition. But I knew as soon as I began teaching that I could live no other way. My girls . . . I'd see myself in them, and I'd wonder who would be sent away and who would die young. There were enough who died young . . . there were enough. I hated to send them home after school, and still do. If there's little enough for the boys to look forward to, there's even less for the girls. It isn't much of a world we have, but such as it is it's a man's world. Even the rich women just sit in windows and sew and think up useless things to do; there's nothing really important they can do. And I look at my girls, and want to keep them with me, they're alive while they're with me, and so am I. It's for them I'm doing this, it's for them I do everything. I don't care about *campesinos* . . ."

We had reached the school, and she looked up at the dark windows as if she were impatient for the morning sun to send in light and warmth and her girls. Then she looked at us; it was an unfriendly look, but not a personal one—we only had meaning to her insofar as we could help her girls. We were, as persons, superfluous. "My husband was a *campesino* . . ." (Was there a suggestion in her voice that he too had been superfluous?) "He tried to be more, but he was not. He tried to teach, but he could not. I don't blame him for that, or for what he was, or for what he was not. I think he was almost a good man, but I was never sure. I don't know men, I don't understand them, and so I have no right to judge them. If my husband drank too much, it's pointless to say he failed me, since I never expected him not to drink too much. More probably I failed him, and I'm sorry for that, I never meant to hurt anyone. It hurt him, I think, that I loved my girls so much, and it hurt him, I'm certain, that the merchant and his son had done what they did, and that I had neither loved them nor stopped them." She leaned against the school wall and closed her eyes. "I'm tired of hurt, tired of myself. You mustn't count on me too much in all this. I can't say I won't fail you."

"There's no question of failing me," Peter said. "You won't fail the children, will you?"

Her eyes were instantly open, and she looked angrily at him. "You have a way of touching people, child." She moved toward the door, then stopped. "I shouldn't call you child, should I? But it's probably that in you that lets you touch me. I don't understand you, but I understand that in you." She watched him quietly, as if somewhere inside him there was a small boy she could draw to her only in silence; with the first word the man would be thrown up to hide him, to answer for him. Up the road the pueblo candles were dying, some slowly and some abruptly. The moon was dim and far, and the *maestra*'s face seemed oddly split and broken, a thing of muddy patches, like a botched paint-by-number portrait. I realized that part of her drabness was her smell, musty and remote, like a book long put away. The smell was, in fact, strongest in the first minutes of class, when the book, incredibly, was opened; then life streamed forth, and the air was bittersweet. Finally, so slowly one wondered what it cost her to speak at all, she said, "No, I won't fail the children."

"And you," Peter said to me as we walked along the road, "doesn't it seem wrong to you just to be an observer, without trying to *do* anything about what you see?"

"Now look, Pete," I said, "I never had to fix chicken coops before you came. I've been so useful I'll be afraid to talk about it when I get back. You should see the job I did on Alejandro's outhouse."

"You know what I mean."

"Yes," I said, "I know what you mean. And I'm not sure I know how to answer. By and large, anthropologists are supposed to find out about things, not to interfere with them or change them the way they think they ought to go. If they tamper with the very situation they're trying to study, they've added themselves to it, and what they set out to study isn't there any more. It's something like putting your thumb on the microscope plate."

"But these aren't bugs or chemical solutions. They're people."

"So they are, Pete. And no matter how hard anthropologists try—and some try pretty hard—they can't forget it. So while they strain toward science with one hand, they can't quite bring themselves to take the other hand out of the humanities. Some think that makes them a kind of bridge, but I don't know about that. What it adds up to is that they don't like to meddle—even the applied anthropologists don't feel quite respectable—and that they believe they have to walk more than a mile for an answer, and that they not only analyze human values but tend to be sensitive to them . . . especially the other fellow's, some might say. They're not as detached about things as their reports might suggest. They're not apt to be much impressed by what a tourist or junketing congressman might see as terrible or wonderful, but they do see beauty, they do see pain, they even see— though they hate to admit it—love. Most of all, they try to understand, not to manipulate. Oh, if they're invited to take part here and there, they do it, but they try not to be intrusive, or to attract power to themselves."

"I don't try to attract power to myself."

"No, Pete, that's true, and it's one reason why I like you. But it could happen, all the same, whether you try or not; people could become pretty dependent on you. I don't say that's bad; but if it's your role to serve as a leader, it's our role to see how it happens and how it affects the other people. Some say that what anthropologists do is hold up a mirror, so man can look at himself. In a way that's so, though we don't always do it well, and sometimes we seem to bend over so far backwards to catch all sides of a thing we fall flat on our ass. But don't judge anthropology by what I am, or by what I say about it. I'm probably a lousy anthropologist."

He shook his head. "I just don't know what to make of you," he said.

"That's because you're dedicated," I said. "I'm not dedicated. Every now and then I surprise myself by having a conviction, but like the sedentary man with an urge to exercise, I lie down until it goes away. Anyway, you don't have to worry about what I do. It's more important what the School Council does."

The School Council met every afternoon for a week, with the *maestro* sitting in and reporting back to the *maestra*. Most of the suggestions that were ultimately adopted came from the *maestra*. "For someone who isn't even here," Alejandro said wonderingly, "she has a lot to say." Yet no one who presented an idea expected anything to be done about it until Ernesto had tried it out on her and brought back her reaction. Unworkable ideas were often reshaped by her, and workable ideas given a little twist or two to make them even more workable, so that those who submitted them were neither deflated nor overinflated. Peter was busy with his crops, but managed to get together with the *maestra* for an hour every day. She did the same thing with his ideas. "She has a sort of 'Down, boy!' effect on me," he told me with a somewhat chagrined smile. "But there's no question she's the one to work through. Even so, it's going to be their program, not mine. All I've really done is provide a kind of stimulus, but they're the ones who are carrying through. Sometimes she makes me feel like no more than a spare tire, but when I think it over I realize I don't mind at all!"

XII

Easter week came and went, and the pueblo seemed to empty and fill up again accordingly. By donkey, foot, and bus people streamed to the city or the *cabecera* for the *Semana Santa* processions and services. The pueblo church was open, but there were few left to use it. Procopio, who was immobilized by dysentery ("The Lord has sent me a sign to stay"), said there had not been such an exodus in years. "It is because the priest could not come before," he said. As it happened, the priest visited the pueblo unexpectedly on Good Friday. José, who was looking after the church, swore that when the priest entered he muttered, "Jesus Christ, where is everybody?" He spent the day visiting the sick and infirm, and Doña Victoria confessed an amazing assortment of sins to him at the top of her voice. He kept trying to shush her, but she shouted, "They all know anyway, they all know anyway!" Her confession was wildly disjointed and often incoherent, but periodically phrases of shocking precision and lucidity burst through the walls and flashed up and down the road.

I talked to him briefly before he boarded the bus to the city. He had put on a few pounds since I had last seen him, but they were convalescence pounds, lumpy and loose, and his face, full of fatigue, seemed to stretch and strain away from his body, as if it were trying to thin itself out and dissociate itself from the puffiness below.

"You don't look well yet, *Padre*," I said.

234

"I'm not interested in how I look," he said curtly. "I had no right to be sick at all. What I want to tell you is that I saw your young friend in the city. He came to see me . . ." A government car passed, heading toward the *cabecera*, motor racing and wheels spitting back dust and gravel. The priest coughed out part of the dust cloud and glared after the car. If I had been the driver just then, I would have been concerned about lightning bolts. I thought of making some comment on the devious ways leading to the separation of Church and State, but while I was wrestling with it, the priest dropped a dry terminal cough and resumed. "What disturbs me is how *he* looks. Even saints in the wilderness had more flesh than that. Don't you have any eyes, Don Guillermo?"

"I stop seeing things after awhile," I said. "It's a great weakness of mine."

"I'm surprised you don't keep bumping into things."

"As a matter of fact, I do."

"Pah!" He whacked at his robes so vigorously the dust squirted halfway across the road. Then, as if he had knocked out his own stuffing, he sagged against my arm.

"Would you like some water, *Padre?*"

"No, *hijo*," he said shakily. He breathed deeply, pumping himself up again. "We had a terrible time together," he said. "He kept trying to prop me up, and I kept trying to prop him up. We ended up . . ." He looked sternly at me. ". . . laughing!"

"Outrageous, *Padre.*"

"Mmmm." He frowned at a pair of dogs sniffing each other in the road: Should Catholic dogs be doing that? "He told me about the new plans, and I . . ." He seemed embarrassed.

"You disapprove, *Padre?*"

"Disapprove? Disapprove? *Pues*, not at all. In fact, I . . . I want to set aside a little money and send it along to help out—for paper, crayons, whatever's needed. It won't . . . it won't offend the *maestra*, will it? I don't know why, but she never stops to pass the time of day with me."

"I suspect she isn't the sort who passes the time of day, *Padre*."

"I'm not either, really," he muttered. "*Así*, no wonder we shoot by each other so quickly. But it won't offend her?"

"As long as it's for the children, *Padre*, it won't offend her."

Peter had never been busier. What the priest had said about his appearance was doubtless true, but he always seemed to be moving, however slowly, from field to school to city and back, so that it was difficult to look at him closely. Yet, when I did, he seemed no less healthy and possibly healthier, and I reminded myself that the priest had not seen him for some months before the city visit. If Peter had walked in on him when he still had his beard, the priest might have been even more shocked. Perhaps, I thought, there was a limit to how drawn one could look, and Peter, having reached it, would look progressively better to observers like myself simply because he no longer looked progressively worse.

In time, however, I realized I had been judging too much on the basis of face and frame. It was not from the outside in but from the inside out that he was being consumed, and while a shell of constancy clung to the exterior, sign was added to sign that the inner demands, the inner burning, were more intense than ever.

He linked his latest work projects to the expanded education program by starting adult classes in techniques of developing a community drainage system, of resurfacing roads, and of improving sanitation arrangements. "I guess I should be more of a specialist to tackle some of the things needed," he told me. "But I know enough to work it out with all the pamphlets and manuals and other materials I can have sent to me, and with the help I can get here. The men here have a pretty good idea of what can be done and what can't, and the way we're going about it is to pool my ma-

terials and theory with their experience and common sense
to get us all to the point where we can go ahead and do these
things right."

Interest in the classes was initially low, but rose when
José suggested calling them meetings instead of classes, and
rose still further when Romelio formally designated them
as meetings of the Junta on Community Improvement. "It
seemed deceptive to me at first," Peter said, "but then I realized that's really just what the classes were."

On his trips to the city, he typically took produce in and
brought materials for his classes back. He stayed up late at
night going over the correspondence materials and planning new units. Early in the morning he was in the field, hoe-
ing, digging, planting, pruning, cutting, picking, stacking,
thinning, spraying, keeping to his crop schedule. By the time
school was under way he had bathed (the *maestra* had
insisted on this—"Schools are meant to hold many
things," she had said, "but certain smells are to be left outside") in the river, put on his teaching suit, and was ready
to help out where he was needed. Sometimes he was called on
to lecture to the regular classes; he was starting a series on
men of history who, from humble beginnings, had gone on to
make enduring contributions to their times and their people.

"You think that's corny, don't you?" he challenged.

"Not if you believe in it," I said.

"Well," he said simply, "I believe in it."

Sometimes he took over the special classes; a third and
fourth grade had been formed, with six pupils (sent on a
trial basis by dubious but curious parents) in each, and a
fifth grade was being planned.

Sometimes he coached the boys in basketball. "It's the
only sport I was ever any good at," he told me, "and I only
got into that because I was fairly tall."

Sometimes, with José, he made repairs in and about the
schools. Once José, trying to fix a leaky ceiling, brought

down part of it on Ernesto's head in the middle of a discourse on the future tense. "What did I say to deserve that?" Ernesto asked wonderingly, brushing away the pieces. Subsequently repairs were made when classes were out.

When Peter was through with his work at the school, he changed back into old clothes (unless he had already changed to do repairs) and returned to the field until supper. After supper he held his adult classes (though he soon began to speak of them regularly as meetings of the Junta), and then took up his late studies, with manuals, books, pamphlets, papers, pencils, compass, triangle, ruler, and other materials piled around him on the bed. "I save on energy that way." he told me. "I just keep reaching into the pile until I fall asleep." José said that he was often waked in the early morning hours by the clump and thump of the materials as they fell from Peter's bed.

The daily round of activities was interrupted by trips to the city, by rain (when he could not work in the field), and by weekends or holidays when the schools were closed. The interruptions meant not that he rested, but that he turned to something else: on rainy days he spent more time in the schools, on weekends he spent more time in the field, and on rainy weekends he spent more time in his room with his books and manuals. On Saturday evenings he usually dropped into Alejandro's *cantina* to try to unwind. But he no longer seemed to be able to relax, and almost always ended up talking earnestly about latrines, fertilizer, bugs, the low price of cabbage or the high price of crayons. Pamphlets and diagrams regularly poked from his pockets, so that he looked like a scarecrow stuffed inadequately with paper. "It's no good trying to be just like everyone else," he told me over a beer he never finished. "I'm not, and I might as well face up to it and go on from there. There's no point in losing yourself if you don't come out somewhere. I feel I've learned a lot; I can understand better how it is not to care any more, how it is not to *want* to care any more, because you only get hurt when you do. But once you focus on the children, there's a reason for caring you can't shut out. Other things fall into place then, and progress makes sense."

"So you're building an empire."

"No," he said seriously. "I'm not really building anything. The more I do, the less important I am. If I have a part in all this, it's to work like hell to make myself unnecessary."

He ate so little at mealtimes José persuaded him to tuck a roll in with the papers he carried, so that, reaching for a pamphlet, he occasionally came up with the roll and abstractedly took a bite or two before dipping back in for the pamphlet. The *maestra* complained that he left a trail of dropped papers and crumbs, but did not seem to mind picking up the papers or sweeping inside crumbs outside. Nor did anyone else. In fact, if he had his trail, he also had his trailers. Wherever he went now, there seemed to be someone tagging along. Children watched him work in the field, and adults watched him work around the school, and more and more the watching led to helping. "I don't know what I intended to do today," Procopio told me, "but it wasn't to paint a school outhouse. *Cierto!* But there he was, ready to fall apart, and there I was, also ready to fall apart, helping him. If I hadn't been so proud of myself, I would have been ashamed."

At first I thought it was largely curiosity that gave him so much company, and perhaps at first it was—"They've never seen anyone who moved so slowly and got so much done," Ernesto pointed out. But it was increasingly obvious that far more than curiosity went with him. When he stumbled, there was a hand at his elbow. When he fell, other hands raised him and brought him water. When he reached for something, it was brought nearer. When the day was very hot, and his straw hat had taken on its share of dust and perspiration, it was quietly replaced with a dry cool one. When the day was cold, an extra *ruana* was draped over his shoulders. He did not protest. It was as if, for him, there was no time for protesting.

They're holding him up, I thought. They're holding *him* up.

He had once been almost invisible. Now he was part of a cluster, a growing cluster.

I asked María what was happening. "He's ours now, that's what's happening," she said.

Things were booming. In one of my notebooks I wrote, "They're off in a cloud of dust," then added, "No, not really." It was the same dust as before, and the only racing motors belonged to the buses and the government cars. Yet, if people wore the same dust, they wore it differently. One might have thought they were sharing in an abundance which, if not very useful, was at least something they could be as generous as they pleased with: "Won't you have some more dust?" "Thanks, I've plenty." Another notebook entry reads, "Everyone seems to be doing more than he's doing. What's been added? Purpose." When I made the entry, I started to write, "A purpose," but realized it was more general than that. People wore it with the dust.

Romelio was able to report that traffic over the renovated bridge had increased so much that "on Saturdays a market occurs there." The *cabecera* office acknowledged this report with an elaborate commendation "to be inserted in your permanent file," and Romelio was so pleased he spent three days writing out copies of his copy, to be sent to relatives and friends in nearby pueblos. He also had his wife take a basket of rolls to the bridge every Saturday, so that even if no one else came along there would still be a market for reporting purposes. Actually, in successive weeks the market flourished, and there was a brisk trade that brought more meat (especially mutton from the highlands to the west) into the pueblo in exchange for local vegetables.

The new market stimulated interest in trying for higher

crop yields ("Larger goals are all well and good," Ernesto observed, "but they lack the immediacy of fresh mutton."), and there were more and more converts to Peter's methods. As yields in fact began to rise, not only local trading but city trading was spurred. Through the Junta and School Council, whose membership overlapped, some of the extra centavos were diverted to the purchase of school supplies for the children as well as materials for the adult classes.

The *maestra* started a late afternoon class in nutrition and hygiene for the women. The first session, on the preparation of mutton, attracted twelve and offended none. The second session, on feminine hygiene, attracted fourteen and evidently shocked them all. "They're so scandalized," the *maestra* told Peter, "that I suspect we'll have either a big turnout next time or none at all." Thirty-seven women, many of whom were patently prepared to be outraged, came to the third session, and the *maestra* predicted flatly that attendance at future sessions would be forty and up. "It's exciting for them," she said. "It's about the only chance they've had to get out from under. Gossip's important to them, and even when they think the subject's shocking, what's hardest for them is not to have been there."

One morning I collared Peter on his way back from the field—technically this was not easy, since his collar was in shreds—and congratulated him on the way everything seemed to be working out. "Things *are* falling into place, aren't they?" he said. "Even the bridge fits in now. And we're moving in the right direction now, I'm sure of it. But . . ." He looked back at the two boys who were helping him carry tools. They grinned and made a clatter of a wave: machete and hoe knocking against rake and spade. "But I wish I could hurry everything along. I guess I should have learned patience by now, and I thought I had, but I suppose the kind I felt only works when you don't really expect to get anywhere. It's comforting then; you can draw it around you like a blanket and keep a lot of things out. But now that we're going somewhere, I can hardly wait to get there.

It's something like the way I used to look forward to Christmas; patience was a lot easier in August than in December. Only now I feel I'm giving as well as getting, and that makes it even harder to wait. I want it all to happen right away!" He smiled at the two boys. His eyes seemed painfully tired. An infection had developed in his left eyelid, which was really not greatly swollen but, on the thin wasted face, looked enormous and grotesque. "But it's going to take years . . ."

"So what if it does?" I said. "You'll have a good reason to come back."

"Come back?" he said, startled. "Who said anything about leaving?"

"Well, you're not going to stay here forever, are you?"

"I haven't even thought about it. There's been too much to do. How can I leave?"

"I thought you were supposed to be making yourself unnecessary."

"Yes, but . . . look at all the things that . . . I won't be ready to leave for a long time."

"Maybe you never *will* be ready. Maybe you'll just go on and on, putting it off. Maybe what you'll really be doing is making yourself more and more necessary."

"Oh no," he said hastily. "I . . . I guess I'll be leaving *some* day. But I won't have to think about that for a long while yet."

He was wrong.

XIII

It was on a Saturday morning that it happened. I was down by the bridge, watching the market stalls being set up, listening to the early haggling, and sniffing—almost tasting—an incredible hash of odors: cheese, mutton, cabbage, *chontaduro*, guava, enchiladas, tamales, chicken, onions, chocolate, cigars, soap, rum, coffee, *panela* (crude brown sugar sold in blocks wrapped in *platano* leaves), and burros. *Ruana* and dress colors were brighter than usual, movements quicker and voices sharper. Far more than buying or selling was and would be going on. *Campesinos* were brought together chiefly by their markets. When it comes to communication, I thought, what Telstar lacks, markets have.

"No nails," José was saying. "You'd think *someone* would be selling nails."

"I wouldn't," I said. "But I've never really thought about anyone selling nails anywhere. I suppose it's different for a carpenter."

"It's always different for a carpenter," José said. "I'm not complaining, but it's more than nails with me. Who cares about coffins anymore? Who *really* cares?"

"I don't know," I said. "There must be a few."

"There's only the dead to care, and they can't. If the bottom dropped out of coffins tomorrow, Don Guillermo, no one would cry."

"Are you talking about the bottom dropping out of the coffins themselves or out of the coffin business?"

"Either one, Don Guillermo, either one." He sat beside me on the slope overlooking the market. "I've been thinking about trying something else."

I looked hard at the frozen face. "You *are* José, aren't you? The one who told me there was nothing else for him?"

"The same, yes, the same, no." He sighed and began to chew on a blade of grass. "The truth is, I'm restless. I'm not the only one, Don Guillermo. The whole pueblo's restless, like the market down there." We watched the milling; colors flashed and voices rose. Children raced in and out, laughing. It was, after all, only market life, but a life brought closer than ever. Was this the kind of spirit that . . . ? "Coffins," José said. "The dead are becoming dead. People don't think about them so much anymore. Soon they'll be left to bury themselves. What's stirring is what's important now, Don Guillermo. People want to *do* things, different things. It's your friend's fault. The mosquito bites, and there's no end to the scratching. Oh, it's not so much like that. But a little, a little."

"I can't tell whether you approve or disapprove, Don José."

He shrugged. "What does that have to do with it? Do I approve or disapprove of getting up in the morning?" He sat quietly for a minute or two, then said, "We feel less comfortable now, I think, but there's more . . ." He stood up. "There's more pride," he said.

"What about purpose?" I said.

"Yes," he said. "There are many names for what's happening. Purpose, hope . . . all in an itch. But there is nothing more important than a reason to be proud. My uncle used to say the best thing you could do for *campesinos* was give them a reason to be proud. Even a jailbird can have purpose and hope—to get out of jail. But if he has no pride, there's no real point in being free. *Entiende?*"

I nodded.

"You *gringos* are good at dumping money. But those you dump it on have no reason to feel proud about it. *Al con-*

trario. You can take care of people, but who is proud at being taken care of? Our jailbird is being taken care of, *verdad?* But Pedro—he is more than money. Is he helping us now, or are we helping him? Or are we all helping one another? It's all one now, and we have a reason to be proud."

"He doesn't want to leave," I said.

"It's because he needs us a little, I think. Who would have thought a *gringo* would come, and end up needing *us?* Not for what he can get out of us, but for what we are to him. In some ways, that's the best part." José's frozen face softened. "It's why we love him."

"So you're pleased?"

"Pah! I've never claimed to be pleased. It's not easy to have to start thinking about things in a different way. It was bad enough having you sitting around listening and watching instead of talking and turning up your nose. What kind of a *gringo* is that? people said. And just when we were getting used to you, Pedro had to come along. No, there's nothing you can count on anymore."

As we hurried back toward the pueblo—I rarely ran, but I was running now; if I had slowed down, José, who also ran rarely, would have gone right over me—as we rushed, I thought of those last words of his. Had I been counting on Peter to go on and on? There had been signs enough that he could not. Yet, when the boy had brought word of his collapse, I was as surprised as I would have been to hear that old Doña Victoria was doing wind sprints in the plaza. I had been like a man too easily persuaded that drained toothpaste tubes are always good for another squeeze and that gasoline tanks registering empty are always good for another mile; the day comes when he learns at last that one can run out.

Peter was in his bed, with a thin blanket over him and a folded *ruana* under his head. His face was a curious gray, as if the weathered ruddiness had lost its color to a black-and-white photograph, and for the first time the unfinished coffin that held his shirts and papers seemed ominous to me. Following my eyes with his, he smiled feebly and said, "I'm not ready for *that* yet."

"Hell no," I said. "You never looked better."

Visenta came in from the patio with a pitcher of water. "So," she said, "You two finally crawled back. The boy I sent must be an old man by now."

"Crawled!" José said. "I haven't moved so fast since Don Paco's funeral."

"Don Paco?" Peter said.

"Don Paco Calderón," José said. "Everyone called him Tío Paco. He lived on top of a hill just the other side of your bridge, Pedrito. He used to live near the bottom, but the little brook he got his water from carried the garbage from all the huts farther up the hill. Since his was the downhill hut, he was getting the worst of it, so after awhile he moved to the top. He had his hut right next to the spring that fed the brook, and his garbage went in *first*. He was so high up he was almost cut off from everybody else, and everything was so up and down there he almost never went out for exercise. He had a little pension to live on, and a wife to go get it for him and bring in supplies, so he mostly stayed up there in his hut, getting fatter and fatter."

"What was the pension for?" Peter asked.

"He was shot up some in the last war, which was another reason he didn't get around much. *Así*, almost no one ever saw him, but all the people farther down the hill came to feel they knew him well, from his garbage. So they called him Uncle Paco. '*Pues*, Uncle Paco never tires of cabbage,' they'd say, or 'Poor Uncle Paco, the fish didn't agree with him.' "

"What a revolting story!" Visenta said.

"You'd call the many ways of friendship revolting, witch? *Pues*, not I. When he died, there was a great turnout for his funeral. True, many were curious to see him; they never had. But there were more than a few—even among those who had never seen him—who felt on intimate terms with him. In a sense, he had supped with them for years.

"I was one of the pallbearers, and while the priest waited at the foot of the hill, we went up to get Uncle Paco. Ah, but he was enormous! He almost filled the hut. We had brought up twice as many boards as I had thought might be necessary, but we had to send back down for more boards and more pallbearers. When the reinforcements had come, we worked him through the doorway—he came out with a pop—and I whacked together a coffin around him. Then we started down the hill with him.

"We tried to go very slowly, step by step, but little by little we picked up speed, and soon enough we were all tearing down the hill, faster and faster, Uncle Paco riding us all the way. *Carajo!* We reached the bottom and shot right by the priest. 'Where are they going with him?' I heard the priest say. 'Perhaps they're stealing him,' someone suggested. I thought I heard the priest say, 'But why?' though we were almost out of earshot by then."

"Didn't you ever get any thin ones?" Visenta asked.

"Most of them were thin ones," José said. "At least by the time they died. That's why the fat ones stand out. I don't think I'll ever forget Uncle Paco."

Peter was groaning and trying to smile all at once.

"Just the sort of story to cheer him up," Visenta said reprovingly.

"It does, it does," Peter said weakly. "What finally happened?"

"*Pues*, we went right into the river with him, just about where your bridge is. We floated him most of the rest of the way. I remember so clearly the priest walking along the bank, chanting."

"Enough!" Visenta said. "Too much!"

"But I haven't yet told of the frog who got trapped in the coffin, and croaked the Ave María—or so the sexton said—until . . ."

247

"Stop!!" Visenta said. "It wasn't for your disgusting stories that I sent for you. I want you . . ."

"A miracle, the sexton said it was," José went on imperturbably. "I recall his words . . . 'How humble the frog,' he said . . . I know those were his words, because one of the pallbearers—the one who could swim—was letting air at the time, and there was such a bubble I had to ask the sexton to repeat himself. 'How humble the frog,' was what he said, 'and yet it respects the Lord.' 'The what?' I asked —I was closest to the bubble. 'The Lord,' he said. 'Ah,' I said . . ."

"Silence!" Visenta said. "I want you two to arrange to get him out of here."

"Get who?" José asked. "The Lord?" He looked innocently at Visenta. "The frog? Which one?"

"Which one, which one," Visenta muttered.

"Surely you don't mean Pedro?" José said. "I thought you could cure anything. What kind of evil spirit could defeat you?"

"Spirit!" Visenta glowered at him and murmured interesting words.

"Ah, the spirit speaks," José said respectfully.

"The only spirit here is the spirit of your stupidity," Visenta said. "What he's got is yellow jaundice. Look at his eyes, fool!"

"Is it safe?" José asked.

"Safe enough for a fool," Visenta said.

"You look first, Don Guillermo," José said.

"Thanks, I've looked," I said. "It must be safe."

Alejandro came in, followed by Ernesto.

"Yellow jaundice," José explained, as if the diagnosis had been his.

"It's what comes of drinking water," Alejandro said sadly.

"Once you start criticizing water," José said, "who knows where it may lead, *compadre?*"

"True," Alejandro said. "Everything else follows. I

248

apologize to water everywhere. What I should have said was, It's what comes when things *get into* water."

"Disgusting," Visenta said. "Your friend's sick, and you talk in this disgusting way."

"It's *our* way," José said. "What would you have us say? Goodbye, Pedro?"

"I have a little pennant we could wave bravely at him," Ernesto suggested.

"Why don't we get him drunk?" Alejandro said.

They were all crowded around the bed now, and their words had so little to do with their troubled faces that I kept expecting them to adjust either the one or the other. But this, as José had said, was their way. Perhaps, I thought, an adjustment would be made if he turned better or worse. But I was reminded of stories Romelio had told me of men who had joked—poorly, perhaps, but persistently—at death as it drew near. "They joked cruelly," he had said. "But it was not cruel at all."

The *maestra* came in. A look passed between her and Visenta that surprised me. Was it jealousy? What kind of jealousy?

"There are too many in here," Visenta said.

"Who would you turn out?" asked the *maestra*. Visenta was silent.

A light rain began to fall. I thought, irrelevantly, It will hurt the market. The *maestra* went to the bed and said, "Yes, it had to happen." She touched Peter's face, as if he were a pupil who had fallen in the schoolyard. "What now, child?" she asked. "Are you to be sent home?"

"I believe so, Doña Margarita."

"Yes, you should be," she said gently.

"I have said so," Visenta informed her, and the world at large.

"Ah, you have said so. Of course, if you have said so . . ." The *maestra*'s voice trailed away—"So you've done somebody else's homework," it suggested. She and Visenta looked at each other again: the one face drab, mild, passive, seem-

249

ing ever about to slip away; the other bold, compelling, challenging, predatory. There was no doubt who had the stronger face. But who, I wondered, was the stronger woman?

Sebastian came in. He glanced suspiciously around the room, then went to the bed. His oversize *ruana* caught momentarily on a chair, but he swept it away with dignity. He poked his round little face close to Peter's, and said, as if he hoped no one else would hear, "I'm sorry, *mono*."

"Thank you, Don Sebastian."

"It doesn't change all that's between us, you understand, but for what you feel, I'm sorry."

"Thank you."

The rain was heavier now, and we listened to it drum on roof and shutters. I thought of the first time Peter had been in this room, and had been so taken with the smell of earth under rain. It *did* smell good, damn it.

Romelio bustled in, all efficiency and forms. He shook himself with the briskness of a bulldog, frowned at Sebastian and Visenta, and went to Peter. "Who gave you permission to get sick?" he said gruffly. "Foreigners aren't allowed to get sick without my permission."

"Are you going to put me in jail, Don Romelio?"

"I'm going to have you deported. That's the penalty."

"Can't I come back?"

"Only when you're well. You must weigh thirty pounds more at least. We want no one here who doesn't bring his own flesh." He cocked his head toward Alejandro. "Don't put on more than your share; some go too far."

"If I could give him some of mine, I would," Alejandro said. "If everyone in the pueblo took some of mine, I'd still have enough."

"Don't worry, Alejandrito," José said. "You're still only a radish compared to Tío Paco."

"Ah, Tío Paco," Alejandro said. "He had enough for the whole *Departamento*. But his came from eating; a terrible way to get fat." His great dry lips drooped disdainfully.

Old Procopio came in, with Rosa Linda at his elbow. They stood hesitantly by the doorway when they saw all the others.

"Too many," Visenta muttered. "Far too many for a room this small."

"My aunt wanted to come," Sebastian said. "If her legs weren't so stiff . . ." He pulled a small packet from his *ruana*. "She sent over some tobacco."

"It's what I get for telling anyone," Visenta said. "A word, only a word, and the world wants to come in. Why don't you all leave?"

"No, please," Peter said. "I want to see Don Procopio, and thank Rosa Linda for Christmas again, and . . ."

"Too many," Visenta said. "Too many."

"No," Peter said, weakly but fervently, "not too many. Never too many. Please . . . all of you . . . come . . ."

The bus was ready to leave. Peter, wrapped in blankets, sat in the back with Romelio, who had insisted on making all official arrangements for his admission to the hospital in the city and his subsequent return to the States for a rest as prolonged as prescribed. The prospect of filling out so many forms delighted Romelio, but—his gruffness betrayed him—it was not the only reason he was now sitting next to Peter, keeping the blankets tucked in and flies from riding on Peter instead of the produce. It seemed to take all Peter's strength to hold his head up, but he was using it for that.

The pueblo had turned out as for his arrival almost a year ago. Young, old, all who could had come. I remember particularly a woman of perhaps thirty with an immense tumor on the right side of her head, who approached the bus from her left with a piece of toilet paper—a luxury item —over the tumor. Before, most had waited along the road rising into the pueblo. Now there was a great crowd around the bus, with many pressing close to speak softly to him and touch him.

"*Vaya con Dios, Señor.*"

251

"Buen viaje, mono."

"Hasta luegito, joven."

And most often: "Come back . . ." "Come back . . ."

Doña Victoria was perched on a barrel (it reeked of rum) so close to the bus she could kick one of the tires, which she did from time to time. ("So," she would say—thump!—"So you'd take him away, would you?") She was not consistently clear that it was Peter who was leaving: as her grumbles indicated, at any given moment it was apt to be her dead husband, Sebastian, Wally Frank, herself, or a relative she identified only as Cousin Bushy. But when Peter's turn came, it was then she kicked the tire.

I went up to say goodbye. "Well, Pete," I said, "you did all right."

He looked puzzled. "*I*?" he said.

"Sure," I said. "You even found a few answers."

He nodded. "But the questions change. There's never . . ." His voice slipped away with his thoughts, then came back as a warm whisper, drained of sound but not spirit. "Anyway, it's moving. I hope it doesn't stop."

"You've friends enough who hope *you* don't stop, Pete. Rest up."

"Yes . . . yes . . ." His eyes misted, and he turned his exhausted face away.

"Drop me a card about the unruly natives up north. They seem to be pretty restless these days."

"Yes . . ."

When the bus had pulled out—with a wild clatter of squawking hens and yelping dogs—I stood watching it with José, Ernesto, and most of the pueblo until it was only dust.

"So," José said. "He's gone. Somehow I did not think the bus meant it. I thought it might go for a little way and come back, or break down completely. It has happened before; it knows how."

"I'm wondering about a different sort of breakdown," I said. "What he's done . . . what he's started . . . will it all collapse now?"

"No," Ernesto said. "It's ours to do now."

"An opinion I respect," José said. "But only an opinion. For myself, I am doubtful. In a few months, in a year or so, who knows? Perhaps things will be as they were, after all."

"No, Don José," Ernesto said. His voice seemed to have a new force to it. "Things will not be the same again."

"Ah," José said, looking carefully at his friend. "Who let the teacher out?"

María had just swept the black snake from the patio. "And you," she asked me, "will you go soon?"

"Very soon," I said. "My report's almost finished."

"Is it very heavy?" she asked.

"Heavy enough, Doña Maria."

"Will anyone read it?"

"I don't know."

She offered me one of her beautiful smiles. "If I could read, I would read it."

"If you keep going to the *maestra*'s classes, perhaps you'll learn."

"I might," she said. "But there are so many terrible things going on to read about, I'm not sure I want to. If I learn and don't like it, can I unlearn again?"

"Not very well. For better or worse, you'll know how."

She sighed and picked her nose. "There are so many peculiar things to know. Who set out to learn such things in the first place?"

"All of us together, a long time ago."

"Together? But we're so far apart."

"We've taken different ways. But perhaps we can come together again."

"That would be nice." She flicked a spider from the broom. "Poor little Pedro. It wasn't much of a gift we gave him, was it?"

"It'll do," I said. "It'll do."

About the Author

William Sayres received his doctorate in social anthropology at Harvard. He has taught at Yale and is presently Visiting Associate Professor in Anthropology and Education at Teachers College, Columbia. As a lecturer, he participated in the training program for the first contingent of Peace Corps volunteers destined for Colombia, S.A. On the basis of five years of work and research in Colombia, Peru, Ecuador, and Bolivia, he has a first-hand familiarity with the types of communities to which members of the Peace Corps have been assigned.

Mr. Sayres lives with his wife and twelve-year-old son in North Chatham, New York. He is the author of numerous articles and monographs for learned journals, two non-fiction books, and the novel, *Sonotaw*.